THE
SILVER
ROAD

STINA JACKSON

Translated from the Swedish
by Susan Beard

CORVUS

Originally published in Sweden as *Silvervägen*
by Albert Bonniers Förlag in 2018.

First published in Great Britain in 2019 by Corvus,
an imprint of Atlantic Books Ltd.

10 9 8 7 6 5 4 3 2 1

A CIP catalogue record for this book is available
from the British Library.

Hardback ISBN: 978 1 78649 730 7
Trade Paperback ISBN: 978 1 78649 732 1
OME ISBN: 978 1 78649 822 9
Ebook ISBN: 978 1 78649 731 4

Printed in Great Britain by TJ International Ltd, Padstow, Cornwall

Corvus
An Imprint of Atlantic Books Ltd
Ormond House
26–27 Boswell Street
London
WC1N 3JZ

www.corvus-books.co.uk

To Robert

PART I

It was the light, the way it stung and burned and tore at him, hung over the forests and the lakes like an incentive to go on breathing, like a promise of new life. The light, that filled his veins with an urgency and robbed him of sleep. It was still only May, but he lay awake as dawn filtered through fibres and gaps. He could hear the melting frost seeping out of the ground as winter bled away, and streams and rivers rushing and surging as the fells shed their winter covering. Soon the light would consume every night, invading, dazzling, shaking life into everything that slumbered beneath the rotten leaves. It would fill the buds on the trees with warmth until they burst open, and the forest would fill with mating calls and the hunger cries of newly hatched life. The midnight sun would drive people from their lairs and fill them with longing. They would laugh and make love and become crazy and violent. Some might even disappear. They would be blinded and disorientated. But he didn't want to believe that they died.

*

He smoked only while he was searching for her. Lelle saw her in the passenger seat every time he lit another

3

cigarette, the way she grimaced and fixed her eyes on him over the rim of her glasses.

'I thought you'd given up?'

'I *have* given up. This is just a one-off.'

He could see her shake her head, scowl and bare her teeth, the pointy canines that embarrassed her. Her presence was more palpable then, as he drove through the night and the daylight clung on. Her hair that was almost white when the sun caught it, the dark splash of freckles on the bridge of her nose that she had tried to disguise with make-up in recent years, and her eyes that saw everything, even though she gave the impression she wasn't looking. She was more like Anette than she was him, and that was just as well. The beauty genes certainly hadn't come from him. She was beautiful and that wasn't just because he was biased, people had always turned to look at Lina, even when she was very little. She was the kind of child who would bring a smile to the most jaded of faces. But these days nobody turned to look at her any more. No one had seen her for three years – at least, no one who was prepared to say it openly.

His cigarettes ran out before he reached Jörn. Lina was no longer sitting in the seat beside him. The car was empty and silent and he had almost forgotten he was driving, eyes on the road but taking nothing in. He had been travelling along this main road, known as the Silver Road, for such a long time that he knew it like the back of his hand. He knew every bend and every gap in the wildlife fencing that allowed moose and reindeer to cross if they had a mind to. He knew where rainwater collected on the surface and where mist drifted up from the tarns and distorted his vision. The road's sole purpose had disappeared with the closure of the silver mines, and it had become treacherous after years of neglect and deterioration. But it was also the only road that connected Glimmersträsk with the other inland communities, and however much he detested the cracked tarmac and the overgrown drainage ditches that stretched out behind him, he would never abandon it. This was where she had disappeared. This road had swallowed up his daughter.

No one knew that he drove at night, searching for Lina. Or that he chain-smoked and put his arm round the passenger seat and chatted with his daughter as if she were actually there, as if she had never disappeared. He had no one to tell, not since Anette left him. She said it was his fault from the very beginning. He was the one who had given Lina a lift to the bus stop that morning. He was the one to blame.

He reached Skellefteå at about 3 a.m. and stopped at Circle K for fuel and to fill his flask with coffee. Despite the early hour, the lad behind the counter was bright-eyed and cheerful, with red-blond hair combed to one side. He was young, maybe nineteen, twenty. The same age Lina was now, although he found it hard to imagine her so grown up. He bought another pack of Marlboro Lights, despite his guilty conscience. His eyes fell on a display of mosquito repellent beside the till. Lelle fumbled with his bank card. Everything reminded him of Lina. She had reeked of mosquito repellent that last morning. It was actually the only thing he remembered, the way he had wound down the window to get rid of the smell after dropping her off at the bus stop. He couldn't recall what they had said to each other that morning, whether she was happy or sad, or what they had eaten for breakfast. Everything that happened afterwards took up too much room, and only the mosquito repellent remained. He had said as much to the police that evening – that Lina stank of mosquito repellent. Anette had stared at him as if he were a total stranger, someone to be ashamed of. He remembered that, too.

He opened a new pack and kept the cigarette in his mouth until he was back on the Silver Road, going north this time. The homeward stretch always went faster, felt bleaker. Lina's silver heart hung from its chain over the rear-view mirror and reflected the sun. She was sitting next to him again, her blonde hair falling like a curtain over her face.

'Dad, you do know you've smoked twenty-one cigarettes in only a few hours?'

Lelle knocked the ash out of the window, blowing the smoke away from her.

'That many?'

Lina rolled her eyes as if she were calling on higher powers.

'Did you know every cigarette takes nine minutes off your life? So this evening you've shortened your life by one hundred and eighty-nine minutes.'

'You don't say,' said Lelle. 'But what have I got to live for, anyway?'

The reproach clouded her pale eyes as she looked at him.

'You've got to find me. You're the only one who can.'

Meja lay with her hands on her stomach and tried not to listen to the sounds. The hunger that growled under her fingers, and the others, the nauseating sounds that came up through the gaps in the floorboards. Silje's heavy panting and then his, the new man's. The squeaking of the bed and then the dog barking. She heard the man yell at it to go and lie down.

It was the middle of the night by now, but the sun was still shining strongly in the little triangle-shaped room. It fell in warm, gold shafts over the greying walls and revealed the pattern of capillaries under her closed eyelids. Meja couldn't sleep. She kneeled beside the low window and brushed away the cobwebs with her hand. There was only blue night sky and blue tinted forest as far as the eye could see. If she craned her neck she could see a slice of lake down there, black and still. Enticing, almost. She felt like a captured princess in a fairy tale, locked inside a tower surrounded by deep, dark forest, doomed to listen to the sex games of her wicked stepmother in the room below. Except Silje wasn't her stepmother, but her mother.

Neither of them had been to Norrland before. During those long hours on the train heading north the doubt had plagued them both. They had argued and cried and sat in lengthy periods of silence as the forest thickened outside the window and the distance between stations became longer and longer. Silje had sworn that this would be the last time they moved. The man she had met was called Torbjörn and he owned a house and some land in a village called Glimmersträsk. They had met online and talked forever on the phone. Meja had heard his monosyllabic Norrland way of speaking and seen pictures of a man with a moustache and thick neck, and eyes like slits when he smiled. In one photo he was holding an accordion and in another he was leaning over a hole in the ice, holding up a fish with red scales. Torbjörn was a *real man*, according to Silje. A man who knew how to survive in extreme conditions and who could look after them.

The train station where they eventually got out was nothing more than a hut among the pines, and when they tried the door it was locked. No one else had got out and they stood feeling helpless in the slipstream of the train as it pulled away and vanished among the trees. The ground vibrated for a long time under their feet. Silje lit a cigarette and started to drag the suitcase over the crumbling platform, while Meja stayed where she was, listening to the rustle of the trees and the whine of a million mosquitoes. She felt a scream begin to take shape in the pit of her stomach. She didn't want to follow Silje, but she didn't dare stay where she was. On the other side of the track the forest loomed, dark green verging on black, like a curtain against the illuminated sky, and a thousand shadows moved among the branches. She couldn't see any animals, but the feeling of being watched was as powerful as if she had been standing in the middle of a town square. There was no doubt they saw her, hundreds of pairs of eyes, taking her in.

Silje had already made her way to the neglected car park where a rusty Ford was waiting. A man with his face shadowed by a black cap was leaning against the bonnet. He stood up when he saw them coming, revealing the wad of snus tobacco in his mouth as he smiled. Torbjörn looked bigger in real life, more solid. But there was something awkward and inoffensive about the way he moved, as if he were unaware of his own size.

Silje dropped the case and clung to him like he was a lifebuoy in the middle of this sea of forest. Meja stood to one side and looked down at a crack in the asphalt where some dandelion leaves had found a way through. She could hear them kissing, hear the tongues rooting around.

'This is my daughter, Meja.'

Silje wiped her mouth and waved her hand in Meja's direction. Torbjörn studied her from under the peak of his cap, saying in his abrupt way that she was welcome here. She kept her eyes pinned to the ground to emphasize that this was happening against her will.

His car stank of wet dog, and a rough greying animal skin was spread out in the back. Yellow stuffing had started to bulge out of one of the seat backs. Meja sat on the very edge of the seat and breathed through her mouth. Silje had told her that Torbjörn was well-off, but judging from appearances so far that was an exaggeration. There was nothing but gloomy pine forest lining the road to his house, interspersed with areas of ground bare from felling. Small, isolated lakes shone like teardrops among the trees. By the time they reached Glimmersträsk there was a burning lump in Meja's throat. Torbjörn had his hand on Silje's thigh, lifting it only to point out things he thought were of interest: the small ICA supermarket, the school, pizzeria, post office and bank. He appeared immensely proud of it all. The houses themselves were large and scattered. The further they drove, the greater the distance between the buildings. Forest and fields and pastures lay in between.

From time to time there was the sound of a dog barking in the distance. In the front seat Silje's cheeks had turned red and shiny.

'Look, how lovely, Meja. Like something out of a story!'

Torbjörn told her not to get excited, that he lived on the

other side of the swamp. Meja wondered what that meant. The road in front of them narrowed and the forest crept closer, and a heavy silence filled the car. Meja found it hard to breathe as she watched the soaring pines flicker past.

Torbjörn's house stood alone and isolated in a forest clearing. The two-storey building might have been impressive once, but now its red paint was peeling and it gave the impression of sinking into the ground. A scraggy black dog stood at the end of its chain and barked at them when they got out of the car. Meja's legs felt unsteady as she looked around her.

'Here she is,' said Torbjörn, flinging his arm wide.

'So silent and peaceful,' Silje said, but the delight had gone from her voice.

Torbjörn carried in their bags and put them on the filthy black floor. It stank in there, too, of stale air and soot and ingrained fat. Shabby upholstery on furniture from a forgotten decade stared back at them. The brown-striped wallpaper was hung with animal horns and knives in curved sheaths, more knives than Meja had ever seen, and the place was full of dust and inescapable smells. Meja tried to catch Silje's eye, but failed. She had glued that smile to her face, the one that meant she was prepared to put up with almost anything, and that she was far from admitting she had made a mistake.

The moaning from the ground floor had stopped, leaving space for the birds. Never before had she heard such birdsong. It sounded hysterical, unsettling. The roof sloped and formed a triangle above her head, and hundreds of knotholes were watching her. Torbjörn had called it the triangle room when he stood on the stairs indicating where she was to sleep. Her own room on the upper floor. It was a long time since she'd had a room of her own. Mostly she'd had only her own two hands to stop the noises. The noises of Silje and her men – the loud sex and the arguments. Always the arguments. It didn't matter how far away she and Silje moved, the noises always caught up with them.

Lelle didn't notice the tiredness until he swerved off the road and the tyres rumbled under him. He lowered the window and slapped his face hard, making his cheek sting. The seat beside him was empty. Lina had gone. All this driving about at night – she really wouldn't have approved of that either. He put another cigarette in his mouth to keep himself awake. His cheeks were still glowing from the slap when he arrived home in Glimmersträsk. He pulled up by the bus stop and parked, looking disapprovingly at the innocuous-looking bus shelter that was embellished with marker-pen graffiti and bird droppings. It was early dawn and the first bus wasn't due for a while. Lelle climbed out of the car and walked over to the wooden bench covered in scratches. There were sweet wrappers and globs of chewing gum on the ground. The night sun shone in the puddles, but Lelle couldn't recall it raining. He trudged a couple of times around the shelter, then positioned himself as usual where Lina had stood when he had reversed the car. Then he leaned his shoulder against the dirty glass just as his daughter had done. Nonchalantly, almost, as if she wanted to emphasize that this was no big deal. Her first real summer job. Planting spruce trees up in Arjeplog, earning good money until the autumn term started. Nothing special about that.

It was his fault they were early. He was the one who was afraid she would miss the bus and arrive late for her first day at work. Lina hadn't complained, because the June morning warmed and was alive with the chorus of birds. All alone she had stood there at the bus shelter, with the sun reflected in his old aviator sunglasses she had nagged him to give her, even though they covered half her face. She had waved, possibly. Maybe even blown a kiss. She used to do that.

The young policeman had been wearing similar sunglasses. He pushed them up on to his head as he stepped into the hall and fixed his eyes on Lelle and Anette.

'Your daughter didn't get on the bus this morning.'

'That can't be right,' Lelle said. 'I dropped her off!'

The police officer shrugged and his pilot sunglasses slipped.

'Your daughter wasn't on the bus. We've spoken to the driver and the passengers. No one has seen her.'

They had looked at him knowingly, even then, the police officers and Anette. He could feel it. The reproach in their eyes pierced him and all his strength oozed away. After all, he was the last person to see her. He was the one who had given her the lift, the one who was responsible. They asked the same detestable questions over and over again, wanting to know the exact time he'd left her and how Lina was feeling that morning. Was she happy at home? Had they quarrelled?

In the end it got too much for him. He had grabbed one of the kitchen chairs and hurled it fiercely at one of the officers, a spineless bastard who raced out and called for backup. Lelle could still feel the cool, wooden floor against his cheek as they held him down and fastened the cuffs, still hear Anette crying as they took him away. But she hadn't come to his defence. Not then, not now. Their only child was missing and she had no one else to blame.

Lelle started the engine and reversed the car away from the solitary bus shelter. Three years had passed since she stood there, blowing him kisses. Three years, and he was still the last person to have seen her.

Meja would have stayed forever in that triangular room if it hadn't been for the hunger pangs. She could never escape the hunger, wherever they lived. She kept one hand on her

14

stomach to silence it as she pushed open the door. The stairs were so narrow she practically had to walk down them on tiptoe, and some of them creaked and groaned under her weight. It was useless trying to be quiet. There were no lights on in the empty kitchen. The door to Torbjörn's bedroom was shut. The dog lay stretched out beside it, watching her guardedly as she passed. When she opened the front door it got to its feet and slipped out between her legs before she had time to react. It lifted its leg by the lilac bush and then made a few circles in the long grass with its nose to the ground.

'Why did you let the dog out?'

Meja hadn't seen Silje sitting in a camping chair against the wall. She was smoking a cigarette and wearing a flannel shirt Meja didn't recognize. Her hair was like a lion's mane around her head and it was plain from her eyes that she hadn't slept.

'I didn't mean to, he slunk past.'

'It's a bitch,' Silje said. 'Her name's Jolly.'

'Jolly?'

'Uh-huh.'

The dog reacted when it heard its name and was soon back on the veranda. It lay down on the dark wood with its tongue out like a tie and gazed at them. Silje held out the packet of cigarettes and Meja noticed she had red marks round her neck.

'What have you got there?'

Silje gave a lopsided smile.

'Don't pretend to be stupid.'

Meja took a cigarette, although she would have preferred food. She hoped Silje would spare her the details and squinted towards the forest. She thought something was moving about among the trees. There was no chance she would ever set foot there. She drew on the cigarette and felt that suffocating feeling again, like being locked in and surrounded.

'Are we really going to live here?'

Silje dangled one leg over the armrest, showing her black underwear. She jiggled her foot impatiently.

'We've got to give it a chance.'

'Why?'

'Because we haven't got a choice.'

Silje wasn't looking at her now. The shrillness and euphoria in her voice had gone, her eyes were matt, but her voice was determined.

'Torbjörn's got money. He's got a house and land, a steady job. We can live well here without worrying about next month's rent.'

'A run-down shack in the middle of nowhere isn't what I call living well.'

Red streaks flared up on Silje's neck and she put a hand over her collarbone as if to control them.

'I can't cope any more,' she said. 'I'm sick and tired of being poor. I need a man to look after us and Torbjörn is willing to do just that.'

'You sure of that?'

'What?'

'That he's willing?'

Silje grinned.

'I'll make sure he's willing, don't you worry.'

Meja crushed the half-smoked cigarette under her shoe.

'Is there anything to eat?'

Silje inhaled deeply and smiled as if she meant it.

'There's more food in this old shack than you've seen in your entire life.'

∗

Lelle was woken by his mobile vibrating in his pocket. He was sitting in a sunlounger beside the lilac bushes and he could feel his body aching as he put the phone to his ear.

'Lelle? Were you asleep?'

'Shit, no,' Lelle lied. 'I'm out here working in the garden.'

'Are there any strawberries yet?'

Lelle threw a glance at the overgrown patch.

'No, but they're well on their way.'

Anette's breathing was loud on the other end, as if she were trying to compose herself. 'I've put the information on the Facebook page,' she said. 'About the memorial service on Sunday.'

'Memorial...?'

'For the third anniversary. You can't have forgotten.'

The chair creaked as he stood up. A wave of dizziness made him reach for the veranda railing.

'Of course I haven't bloody forgotten!'

'Thomas and I have bought candles and Mum's sewing group have had some T-shirts printed. We thought we'd start at the church and walk together to the bus shelter. Perhaps you can prepare something, in case you want to say a few words?'

'I don't need to prepare. Everything I want to say is here inside my head.'

Anette sounded weary as she replied: 'It would be good if we could show a united front, for Lina's sake.'

Lelle massaged his temples.

'Are we going to hold hands, too? You, me and Thomas?'

A deep sigh reverberated against his ear drum.

'I'll see you Sunday. And Lelle?'

'Yeah?'

'You're not out driving at night again, are you?'

He rolled his eyes up to the sky, where the sun was hiding behind the clouds.

'See you Sunday,' he said and rang off.

It was 11.30. He'd had four hours' sleep outside in the sun-lounger. That was more than he usually got. He scratched the back of his head and saw blood under his fingernails from the mosquito bites. Inside, he put on some coffee and rinsed his face in the sink. He dried himself with the fine linen tea towel and could almost hear Anette's protest break the silence. Tea towels were for china and glass, not unshaven human skin. And it was the police who should be looking for Lina, not her obsessed father. Anette had slapped him full in the face and screamed that it was his fault; he was the one who should have made sure she got on the bus; he was the one who had taken her daughter away from her. She had hit and clawed at him before he managed to grab her arms and hold her as hard as he could until her muscles relaxed and she crumpled under him. The day Lina disappeared was the last time they touched each other.

Anette looked for answers outside, turned to friends and psychologists and newspaper reporters. To Thomas, the occupational therapist who stood ready and waiting with open arms and a throbbing erection. A man who was willing both to listen and screw away the problem. Anette self-medicated with sleeping tablets and sedatives, which took the focus from her eyes and made her talk too much. She created a Facebook page dedicated to Lina's disappearance, organized meetings and gave interviews that made the hairs on his arms stand on end. The most intimate details of their life together. Details about Lina that he hadn't wanted anyone to know.

As for him, he spoke to nobody. He didn't have time. He had to find Lina. Searching was the only thing that mattered. The trips along the Silver Road began that summer. He lifted the lid of every rubbish bin and dug his way through skips and marshes and disused mines with his bare hands. He sat at home with his computer, reading long threads on internet forums where total strangers discussed their theories about Lina. A long, sickening tangle of suggestions: she had run away, been murdered, kidnapped, dismembered, lost her way, drowned, run over, forced into prostitution, and a whole catalogue of other nightmare scenarios he could hardly bear to think about, but made himself read anyway. On an almost daily basis he rang the police and yelled at them to do their job. He didn't eat or sleep. He would come home after long days and nights on the Silver Road with his clothes dirty and scratches on his face that he couldn't explain. Anette stopped asking. Maybe he was relieved she had left him for Thomas, so that he could devote himself to the search. The search was all he had.

Lelle took his coffee to the computer. Lina smiled at him from the screen saver. The air in the room was heavy and stale. The blinds were down and dust whirled in the light that seeped in between the slats. A half-dead pot plant drooped on the windowsill. Everywhere sorrowful reminders of his decline, of what he had become. He logged into Facebook and saw the post about Lina's memorial service. One hundred and three people had liked it and sixty-four had registered to attend. *Lina, we miss you and will never give up hope*, one of her friends had written, followed by exclamation marks and crying emojis. Fifty-three people liked this comment. Anette Gustafsson was one of them. Lelle wondered if she was ever going to change her surname. He went on clicking, past poems and photos and angry comments. *Someone knows what happened to Lina, time you stepped forward and told the truth!* Angry, red-cheeked emojis. Ninety-three likes. Twenty comments. He logged out. Facebook only made him depressed.

'Why can't you get involved on social media?' Anette used to nag him.

'Get involved in what? A virtual pity-party?'

'It actually concerns Lina.'

'I don't know whether you've noticed, but my focus is on *finding* Lina, not grieving for her.'

Lelle sipped his coffee and logged into Flashback. Nothing new had been added to the thread about Lina's disappearance. The last entry was dated December the previous year and was from a user with the name 'truth seeker'.

The police need to check out the HGV drivers using the Silver Road that morning. Everyone knows it's a serial killer's favourite job, just take a look at Canada and the USA. People disappear every day on the highways over there.

All one thousand and twenty-four contributors to the Flashback forum seemed touchingly unanimous in their belief that Lina had been picked up and abducted by someone driving a vehicle before the bus arrived. The same theory as the police, in other words. Lelle had phoned round couriers and haulage companies, asking which drivers had passed through the area at the time of Lina's disappearance. He'd even met some of them for coffee, searched their vehicles and given their names to the investigation team. But none of them seemed to be a suspect and no one had seen anything. The police didn't like his persistence. This was Norrland, not America. The Silver Road wasn't a state highway. No serial killers lurked there.

He got up and began rolling up the sleeves of his shirt. It reeked of smoke. He stood facing the map of northern Sweden and peered at the cluster of pins blooming across the interior. He took another pin from the desk drawer and punctured the map yet again, to mark the place where he had been the night before. He wouldn't give up until every millimetre was covered, until every strip of road and dead-end track and despoiled forest clearing was turned inside out.

He moved a blood-stained fingernail over the map, hunting for the next obscure track to investigate. He saved the coordinates on his mobile and reached for his keys. He had wasted enough time already.

*

Silje's eyes had that glint of mania, as if all of a sudden everything was possible, as if a run-down house in a forest was the answer to her prayers. Her voice rose a couple of octaves, becoming clear and melodious. Words tumbled out of her, as if there wasn't enough time to say everything that needed saying. Torbjörn seemed to be enjoying it. He sat in contented silence as Silje raved on, saying how happy she was with him and his family home, how she loved everything from the patterned vinyl flooring to the huge floral design of the curtains. Not to mention nature, the way they were surrounded by it. Just what she'd dreamed of all these years. She made a big show of getting out her easel and paintbrushes, swore she would do her best work, thanks to the exceptional light of the summer nights. It was here in the fresh air that her soul would find rest, it was here she could really be creative. This new ecstasy made her overly demonstrative. Her frenzied outbursts had to be emphasized with kisses and strokes and long hugs, all of which sent fear surging down Meja's backbone. This mania was always the beginning of some fresh new hell.

On the second evening the medication went in the bin. Half-empty blister packs stared up at Meja through the potato peelings and coffee grounds. Powerful tablets in harmless pastel shades. Small chemical miracles which could ward off both the insanity and the darkness, and keep a person alive.

'Why have you binned your medication?'

'Because I don't need it any longer.'

'Who says you don't need it? Have you talked to your doctor?'

'I don't have to talk to a doctor. I know myself that I don't need it any more. Out here I'm in my element. Now, finally, I can be who I really am. The darkness can't reach me here.'

'Can you hear yourself?'

Silje gave a peal of laughter.

'You worry too much. You should learn to relax, Meja.'

Through the long, luminous nights Meja lay staring at her backpack, which was still full of all her things. She could steal some money and get the train back south, stay with friends while she looked for work. Go to social services for help if it came to that. They knew what Silje was like, how destructive she could be. But she knew she wouldn't do it. She had to keep an eye on Silje, who had become full of platitudes.

I've never breathed such fresh air before!

Isn't this silence wonderful?

But Meja didn't experience any silence. Quite the reverse: the forest was full of sounds that drowned out everything else. Night time was worst, with the whining mosquitoes and twittering birds, and the wind rushing and howling, making the spruces curtsey. Not to mention the sounds from downstairs. Shrieking and panting and phony voices. Mostly Silje, naturally. Torbjörn was a more reserved kind of person. Not until they had gone quiet did Meja dare go down to the kitchen, when only the sound of Torbjörn's snoring echoed through the room, to drink up the dregs of Silje's wine. The wine was the only thing that helped against the light.

Lelle didn't sleep in the summertime. Not any more. He blamed the light, the sun that never set, that filtered through the black weave of the roller blind. He blamed the birds that chirped all night long and the solitary mosquitoes that buzzed above him as soon as his head hit the pillow. He blamed everything apart from what was really keeping him awake.

His neighbours were seated on their patio, laughing, their cutlery clinking. He ducked to avoid them seeing him as he walked towards the car. He rolled down the driveway as far as he could before turning on the engine, just so they wouldn't hear. But he was pretty sure the neighbours knew that he disappeared in the evenings, that they saw his Volvo glide over the gravel at the very quietest time of night. The whole village was quiet as he passed, houses silent and glowing in the midnight sun. He passed the school where he worked, although he'd been on leave so much in the past few years he could barely call himself a teacher any more. As he came closer to the bus shelter his pulse began to pound in his temples. There was a hopeful little devil inside him that expected to see Lina there, arms crossed, waiting, exactly as when he had left her. Three years had passed, but that damned bus shelter still haunted him.

The police had a theory that someone who was travelling the Silver Road had pulled up at the bus stop and abducted Lina. Either the person had offered her a lift or forced her into the vehicle. There were no witnesses to support that theory, but it was the only explanation. How otherwise could she have disappeared so fast and without trace? Lelle had dropped Lina off at about 5.50. The bus had arrived fifteen minutes later, according to the bus driver and the passengers, and by then Lina wasn't there. It was a fifteen-minute window. No more than that.

They had gone through the whole of Glimmersträsk with a fine-tooth comb. Everyone had joined in the search. They had dragged every lake and river and formed human chains that walked for miles in every direction. Dogs and helicopters and volunteers from the whole county had helped in the search. But no Lina. They never found her.

He refused to believe she was dead. For him she was just as much alive now as she was that morning at the bus stop. Sometimes he was asked questions by scavenging reporters or tactless strangers.

Do you think your daughter is alive?
Yes, I do.

Lelle had time to smoke three cigarettes during the thirty-minute drive up to Arvidsjaur. The petrol station was closing as he walked in. Kippen was mopping the floor, facing the other way. His bald head shone under the fluorescent lights. Lelle tiptoed to the coffee machine and filled a disposable mug to the brim.

'I was just wondering where you'd got to.'

Kippen leaned the heavy bulk of his body on the mop.

'I made fresh coffee especially for you.'

'Cheers,' said Lelle. 'How's it going?'

'You know, can't complain. You?'

'Still breathing.'

Kippen took the money for the cigarettes. He didn't charge Lelle for the coffee and handed him a day-old cinnamon bun in a bag. Lelle broke off a dry corner, which he dunked in his coffee as Kippen returned to his mopping.

'You're out driving tonight, I see.'

'Yep, I'm out driving.'

Kippen nodded and looked sad.

'The anniversary is almost here.'

Lelle looked down at the wet floor.

'Three years. Sometimes it feels like it was yesterday, and sometimes it feels like a whole lifetime has passed.'

'And what are the police doing?'

'I wish I bloody knew.'

'Surely they haven't given up?'

'Nothing much happens, but I'm keeping the pressure up.'

'That's good. I'm here if ever you need any help.'

Kippen dipped the mop into his bucket and wrung it out. Lelle balanced the bun on his coffee mug, shoved the cigarettes into his pocket and patted Kippen's shoulder with his free hand on the way out.

Kippen had been there from the beginning. In the days after the disappearance he had gone through the petrol station's CCTV footage, covering the hours before and afterwards to see if there was any trace of Lina. If she had been given a lift or been snatched by someone there was a possibility the person had stopped to fill up. They hadn't found anything, but Lelle had the feeling that Kippen never stopped checking, even after all this time. He was a rare friend, someone to treasure.

Lelle sat behind the wheel again and dipped the last piece of his bun in the coffee, studying the desolate pumps as he ate. He had calculated how far Lina's abductor could have driven if he'd had a full tank when she was taken from Glimmersträsk. Depending on the car, they could have driven further into the mountains, maybe all the way to the Norwegian border. If they'd stayed on the Silver Road, that is. It was also possible they had turned off on to smaller, rarely used roads without traffic or houses. They hadn't realized until the evening that she was missing, of course. That was more than twelve hours later. So the kidnapper or kidnappers had been given a good head start. He wiped his hands on his jeans, lit a cigarette and turned the key in the ignition. He left Arvidsjaur behind and was alone with the forest and the road, winding down the window so he could breathe the smell of the pines. If trees could speak, there would have been thousands of witnesses.

The Silver Road was the main artery that linked him to a wide network of smaller veins and capillaries that pumped through the countryside. There were overgrown timber tracks, snowmobile trails and well-worn paths that wound their way between abandoned villages and shrunken communities. There were rivers and lakes and sour little streams that flowed both above and below ground, steaming marshes that spread out like weeping sores, and bottomless, black-eyed tarns. Searching for a missing person in this kind of terrain was a lifetime's work.

There were vast distances between communities and between people travelling here. On the few occasions a car overtook him his heart would hammer, almost as if he expected to see Lina through the rear window. He stopped at remote lay-bys and lifted the lids of the rubbish bins, as so many times before, his heart in his mouth as if it were the first time. He would never get used to it. Just before Arjeplog he turned off on to one of the smaller capillaries, a road that was no more than two tyre tracks running between the firs. Lelle smoked without taking his hands off the wheel. Veils of mist drifted like spectres among the trees and he squinted through the faint light to get a better idea of where he was. The track was too narrow to turn around, and if he wanted to go back he would have to reverse. But these days Lelle wasn't the kind to reverse. The Volvo had to bump over the scrubby undergrowth, while ash flickered down the front of his shirt. He pressed on until he glimpsed the first building between the tree trunks, a disintegrating house up to the windowsills in brushwood. Where there had once been windows and doors there were now gaping holes. Further down the road another wooden skeleton was being consumed by the forest, and then another. Decaying homes where no one had lived for decades. Lelle stopped the car in the middle of this desolation and sat for a long while before filling his lungs with air and taking the Beretta from the glove compartment.

*

Meja had learned to keep out of the way of Silje's men. She avoided being alone in the same room as them, because she knew it was seldom only Silje they wanted. They liked to press up against her, slap her backside, give her breasts a small, sly nip. It had been like that even before she'd had any breasts to nip.

But Torbjörn would never touch her. She realized that the third evening after their arrival, when she came down to the kitchen and found him alone, slurping coffee from his saucer. She slipped past him as quietly as she could and went out to the veranda as if she hadn't seen him. Meja had only just lit a cigarette when he stuck out his head and asked her if she wanted a late snack. The skin on his face was creased and she realized he was older than she thought, considerably older than Silje. Old enough to be her grandfather.

He disappeared back inside and she could hear him whistling as he smoked. She kept her eyes on the forest, mainly to hold it back from her. She couldn't understand how anyone would live like this of their own free will. Disturbing rustlings came from under the spruce branches where the shadows danced. A smell of mould rose up from the veranda, and the dog's claws clicked against the greying wood when it came out and lay at her feet, so close she could feel its rough coat under her toes. From time to time it lifted its head and looked towards the forest, as if it had heard something deep inside there. Meja felt her heart contract every time. Finally, she couldn't stand it any longer. The stranger in the kitchen was better than all the things she couldn't see.

Torbjörn had laid the table with coffee cups, bread, cheese and ham.

'I don't have anything else.'

Meja hesitated in the doorway, glanced at the room where Silje was sleeping, and then at the food.

'Bread's fine.'

She dropped into the chair opposite Torbjörn, but kept her eyes on the scratched tabletop. A camera with a huge lens was resting there, its wide shoulder strap nearly touching the floor.

'Are you a photographer?' she asked.

'Oh, I just play around.'

Torbjörn poured out coffee that was so hot the steam hung like a veil between them.

'You do drink coffee, don't you?'

Meja nodded. She had been drinking coffee for as long as she could remember. It was either coffee or alcohol, but that wasn't something she'd admit to outsiders. The bread was white and soft and dissolved on her tongue, and she spread slice after slice, because now her hunger was so intense she couldn't stop herself. Torbjörn didn't appear to notice, because he was sitting facing the window, talking to her and pointing. He indicated the forest paths and the woodshed in the corner, where there were bikes and fishing rods and other things she might like to use.

'Everything here is at your disposal. This is your home now. I want you to know that.'

Meja heard this as she chewed and suddenly found it hard to swallow.

'I've never done any fishing.'

'That doesn't matter. I'll teach you in no time.'

She liked the way his face crinkled when he smiled and the stilted melody of his words. He looked at her only briefly, as if he didn't want to impose, and she felt comfortable enough to pour herself another cup, even though that meant leaning across the table for the coffee pot. Meja knew she shouldn't really be drinking coffee this late, but with the sun shining all night, she wouldn't be able to sleep anyway.

'Well, well, here you are, all cosy.'

Silje was standing in the doorway wearing only her panties, her sagging breasts deathly pale in the sharp light. Meja turned away.

'Come and sit down before this girl of yours eats the lot,' said Torbjörn.

'Oh, Meja will eat you out of house and home if you let her.'

Silje spoke in that kind of sharp voice that made Meja's stomach muscles contract. She shuffled across the floor and stood by the kitchen fan, clicked her lighter and dragged deeply on her cigarette, as if she were trying to draw the tobacco down into her toes. Meja saw her in the glass of the grandfather clock. The glint in her eyes, the ribs heaving under her skin. She wondered if she had withdrawal symptoms after stopping the medication, but didn't want to ask while Torbjörn could hear. He held up the coffee pot to Silje.

'I was just telling your daughter she can have a look around the place. There are bikes if she wants to go to the lake or into the village.'

'Hear that, Meja? Why don't you go outside and have a look?'

'Later, maybe.'

'You've got nothing else to do, have you? Cycle to the village and see if you can find some kids your own age.'

Silje crumpled up the cigarette packet, reached for her purse and took out a twenty-kronor note, which she handed to Meja.

'Buy yourself an ice cream or something.'

'Nothing's open this late,' Torbjörn said. 'But the kids tend to hang out in town anyway. They'd like it if someone new joined them.'

Meja got up unwillingly from the table and held out her hand for the money. Silje followed her on to the veranda.

'Torbjörn and me need some time alone, that's all,' she said. 'You can stay away for a few hours, can't you? Go and have some fun!'

She leaned over and brushed Meja's cheek with her lips, handed her two cigarettes and then shut the door. Meja was left staring at it. Behind her the trees rustled as if they were laughing at her. She could feel the old resentment stirring in her gut. This wasn't the first time Silje had pushed her out into the cold, but she vowed that it would be the last. Slowly she turned around, instantly aware that it was only her and the forest, exactly as she feared.

Abandoned plots were the places he visited, places where the houses had fallen into disrepair and the paths were overgrown. A Finnish clairvoyant from Kemi had told him this was where his daughter was. *Among dense forests and wooden ruins that people have left behind.* Lelle didn't have

34

much time for clairvoyants, but there was little else to go on. He had nothing against grasping at straws these days.

He was thankful for the light night as he crossed doorsteps, hunched through doorways with their doors hanging from rusted hinges, and wandered over old, protesting floors marked by damp and time. He ran his eyes over mouldy kitchen sofas, wood stoves, and lampshades painstakingly wrapped in cobwebs and dust. Some houses were empty and echoing, others had been left in a hurry, with fragile porcelain on the shelves and framed tapestries proclaiming words of wisdom:

Love me most when I deserve it least, because that's when I need it the most

It isn't how big the house is, it's how happy the home is.

Give thanks for all we're given every day.

Hardly surprising they had left when they had plastered the walls with these questionable nuggets of wisdom. He thought of all the apple-cheeked women sitting beside their paraffin lamps on winter nights, needle and thread in hand, and wondered if the simple messages had comforted them in their harsh existence or if the fault was with him for finding them smug.

The midnight sun filtered through the empty window frames and made patterns in the dust where mice and

hare droppings lay hidden. He made his way into bed-
rooms, looked under beds and inside wardrobes, moving
as quickly as he dared over the precarious floorboards. By
the time he came to the last house his heart had stopped
throbbing in his eardrums. It was almost over, soon he
would be sitting safely in the car again. The last house
looked in better shape, with glass in the windows and roof
tiles in place. The front door wouldn't give. He had to heave
with all his strength until it came free so unexpectedly he
was thrown to the ground. He swore loudly in the silence
and felt the damp on his jeans and a burning pain at the
base of his spine when he stood up. He threw a backward
glance as if to ensure no one was standing out there in the
emptiness, laughing at him.

His feet were scarcely over the doorstep before the
stench hit him. The suffocating stench of death and decay.
He recoiled so violently that he came close to falling over
again. He put a hand on the firearm in his waistband and
swiftly deactivated the safety device. Over his shoulder
he saw his car fifty metres away, half-hidden by foliage.
He considered running back and climbing in behind the
wheel, forgetting the whole thing. Forgetting that damned
clairvoyant from Kemi and the darkness lurking in forgotten, deserted homes. But he didn't run. Instead, he
covered his face with his free hand and stepped through
the doorway with his weapon in front of him. He could see
the air shimmering. Inside, the stench was unbearable and

the nausea welled up in his throat as he fumbled through the gloom. He was met by human faces smiling down at him from the walls, a collection of framed black and white photographs nailed to the water-damaged wallpaper. Small blonde children with gappy smiles, a woman in a black dress with equally black eyes. Lelle turned away and squinted through the rays of dust. There was a sooty fireplace, some spindly, three-legged chairs and a kitchen table with a flowery plastic cloth. Beneath the table was a bulging shape.

It was a vole. Dead and bloated, with its tail wrapped around its body. Lelle lowered his weapon and walked back out, past the smiling faces and through the front door. He ran to the car and stood there with his hands on his knees, breathing in lungfuls of forest air. The stink of decay had etched itself into his nostrils. He could still smell it as he got behind the wheel and headed back to the road. As if it came from inside him.

Meja was only wearing sandals on her feet and fir cones and roots dug into the thin soles. It was the crying that had driven her in among the trees, so Silje wouldn't see. She ran the first bit, but then stopped, battling with her breathing. It wouldn't calm down. The trees stirred above and around her, waving and rustling and brushing her arms as if they wanted to grab hold of her. The dog had come with her, but kept veering off and disappearing into the undergrowth where she couldn't see it. She wished she had a lead so she could keep it close to her. Her heart pounded in her ears, but she didn't know what she was afraid of, whether it was the shadows between the trees or the wild animals, or perhaps only the isolation. She had never been in a forest quite like this. She could scream without running the risk of anybody hearing her. It was clear the trees were ancient, that they had been left to grow undisturbed. The pines had thick grey trunks covered in wispy lichen like bearskin. When she looked up at the canopy she felt dizzyingly small. It was a place to disappear in.

She reached the lake that up here was called a swamp and noticed it was much bigger up close than it had looked from Torbjörn's car. She walked some of the way along the water's edge, where the ground was marshy and small, shrunken birches hung their heads and scraped the surface with their branches. The dog emerged from the bushes and had a drink from the lake. Meja sat on a rock, pulled off her sandals and stuck her feet into the water, but quickly drew them up again. When she put her feet on the rock the black lichen that covered it made her think of dried blood. The dog set off again and she hurried to follow it. An overgrown path clung to the edge of the lake and only stopped for fallen trees and small, trickling streams. She started to feel hungry and wondered how much time had passed, whether she could go home again without being in the way. She lit one of the cigarettes she'd brought with her and inhaled the smoke to stave off her hunger.

Meja was standing there, smoking, when she heard the voices. The dog had run on ahead and was now barking a warning. She set off again, walking faster, and through the branches saw people sitting beside the lake. They had made a fire and a thin plume of smoke was curling skywards. She heard from the exchange of laughter that they were male. They greeted the dog affectionately and then turned to gaze at her. Her cigarette slipped to the ground, but Meja bent down, picked it up and took a quick puff as if nothing had happened. She could feel her cheeks were red and burning. The men were young, with spotty faces and sharp Adam's apples that bobbed up and down when they swallowed. One of them got to his feet and walked over to her.

He had long, restless arms and a face she couldn't read. All she saw were his eyes, staring down at her. He came so close that she shrank back. He held out his hand as if he was going to shake hers, but went for the cigarette instead, snatching it from her fingers. He threw it into the water without taking his eyes off her.

'What the hell are you doing?'

'Nice girls like you shouldn't smoke.'

'Says who?'

'Says me.'

Sounds of laughter came from over by the fire.

'And who are you?'

There was a mischievous gleam in his pale eyes and Meja saw he was joking with her.

'My name's Carl-Johan.'

He dried his hand on his jeans and held it out to her. The skin was rough and covered in callouses.

'Meja,' she said.

He nodded over his shoulder.

'And that's Pär and Göran. They're not as bad as they look.'

The two young men nodded at her from the fire, suddenly embarrassed. All three had dark blond hair and were dressed in matching T-shirts and jeans.

'Are you brothers?' she asked.

'Everyone thinks I'm the oldest,' Carl-Johan said. 'But actually, it's the opposite.' He pulled a knife from the sheath on his belt and pointed the blade at the fire. 'Come and sit down,' he said. 'We're about ready to start cooking.'

Meja hesitated by the fire. The dog had already flopped down beside the young men and only had eyes for the fish they were holding. She glanced at the path leading back to Torbjörn's house. The sun was warm on the moss and suddenly the forest didn't feel so threatening.

*

North of Abborrträsk he turned off on to yet another forest road, despite Lina's protests.

'That's enough for tonight.'

'Just one more.'

The gravel pattered against the underbelly of the car and gleaming wetlands spread out on either side. He could see steam rising from the moss as if the earth itself were breathing underneath. A few kilometres in, he came to a tarn black with algae and with two decaying houses on opposite banks.

With the cigarette in his mouth and holding his gun in both hands, muzzle pointing down, he walked among wet spruce branches that left dark patches on his jeans. He didn't know why he was armed, because he couldn't imagine actually shooting anyone. But he didn't want to be completely vulnerable, either.

The first of the two houses had that familiar smell of rotten wood and desolation. Cobwebs hung in long threads from wall to wall and brushed his hair as he walked through rooms thick with dust. In the sleeping alcove he knelt down and peered under the narrow bunk, but all he found was a green plastic fishing tackle box filled with hooks and shimmering baits. In the living room he opened the doors of the wood stove and poked around among the charred remains of greying wood. A brown mottled rag rug lay like a strip of dirt across the floor to the empty log basket. On the worn material he saw muddy footprints. Lelle bent down and prodded the mud, feeling it was cold and wet. Someone had been here recently and dragged in fresh mud.

Lelle squatted down with his back to the stove and his

weapon raised. He flashed a look at the streaky window panes and the fir trees swaying outside. He stayed like that until his heart rate slowed and his thoughts cleared. Other people were moving about in these forests. Other people were seeking abandoned houses for warmth or research, or to shelter from the weather. That was all.

He made his way outside and walked round the tarn, where radiant white waterlilies appeared to hover on the darkened surface. Lelle wondered how deep the water was, if the tarn was as bottomless as it looked. If it could be dragged. He flicked his cigarette butt into the water and immediately regretted being there. The surrounding ground was soft and boggy and just made for someone to sink into. The whine of the mosquitoes seemed to grow louder and he lit another cigarette to keep them away. The second house was in better condition. The external walls still bore traces of yellow paint and the front door opened without protest. But that was as far as he got before he felt the muzzle of a rifle on his neck.

He raised his hands in the air and stood perfectly still as the room pulsated around him. He could hear his own heart and the breathing of the man behind him.

'Who are you?' the man said, and his voice was no more than a whisper.

'My name is Lennart Gustafsson. Please, don't shoot.'

The muzzle pressed into his neck and Lelle's mouth filled with bile. The pistol fell from his hand to the ground.

He heard the man reach out his foot and kick it away. The muzzle dug harder into his neck, so hard he was close to falling over. Lelle shut his eyes and saw Lina, her beautiful blue eyes blinking at him. The reproach in her voice. *What did I tell you?*

✳

They gutted the fish and stretched the flesh over sticks across the fire. The dark scales gleamed in the light. The entrails had been thrown behind a rock to the delight of the dog. Bloody hands were washed clean in the lake. Meja had never eaten barbecued perch before and was amazed at the way the fish crumbled like bread in her hands and melted like butter on her tongue. The three guys didn't say much, but watched her all the more. Their staring made her embarrassed. She became aware of every movement, of her own hands pushing her hair back, not knowing what to do with them.

Every time she met Carl-Johan's eyes he smiled. He had lovely teeth and a dimple in his chin. It was hard to eat while he was watching. Hard to do anything at all.

It was clear he was the leader. He spoke on their behalf, while they offered backup in the form of nods, laughter or swaggering as required. He was taller than the other two, but not as muscular. His facial features were as smooth and inoffensive as a boy's. He insisted she ate another perch and said she sounded like she came from Stockholm.

'I've lived all over the place,' said Meja, feeling worldly. 'I haven't got a dialect in particular.'

'How did you end up here, in Glimmersträsk of all places?'

'Mum wanted to move here.'

'Why?'

'She met a guy online. He's got a house up here. And Mum's always dreamed about it. You know, a simple life in the woods.'

Meja felt the blood rush to her cheeks. She hated talking about Silje. But out of the corner of her eye she saw the way Carl-Johan was beaming at her, all eyes and teeth.

'Sounds like you've got a wise mother.'

'You think so?'

'Sure. Everyone should be looking for a simpler life, the way the world is today.'

He sat close, so close their shoulders and knees were brushing. She felt intensely small beside him. But his voice was gentle, almost melodious. It filled her with a kind of intoxication. And he saw her. He really saw her.

'Are you always out and about in the middle of the night?'

'This is when the fish bites.'

Carl-Johan nodded towards the swamp, where the light sky was mirrored in the surface of the water.

'How about you? What are you doing out this late?'

'I couldn't sleep.'

'You can sleep when you're dead. Let's swim!'

Carl-Johan pulled off his T-shirt, revealing hard, sun-tanned skin.

As if on command the others pulled off their clothes and followed him. Only Meja was left by the fire. But Carl-Johan stood in the water, coaxing in that sing-song voice of his, until she relented. She kept her T-shirt on and waded into the ice-cold water. She dipped her shoulders under the surface even though it was so cold she thought her heart would stop. Afterwards they dried themselves on a couple of rocks overhanging the lake, and the dog stayed close to Carl-Johan as if it also felt he was the one in charge. She thought of something Silje had said when they lived with a farmer in Laholm: *A man who has a way with animals is a man you can trust.*

'Do you live in the village?' she asked, as they lay, drying.

'No, not in Glimmersträsk. We're from Svartliden.'

'Where's that?'

'About ten kilometres away.'

Göran, the oldest brother, had a face covered in acne which his fingers couldn't leave alone. Meja tried not to look.

'The whole country's falling apart,' he said. 'Svartliden is our haven.'

'Haven from what?'

'From everything.'

The words sounded profound in the silence. The middle brother, Pär, had put a cap over his eyes and said nothing.

Meja looked sideways at Carl-Johan and saw that he was smiling.

'You'll have to come and visit and see for yourself. Bring your mum as well. If it's the simple life you're after, you'll love Svartliden.'

Meja fingered the last of the cigarettes Silje had given her. She longed to light it, but didn't.

'You're weird,' she said. 'Totally weird.'

They laughed at that.

Carl-Johan insisted on going back with her through the forest and she was grateful not to be alone with the trees. The path was narrow and they had to walk in single file, and she could feel his eyes burning on her neck as he moved behind her. The dog went first, whipping the undergrowth with its tail. Meja walked in the middle and searched for words. Guys didn't usually like her, not really. She was too quiet and unsure. They wanted girls who jeered at them and laughed loudly at their jokes. She wasn't good at either the banter or the screeching laughter. It only sounded false when she tried. She could see it in their eyes. It didn't work.

But Carl-Johan didn't joke. He merely walked behind her, talking about the animals they had on the farm. Cows, goats, dogs. *We've got everything at Svartliden*, he said, several times, in a voice vibrating with pride. When she turned around and looked at him there was a seriousness in his eyes that made him look older than he was. She felt a tingling down her spine and she was grateful for the light that made her squint. He was happy in his own skin, that was clear. So unlike her.

She thought of Silje, how she walked around half-naked and everything that poured out of her mouth when she had been drinking. Meja felt her cheeks growing hot with shame, and she stopped at the edge of the trees, where they could see only the roof and the window of the little triangular room. As much as she wanted to, she couldn't invite him in, not with Silje there.

'My mum's ill. I don't think you should come in with me.'

He stood close and she could smell the lake water and the fish blood that had dried in black patches on his T-shirt. He had eyelashes, she could see that now. It's just that they were so pale they hardly showed. She felt a fluttering in her stomach when he looked down at her, and she could see the thin skin over his collarbone pulsating with every heartbeat.

'See you later,' he said.

She had to hold the dog's collar to stop it following him. It whined plaintively as he disappeared between the trees, and it made her want to cry too.

'Turn around so I can see you.'

Lelle held his breath. Slowly, very slowly, he rotated his body until the muzzle of the rifle was pointing at his midriff. The man behind the weapon took shape among the shadows. His hair hung in matted strands over his shoulders and was tangled up in a beard that reached halfway down his chest. He had a dirty face and piercing eyes. His clothes hung from his body and were fraying at the seams, and a long rip in his T-shirt revealed the pale skin underneath. He gave off an acrid smell of forest and sweat and woodsmoke. Without taking his eyes off Lelle, he lowered the rifle.

'What are you doing here?'

'I'm sorry,' said Lelle. 'I didn't know anyone lived here. I'm looking for my daughter.'

'Your *daughter*?' said the man, as if the word was unrecognizable to him.

'Yes.'

Lelle dropped his left hand and dug out Lina's photo from the inside pocket of his jacket. He held it up to the man's face.

'She's called Lina and she's nearly twenty. She's been missing for three years.'

The dishevelled man leaned closer and took his time studying the picture. Lelle's outstretched arm shook nervously between them. He was keeping his eyes on the man's rifle, which was still hanging under his arm.

'I haven't seen her,' the man said, eventually. 'Did she disappear out here?'

'She disappeared from a bus stop in Glimmersträsk.'

'We're a long way from Glimmersträsk.'

'I know, but my search has brought me here.'

The whites of the man's eyes gleamed in the dim light.

'Well, she's not here, I can tell you that much.'

Lelle slipped the photograph of Lina back into his pocket.

It might have been the tension, but he immediately felt his eyes well up and he cleared his throat to hold back the tears.

'I'm sorry for intruding. I didn't think this place was inhabited.'

He made for the door and the watery light, but was barely through the doorway when he heard the gruff voice call out: 'You'll stay for coffee?'

Lelle sat down on a shaky wooden chair, while the bearded man put down the rifle and started measuring out the coffee with dirt-ingrained hands. The windows were covered with dark canvas, but a solitary oil lamp on the table cast a faint light over the pine-panelled walls. From the way he moved and the muscles under his torn T-shirt, Lelle could see that the man was younger than he looked.

'You'll have to forgive me for pointing that thing at you,' the man said. 'But you scared me.'

Lelle had retrieved his gun from the floor and was keeping it within reach.

'I thought the house was empty,' he said. 'Can I ask what your name is?'

'Patrik,' said the man, after some hesitation. 'But I'm called Pat.'

'Do you live out here?'

'Sometimes. When I'm passing.'

'Not many people pass by here.'

Pat smiled and his teeth shone in the darkness.

He poured coffee into two tin mugs and handed one of them to Lelle. The liquid was as thick as tar, but smelled wonderful in the musty air.

'How did you find your way here?'

'Pure chance. I've been driving up and down the Silver Road for three years, searching for every damn trail and forest track.'

'Looking for your daughter?'

Lelle nodded.

'Aren't the cops helping you?'

Lelle pulled out a packet of cigarettes, put one in his mouth and offered one to Pat.

'The cops are crap.'

Pat nodded as if he understood. They lit their cigarettes and allowed the coffee and tobacco to fill the silence. Lelle looked at the young man and watched him draw the smoke deep into his lungs, holding it there like hash. The skin around his nostrils was red raw and twitched from time to time, but apart from that he appeared to have calmed down.

'So what are you doing out here?'

Pat looked up and stared at him through the coils of smoke.

'I guess I'm also looking for someone.'

'Who are you looking for?'

Pat stood up and walked into an adjacent room. Lelle kept his eyes on the rifle propped up against the wall. Pat returned with a battered photograph and handed it to Lelle. It pictured a young man with a crew cut and a serious expression, dressed in desert camouflage and with an automatic weapon strung across his chest. He was sitting in front of a drab, grey building with gaping window frames and walls covered in bullet holes.

'This was me. Before the war screwed me up.'

Lelle took a closer look, comparing the bearded man in front of him with the scrubbed, clean-shaven youth in the photograph. There was no likeness as far as he could see, apart from the eyes, perhaps.

'The war? What war?'

'Afghanistan.' Pat grimaced slightly when he said it.

'So you were with the UN peacekeeping force?'

Pat nodded.

'No shit.' Lelle leaned back in the chair and drank his coffee, trying not to swallow the grounds. A golden strip of sunlight leaked in around the black canvas and he could hear the birds singing outside as a reminder that there was still joyfulness in the world. Pat had taken out his hunting knife and was cleaning his nails with it. He peered at Lelle over the handle.

'Aren't you going to ask me if I killed anyone over there?'

'Swedish UN troops don't normally get involved in the fighting, do they?'

Pat gave a hollow laugh that quickly turned into a cough.

'That's what you think. The truth is more sordid than that.'

He held up seven fingers. The palms of his hands were chafed and flaking.

'Seven people, that's how many I've killed. And I've seen many more die.' Pat tapped the knife against the side of his forehead. 'Their screams never leave you. I hear it all the time.'

Lelle loosened the neck of his shirt. It was stuffy in the confined room.

'It sounds hideous.'

'It's worst when they don't die straight away. If their legs are blown off, but they're still alive. So you go over and put an end to them at close range. Eye to eye. That's when it seems real. When you see the light go out, the life run out of them.'

He pointed the knife blade at Lelle.

'There's something about death that gets under your skin and destroys you from the inside. Nobody warns you about it before you go. Nobody explains what happens to you once you've seen death first-hand, when you've stared it in the face. The way it kind of gets its claws into you. Becomes part of you.'

'Would you have stayed at home if you'd known?'

Pat looked down. The skin on his face had a life of its own, jerking and grimacing.

'I'm a nosy bastard,' he said at last. 'And we all have to learn about death sooner or later. There's no escaping it.'

Lelle pushed his mug away. The lack of air in the room was making him feel tired. He simply couldn't talk about war and death, not when he was caught up in his own stuff. His legs hurt as he stood up.

'Thanks for the coffee. I'd better be going.'

'There are others like me out here in the forests. Other people who've lost themselves and can't cope with the world any more. Maybe your daughter is one of us. Maybe she's just off-grid for a while.'

'Lina likes the world.'

'Do you think someone's hurt her?'

'She wouldn't leave us of her own free will, I know that.'

Pat went with Lelle to the front door, as if he wasn't quite ready to let him go.

'I'll keep an eye out for your daughter.'

'Thanks, I appreciate that.'

'In my experience it's always the smiling people you've got to watch.'

'What do you mean?'

'People who smile for no reason, fooling people with their grins. They're the ones who are evil.'

'I'll bear that in mind.'

Lelle pushed open the door and Pat lifted a hand to shield his face from the sun.

'I'd help you look,' he said. 'But I can't deal with the light.'

'I understand. It saps your energy.'

They shook hands and stood in silence, looking at each other with some kind of understanding until the door swung shut again. Outside the tarn lay like a pool of black oil between the houses and Lelle moved as fast as he could over the boggy ground.

*

At the weekend they drank, both of them. Torbjörn grew loud and red-faced, and started talking about the mine that had closed down and robbed him of his career. Silje fried pork chops and made a potato gratin, which she served on Torbjörn's mother's best china.

Torbjörn ate, getting the food stuck in his moustache, while Silje sat at the opposite end of the table, chain-smoking. She had black rings under her eyes and complained that she always lost her appetite when it was this hot. There were always new excuses. Her thin shoulders made Meja think of baby birds. Her bra straps kept slipping down.

'You ought to eat. You look like a skeleton.'

'Not everyone is as greedy as you, Meja.'

Silje struggled with the truth. The loss of appetite was relatively recent and at first she had blamed the medication, saying it made her feel as if the food was choking her.

But she wasn't taking the drugs any longer. Now she just got angry when Meja pointed out that you couldn't live on red wine.

Meja took herself up to her room. She lay on the narrow bed, staring up at the pointed roof where the beams met. A fragile spider's web balanced across the middle beam and she could see the shrivelled mosquitoes and flies that had met their fate there. Although they were only disgusting little bugs it brought tears to her eyes.

Soon the sound of Silje's moaning made its way up from the ground floor, low at first, then getting shriller. Torbjörn roared and the furniture scraped against the wooden floor. It sounded like he was trying to murder her. Meja pressed her hands to her ears and looked at the treetops swaying outside. In her loneliness the other voices forced their way into her head. The mocking ones.

Is it true your mum gets paid for it?

You know what that's all about, don't you?

Her mobile was dark and silent on the bedside table. No one had called since she stepped on the train to Norrland. There was no one in the city she had just left who missed her, no one who wondered where she had gone. Even though she was the one to keep them in cigs and tablets at the weekend. She thought they would miss the drugs at least, even if they didn't miss her.

She was asleep when the first thud came. She flew out of bed and looked at the door, at the chair back wedged under the handle, so no one could come creeping in while she was asleep. Even though Torbjörn hadn't tried anything, it was a precaution she always took. With the second thud she realized the sound wasn't coming from the door but from the window. She crouched by the sill and peered out into the light night, catching sight of a shadow moving by the veranda. The dog's chain rattled as it shook itself and she watched as the dark shape bent down and patted and stroked. When it turned its face up to hers she could see it was Carl-Johan.

She opened the window and leaned out.

'What are you doing?'

'I thought I'd go swimming in the lake. You coming?'

'Now?' she whispered. 'In the middle of the night?'

'No one can sleep when it's this light anyway.'

Meja craned her neck towards the door, listening out for Torbjörn and Silje, but all she could hear were the sighs of the old house. Her mobile showed 1.30. She smiled down at Carl-Johan.

'Give me ten minutes, and don't let anyone see you!'

She brushed her teeth and rolled on some deodorant. She left her hair as it was, hanging loose, and rubbed some gloss over her lips. There was no time for anything else. Out of habit she put a packet of cigarettes in her pocket, but immediately changed her mind. Carl-Johan didn't like girls who smoked. Quickly she threw the packet into the waste-paper basket, hiding it under the sweet wrappers.

Then she tiptoed down the stairs, avoiding the third step from the bottom that wailed like a cat if it was trodden on. Torbjörn was sitting on the sofa, asleep, with his head at an odd angle. He was naked and his limp penis protruded from the shadows of the pubic hair under his distended belly. Meja turned her head away and carried on towards the front door. From the bathroom off the hall came the sound of retching, a sound that made her throat constrict. Meja put her feet into her Converse, but that was as far as she got. Silje drank too much, swallowed tablets and threw up, that was nothing new, but that shitty feeling of anxiety was still there. Because what if something happened? She stood rooted to the spot, clenching the door handle, hesitating until the retching stopped. Then she opened the door and ran.

Outside the mist had drifted out of the forest and settled like a trail of smoke over the meadow.

Carl-Johan was standing under cover at the fringe of the forest. He gave off a pungent smell of barns and livestock when he held her close.

'Where are your brothers?'

'They had to stay home.'

Carl-Johan took her hand and led her in among the pines, plaiting his fingers in hers in a way that felt completely natural. The dog whined mournfully after them as they vanished among the trees. Their feet squelched and the dew painted dark streaks on their jeans, and all they could see of the path was a narrow strip before it was swallowed up in the mist. Meja looked at the back of his neck where his hair curled and felt a tingling in the pit of her stomach, as if something inside her had woken from its slumber. Something new and exciting.

The mist hung over the lake and swirled ghost-like among the trees, which were blue in the early morning light. Carl-Johan led her to a campfire, dropped her hand and started to bring life back to the embers. He broke off twigs and made a tower of logs, then took a lighter from his pocket and set light to some kindling, which he used to feed the fire. He blew gently until the flames took hold and soon it was burning vigorously. His face became beautiful in the flickering shadows, defined and alive. Meja looked into the fire and felt every muscle tense up when he came and stood beside her. The nervousness made her desperate for a smoke. She didn't know what to do with her hands, so she held them towards the fire and tried to think of something to say. She could hear the water lapping on pebbles.

'Tell me something about yourself,' Carl-Johan suddenly asked.

'What do you want me to tell you?'

'A secret. Something you've never told anyone else.'

Meja looked at him sideways. The flames were dancing in his eyes. She hesitated, thinking the lapping water sounded like it was mocking her. She looked back at the fire and stared at it for a while before she spoke.

'I was only five years old the first time I got drunk.'

'You're joking, right?'

'No. Silje used to call it grown-up juice. I nagged and nagged to try some, but she said only adults were allowed to drink it. Children would die immediately if they touched a single drop.' Meja snorted. 'It only made me more curious. And one evening, when she'd fallen asleep on the sofa, I decided to try it. And I must have liked it, because next morning I woke up in hospital. They'd pumped out my stomach. I nearly died.'

Carl-Johan looked horrified. 'And you were only five?'

'According to the medical records. According to Silje I was older, but she only remembers what she wants to remember.'

The fire burned her cheeks and Meja turned away, regretting what she had just said. She realized it was scarcely the kind of secret he had expected. The familiar lump of shame grew in her throat and it hurt her to swallow. Carl-Johan stretched out an arm and drew her towards him, resting his cheek on her forehead.

'I'm glad you survived, so I had the chance to meet you.'

His chin felt rough against her skin. An unexpected feeling of joy welled up inside her. She could feel the vibrations in his chest as he went on: 'Do you want to hear one of my secrets?'

She nodded.

'Promise not to laugh?'

'I promise.'

'I've never been drunk in my entire life. Never had one drink, not a drop.'

'What? Honestly?'

'Hundred per cent.'

Meja turned her head and looked up at him.

'You think I'm a complete nerd now, don't you?' he said.

'I think it's brave, going your own way.'

The sun had begun to climb above the forest and it was dazzling them, but she could see he was smiling.

*

Lelle popped the cork of the Laphroaig, raised the bottle to his nose and deeply inhaled the whisky fumes. Woodsmoke and salty sea water burned his sinuses. The thirst sat at the back of his throat and itched, and the longing to dilute his blood with the alcohol was so overwhelming that it made him start trembling. If only he could blot out all thoughts and lose himself in sleep for a few hours. Sink down on the sofa, numb. That's what the craving was all about. But the sharp evening sunlight taunted him through the slats of the blind and Lina was in the doorway. A little Lina in pyjamas and tousled hair, with her one-eyed teddy under her arm and her own eyes gleaming like forest tarns. The little child who would never see him drinking. That was the promise he made when she was born. That she would have a proper childhood.

His fingers were like aspen leaves as he pushed the cork back, and the cold sweat in his armpits made him shiver as he made his way to the hall. Outside, summer was taking its first genuine deep breaths. Everything was blooming, birds were trilling and the smell of barbecues and newly mown lawns hit him like a slap in the face. He never believed he would hate summer, but now all it did was remind him of the happiness that no longer existed.

He climbed into the car, smoked his cigarette with the windows closed and concentrated on not looking at his neighbours. He had become skilled at it as the years passed, steeling himself against all the people playing happy families around him. When he reached Storgatan he swung left, towards the village. The blood began humming inside his head and he wished he'd taken a shot of whisky. For his nerves.

It was the men closest to her who were the most dangerous. Lelle had studied the statistics. If someone had harmed Lina, then it was most likely a man she knew, perhaps even loved. A boyfriend.

Delicate birches with their new leaves swayed after him as he turned into a smaller gravel road. There at the end a typical Västerbotten house sat imposingly on a grassy slope. The red exterior glowed in the sun and the windows were blazing mirrors. Lelle parked the car by the avenue of birch trees, stubbed out his cigarette and lit another. He wound down the window and stayed in the car, leaving the motor running just in case they got it into their heads to throw something at him. It had happened before. He took his binoculars from the glove compartment and scanned the front facade. It was bathed in sunlight, which protected it from anyone trying to look in. A set of garden furniture was folded against the wall and recently planted flowers nodded from their large clay pots. There was nothing particular about the place, but even so he felt a growing anger in his chest. For some people it was easy to move on, to pretend nothing had happened.

There was the sudden groan of a hinge and a figure appeared on the steps. A tall, thin man with a cap on his head and ribs clearly visible through his T-shirt. He headed idly towards Lelle, moving unsteadily across the grass like a young calf. A can of cheap beer glinted in his right hand. Lelle felt his anger turn to bile in his throat. His hand dropped from the wheel and his fingers unconsciously tightened into a fist.

The young man stopped ten metres away and threw his arms wide in a challenging gesture. He almost tripped over his own feet, but he stayed upright and looked at Lelle from under his hooded lids. The corners of his mouth drooped. It looked as if he was going to say something, but instead he raised the empty hand, made a pistol with two fingers and aimed it at Lelle. He shut one eye and jerked his fingers. Then he moved the fingers to his mouth and blew on them without taking his sleepy eyes off Lelle.

Lelle glanced at the glove compartment, where he kept the pistol. He visualized himself stretching over for it and answering the fake shot with a real one: a bullet right through the forehead. Then it would all be over. But he heard Lina's protests beside him and instead put the car into reverse. He revved hard and skidded round, leaving circular tyre marks behind him and sending gravel flying between the birches, until the man faded in the dust.

In the passenger seat Lina had buried her face in her hands.

Mikael would never hurt me, Dad.

You can see for yourself how he behaves.

He's angry because you won't stop blaming him. You of all people ought to know what that feels like.

Lina had met Mikael Varg the year before she disappeared. He was the son of one of the wealthiest men in the village. His parents were well-liked and respected, a couple of powerhouses who belonged to various local organizations and the hunting team, and who invested generously in all kinds of projects that could keep the village alive. Unfortunately, their son was a spoiled brat who had terrorized the community since he was a youngster. At first it was innocent mischief, but as time went on he got involved in more serious trouble, such as theft and illegal driving. Even so, Anette had been charmed by him during the year he and Lina had been together. Mikael Varg had the gift of the gab and stood to inherit some valuable property. A mother-in-law's dream, in other words. Anette had dismissed his behaviour as youthful stupidity, the kind he would grow out of in time.

The police had interviewed him after Lina's disappearance and Varg insisted that he 'was at home, sleeping' on the morning Lina was supposed to be getting the bus. Naturally his parents backed up his statement, although they were hardly likely to have been standing guard over the boy's bed in the early morning hours. That alibi satisfied the police, especially when they had nothing else to go on. No sign of a crime. No body.

But that wasn't good enough for Lelle. He would keep an eye on Mikael until the day Lina came back to him. Several times a week he drove to that godawful avenue of birches just to show the lad that he was still watching him, even if all the others were looking in a different direction. It didn't bother him in the least that the Varg family had long since grown tired of him dogging their footsteps. They could threaten and shout and aim fake shots at him all they liked. He didn't care about neighbourliness and community spirit these days. All he wanted was the truth.

The following night they collected her by car. Meja was in her bed, dressed and ready, when the first stone hit the window. The TV was flickering in the sitting room, but the door to Silje and Torbjörn's room was closed, and his snoring rasped like sandpaper across the walls.

Outside in the damp night Carl-Johan crouched, partly hidden behind Torbjörn's old car. She felt the tingling in her stomach again when she saw him. He took her hand and pointed along the gravel road.

'My brother's waiting round the corner.'

If she was disappointed not to have him to herself, she made sure not to show it. Instead of taking the path down to the lake, they sprinted along the gravel that led to the village. Parked beside the ditch was a red Volvo 240 with its fog lights on. Göran was behind the wheel. His hood was pulled up as if to hide his blemished cheeks, and when Meja sat in the back seat he turned round and grinned at her.

'Best fasten your seat belt, it'll be a wild ride.'

The tyres screeched as he swung the car round in the gravel, and Meja's stomach churned. She clung on to the seat in front of her. Carl-Johan found her eyes in the rear-view mirror.

'What have you done today?'

'Nothing,' she said. 'Tried not to die of boredom.'

'Boredom?' He smiled. 'We can do something about that.'

They drove through the village. Everywhere was silent and sleeping. When they pulled out on to a wider, asphalt road she felt Göran accelerate. He was driving with only two fingers on the wheel. She sunk deeper into the shabby upholstery and watched the pines race past.

She didn't ask where they were going. She was only too

pleased to be going somewhere. Away from Silje.

'What have you all been doing today?' she asked.

'Working,' they said, in unison.

'What do you do?'

'All sorts,' said Carl-Johan. 'Pretty much anything to do with animals and the land.'

'So you're farmers?'

They laughed.

Meja leaned between the two front seats and looked at the deserted road. They didn't meet any cars, and signs of habitation were few and far between. Small communities were slotted in here and there between the trees, but there was no one about. It was as if they were the sole survivors in a world that had gone under. She might have been afraid if it hadn't been for Carl-Johan. His hands drummed against his jeans and she didn't need to see his lips to know he was smiling.

The first vehicle they met was a police patrol car. It was stationary in a lay-by and Meja noticed Göran slowing down.

'Shit, shit, shit!'

'Take it easy,' said Carl-Johan. 'He's just having a nap.'

Göran went on swearing as they cruised past the car. Meja peered through the windscreen, but couldn't see anyone inside. When they had left it behind and it hadn't made any attempt to tail them, Göran banged his fist on the wheel and cheered.

'What are the police doing out here in the back of beyond?' Meja asked, when he had calmed down.

'Good question,' said Göran. 'Corrupt bastards.'

Carl-Johan turned to her and winked. 'Perhaps I should inform you that none of us has a driving licence, so it's always a bit stressful when we run into the cops.'

'Why haven't you got driving licences?'

Göran pulled down his hood, revealing his pockmarked cheeks. He twisted the rear-view mirror so he could see her.

'I've been driving a car half my life,' he said. 'Why should I pay the state a load of money just so they can give their approval?'

Meja leaned back in the seat. 'We've never even owned a car,' she said.

The sun rose in the sky and she noticed they were coming to a larger town. Church towers and rooftops were visible in a valley, and a wide river carved its way between the buildings. They passed a row of single-storey houses and Göran almost ran over a cat that darted across the road.

Meja didn't ask where they were. It didn't seem important. Part of her hoped they would never drive back. Göran swung off into an all-night filling station and parked beside one of the pumps. Carl-Johan asked if she would like an ice cream and when they got out he put his arm round her waist. The brightly lit shop was empty apart from the assistant, who was young and pretty and wore her hair in a thick brown plait over one shoulder.

Göran pulled up his hood again and combed his hair over his forehead. When they had chosen their ice creams, he was the one who offered to pay. Meja heard him say something to the girl behind the till and she smiled at him, but it wasn't a genuine smile.

When they returned to the car, Carl-Johan chose to sit in the back seat with Meja. He leaned forward and slapped his brother on the shoulder.

'How did it go? Did you get her number?'

'No.'

'What are you waiting for?'

'She doesn't want to give me her number.'

'How do you know if you never have the guts to ask?'

Göran put the ice cream in his mouth and turned the key in the ignition.

'I've got eyes to see, haven't I?' he said. 'I can forget girls like that.'

On the way back Carl-Johan sat with his arm around Meja. She shut her eyes against the sunlight and was lulled by the motion of the car. Behind the wheel Göran was utterly silent under his hood.

Lelle parked beside Maravältan and made sure he was alone before getting out of the car. He walked softly to the edge of the massive precipice and stood so close his toes were protruding over the top. The earth was loose after the rain and soft sand trickled like water down into the depths. The place had once served as an *ättestupa* or kin precipice, a legendary place where families rid themselves of useless old relatives who could no longer contribute or lend a hand.

He lit a cigarette and leaned out over the drop. It took his breath away, a feeling he liked. It was proof that the blood was still flowing in his veins, even though he felt more dead than alive. And the thought of jumping felt liberating, as if he had a choice even if that was only wishful thinking. He would never be able to end his life until he found out what had happened to Lina. Otherwise he would have done it long ago.

He heard a car pull up behind him. The door opened and emitted the low murmur of a police radio. There were heavy footsteps in the sand and the rattle of keys. Lelle raised a hand in greeting without having to turn round. He already knew.

'Shit, Lelle, do you have to stand so near the edge?'

Lelle turned his head and looked at the police officer. 'Now's your chance to get rid of me. One push and I'll be nothing more than a bad memory.'

'The thought had occurred to me, I can't deny it.'

Hassan was the closest to a friend Lelle had these days, even though he was part of the local police force. It was an unlikely friendship born out of Lina's disappearance.

Hassan stopped a few metres from the edge and put his hands on his hips as he surveyed the view. Lelle flicked his cigarette over the precipice and raised his head. Beyond the steep drop lay endless miles of black forest. Here and there the landscape was punctuated with rivers and areas left bare from felling. A few wind turbines crested a hill as a reminder of human progress and that nothing could remain untouched.

'Well, here she is again,' Hassan said. 'Summer.'

'Too bloody true.'

'And you've started driving?'

'I started back in May.'

'You know what I think about that.'

Lelle smiled, turned his back on the precipice, reached out an arm and gave Hassan a pat on the shoulder. The dark uniform was hot in the sun.

'At the risk of sounding disrespectful, I couldn't give a shit what you think.'

Hassan grinned and ran his fingers through his curly hair. His neck muscles rippled above the unbuttoned shirt collar. He was the well-built kind, solid and impressive. Lelle felt puny by comparison. Used up.

'I assume you have nothing new to offer?'

'Not at the moment, but we're hoping for something around the third anniversary. Someone might be brave enough to come forward.'

Lelle looked down at their shoes. Hassan's shiny ones and his own, muddy and scuffed. 'Anette has arranged a torchlit parade through the village.'

'So I heard. That's good. The last thing we want is for people to forget.'

'I'm not much for people these days.'

The sun vanished behind a cloud and the air chilled instantly.

'Talking about people,' Hassan said. 'Do you remember Torbjörn Fors?'

'The guy who was getting the same bus as Lina that morning? How would I be able to forget that old devil?'

'I saw him shopping in ICA the other day. With a woman.'

Lelle started coughing. He banged his fist on his chest and looked at Hassan dubiously. 'You mean Torbjörn has met a woman after all these years? That's hard to believe.'

'I'm only telling you what I saw.'

'Don't say he's imported some poor woman from Thailand?'

'She's from down south. And young, too. Considerably younger than him. Looked haggard, but couldn't have been more than forty.'

'Who would have thought it? How has the old fox managed that?'

'No idea. And she wasn't alone, either.'

'What do you mean?'

Hassan's jaw tightened. 'She had a daughter with her. A teenager.'

'You're kidding.'

'I only wish I was.'

✳

Silje's croaky voice made her sound like someone very old or very sick. Meja watched her through narrowed eyes as she poured out the wine with an unsteady hand. The sight filled Meja's chest with dread, making it hard to breathe. It wasn't the first glass, because her eyelids were heavy and she slurred when she spoke. If Torbjörn noticed, he didn't let on, not while Meja was there. He merely looked at her with his kindly eyes.

'You're out and about a lot, Meja. Have you made some friends in the village?'

Silje reached out her hand and stroked Meja's hair. 'Meja's very independent. She's not one for friends.'

'I have met someone, actually. A guy.'

Silje slowly turned her head. There was a sudden glimmer in her dull eyes. 'No! Who?'

'He's called Carl-Johan. We met by the lake.'

'*Carl-Johan*. Is that his real name?'

Meja ignored her. She watched Torbjörn push a finger under his lip, dig out the pouch of snus and drop it on to his plate.

'That's not a name I recognize,' he said. 'Where's he from?'

'Svartliden.'

'Svartliden!' Dirty brown saliva flew over the plates. 'You're joking. Not Birger Brandt's lad?'

Meja felt her heart start pounding. 'Yeah.'

72

'I can't talk, seeing as folk think I'm the village idiot, but Birger and his wife? They're in a class of their own.'

'Why?'

Torbjörn's lungs whistled as he breathed in. 'They run some kind of hippie commune out there. Not that keen on modern technology, live like people did in the eighteen hundreds. Birger didn't want his sons going to normal school and there was an almighty fuss, if I remember right. He wanted to home-school them on the farm, but the council was dead against it.'

'Are they religious?' Silje asked.

'Who the hell knows? But it wouldn't surprise me.'

Silje drained her glass and pointed it at Meja. 'Why don't you invite him over so we can have a look at him?'

'Forget it.'

'Come on, invite him here.'

Meja turned her eyes to the forest, where the sunlight streamed through the trees, its shafts illuminating clouds of dust and midges. She could see the glade where they had stood in the dawn light after Göran had dropped them off. The memory of his lips on hers almost made her feel giddy.

Lelle drove the Silver Road south, stopping to fill the car in Skellefteå, where a solitary night-worker stood behind the counter, tapping on his phone. An HGV driver, cap pulled low over his eyes and mouth full of snus, was standing by the coffee machine, filling two large mugs. Lelle bought a coffee and two packets of Marlboro Red from the preoccupied assistant. Beyond the harsh fluorescent lighting the night was wrapped in blue dusk that reminded Lelle of the sea. He got behind the wheel again, smoked a cigarette and tried to think of anything except the sea. But when he started the engine he knew it was too late and at the junction he steered left, away from the Silver Road. He knocked the ash clumsily out of the window and smelled the salt in the air as he drew closer. He drove until he saw the horizon and the sea spread out ahead of him. The sky glowed where the sun was beginning to break through from behind the clouds. He parked and set off walking along the stony edge of the bay until he reached the overgrown strip of beach where the cabin had been. Not a plank was left, but he could still make out the lines of the cellar under layers of dead vegetation. His feet stumbled and he dropped ash as he walked, feeling his breath catch and his heart lurch at the memories.

It had been his childhood home, the place where his dad had drunk himself to death and where Lelle had been left alone at night while his mother worked. He was only about seven or eight when he started draining the dregs his father left behind. He soon learned to taste the difference between weak and strong alcohol, between home-brewed vodka and the real thing. He wasn't very old when he got drunk for the first time and woke with a pool of vomit beside his bed. He had no memory of throwing up. Naturally his mother noticed the smell of alcohol on him, but she never said a word, not to her son or her husband. Rule Number One: ignore the drinking.

Lina had never seen him drink and he was thankful for that. It was a part of him he had buried beside the sea. She had never seen the cabin where he grew up and she had never met her paternal grandparents. His father was dead by the time Lina was born, and Lelle had lied and said her grandmother was also dead. The questions started coming when Lina grew older, questions about his childhood and his parents, but he always avoided giving straight answers. That was the one thing he had promised himself, that his child would never be left alone. She would never come second to alcohol or anything else. He had sworn a solemn oath to himself, but still he had failed. He had failed miserably.

Lelle carried on to the strip of beach that had once been theirs, crouched down and searched for flat stones he could skim on the water. He threw the stones skilfully and hard, as if it was the sea he was angry with. The very smell of salty air made him heave these days. It followed him into the car, which stank of the ocean when he climbed in. He sat for a long time, smoking and studying the weeds that formed a thick layer over his memories. The old familiar thirst grew in his throat, but his hands were steady on the wheel as he drove back north. Between Skellefteå and

Glimmersträsk it started to rain, and on the approach to Arvidsjaur he was forced to stop twice, because the windscreen wipers couldn't cope with the deluge. He smoked and listened to the rain beating against the metal. Lina had been wearing blue jeans and a white, long-sleeved top the day she disappeared, nothing that would survive this kind of downpour. He had obsessed about that the first summer, that she wasn't wearing suitable clothes, that she would get cold or wet or bitten by mosquitoes. It was the natural elements that worried him. He didn't want to think about the human factor.

A car pulled in behind him as he sat taking a break. Its fog lights shone through the rain and he couldn't see the driver through the torrential downpour. He doubted the driver could see him, either. The rain was coming down in sheets and the wind was blowing hard against the wildlife fence. Lelle only had time to think about how grateful he was for this metal box he was sheltering in before there was a knock on the window. He jumped so violently his cigarette fell to the floor and burned a hole in the mat. The man outside had his hood up and the contours of his face were blurred. When Lelle wound down the window he saw it was an older man with sunken cheeks. He fumbled for the cigarette. The smell of burned plastic was gradually filling the small space.

'Sorry, didn't mean to frighten you,' said the man. 'Have you got a mobile I can borrow? My battery's died.'

Grey strands of hair were plastered to his skin and rain streamed down his eyebrows and the cleft under his nose. Lelle took a quick look at his mobile in the cup-holder.

'You can sit in the car and call,' he said and nodded towards the passenger door. 'I don't want my phone getting wet.'

The man hurried round and slid into the front seat. Water dripped from him and he steamed.

'Thanks,' he said. 'That's good of you.'

Lelle stepped out of the car while the man tapped in the number. His legs had stiffened from all the sitting and he walked around to give them a stretch. He walked a lap around the man's car and peered through the glistening windows, as casually as he could. The man had left his windscreen wipers on and they thrashed over the wet glass. The interior light was on and he could see a coffee cup in the holder. The back seat was covered with a black tarpaulin and diverse rubbish: sweet papers, fishing line, empty beer cans, a handsaw and a roll of gaffer tape. On the passenger seat was a scrap of white cloth, and through the mist he saw the outline of Lina's face. *Have you seen me? Ring 112.* One of the many T-shirts ordered by Anette through the years. Had the man been there? Was he from Glimmerträsk?

His head throbbed as he went back to his car. The man gave him back the phone.

'Thanks for letting me use it. I didn't mean to send you outside in this weather.'

'I needed to stretch my legs anyway.'

The man had a broken front tooth and his tongue showed through the gap when he smiled.

'Blasted weather,' he said. 'I had to call my old lady to tell her where I was. She'll hit the roof otherwise.'

'Have you got far to go?'

'No, no. I live just outside Hedberg.'

'Drive carefully,' Lelle said, drying his face on the arm of his jacket.

'You too.'

The man got out and sprinted back to his car. Lelle locked the door behind him. He took his pistol out of the glove compartment and then entered the man's number plate in his mobile, together with a description: *Man, 50–60, average weight, broken front tooth. Hedberg?*

The clock's red lines indicated 4.30. Was his woman really sitting up waiting for him at this ungodly hour? It sounded unlikely to Lelle. He looked in his rear-view mirror and saw the man leaning back in his seat. It was impossible to see if his eyes were open or not, but his still- ness indicated he was going to sit out the storm that was whipping up a curtain of rain between the two cars. Lelle fumbled with his phone. Hassan answered the call, despite the early hour.

'What is it now?'

'I've got a reg. number for you to check.'

✳

Torbjörn insisted on making breakfast for her. As soon as
Meja came downstairs his face lit up and he wanted her to
sit at the old kitchen table. The radio was on in the background and he busied himself at the stove. In the beginning
he had tried to persuade Silje to keep them company, but
after a couple of fruitless attempts he had given up. Silje
had never been a morning person. Meja couldn't recall a
single time they had eaten breakfast together.

Torbjörn made coffee in a brass coffee pot and laid out
more food than either of them could eat: yoghurt, porridge,
boiled eggs, bread, two kinds of cheese, ham, and some
dark-looking meat that Meja turned down, but he insisted
on offering her.

'You must taste it! It's smoked reindeer. You don't have
tasty things like this down south.'

She tore off a tiny piece and put it on her tongue, trying
not to think where it came from. 'It tastes like salty earth.'

That made him laugh. He had gaps between his teeth
and food fastened in his moustache when he ate. But he
didn't worry her. There was something about the way his
eyes slid past her, as if he wanted to see her, but not stare.
As if he was concerned.

'Your mother likes her sleep.'

'She can sleep all day.'

'Pity she misses breakfast. Best meal of the day, I always
say.'

He was wearing a dirty grey string vest and gave off wafts of unwashed body when he moved. Meja wondered if Silje held her breath when they had sex. She shut her eyes and thought of the forest.

Torbjörn dried his hands on his trousers and wiped his nose with the back of his hand.

'My mother is grinning in her grave right now, I guarantee you.'

'Why?'

'Because you're sitting here. She was always nagging me to have children. More important than finding a wife, in her book. Someone to look after the land when you're too old to do it yourself.'

Meja didn't know what to say, so she stretched across the table for some reindeer meat. She put a slice on her bread and took a huge bite. She hoped it would make him happy. And sure enough, he smiled.

Torbjörn poured the remainder of the coffee in a flask and reached out for his ear defenders. Meja had no idea what kind of work he did, only that he spent his days in the forest wearing a green jacket with reinforced elbows and a hi-vis orange safety vest that flapped over his bulging stomach. Sometimes he brought his camera, telling her the names of the birds and flowers he hoped to catch, names that were wholly unfamiliar to her.

'Remember there are bikes in the log shed if you get bored indoors.'

After Torbjörn left she opened Silje's door a crack and was met by a sour odour of ashtrays and red wine. Silje was lying with her arms flung wide and her head hanging to one side, like Jesus on the Cross. Dead to the world. Her nipples were like bruises against the bloodless skin and Meja could see the ribs heaving as she breathed. It was always the breathing she wanted to check.

'Are you awake?'

Meja walked over to the bed, slipped her hand under Silje's back and turned her on to her side. Silje didn't make a sound; there was no sign that she was even conscious. Meja pulled up her legs until she was in a foetal position and pushed her over the crumpled sheet until her head was close to the edge. It was safest that way. In case she needed to vomit in her sleep. Meja quietly left the room, searching her mind for an escape.

*

The sudden ring of the phone in the room made Lelle's heart leap into his throat and his coffee slop on to the table. He would never get used to that sound. The piercing rings that could mean it was all over, that today was the day his life would fall apart.

'I checked out the guy you met the other night, the one from Hedberg,' said Hassan.

'And?'

'Looks like you can smell a villain. He's called Roger

Renlund, convicted of rape in '75 and domestic violence a couple of times in the Eighties. Now living on a disability pension. Seems he inherited the family home in Hedberg after his parents died and he's lived there alone since 2011.'

'Alone? Are you sure?'

'Well, he's the only one registered at that address.'

'He borrowed my phone to ring his old lady, or so he said. I checked the number and it's for a care home in Arvidsjaur.'

'Maybe she works there. Or perhaps he likes older women?'

Hassan had his mouth full of food while he was speaking. Lelle glanced at the clock: 12.05. Lunchtime for normal people.

'Are you going to contact him?'

'On what grounds? Because he's got a T-shirt with Lina's picture on it? Half of Norrland has got one of those T-shirts by now.'

Lelle's fingers ached from gripping the receiver.

'OK,' said Lelle, bluntly. 'I get it.'

'Lelle,' Hassan said, reprovingly. 'Don't do anything stupid, now.'

Lelle sat with the venetian blinds closed, studying the satellite view of Roger Renlund's farm. It was in an isolated spot with thick forest to the rear and overgrown fields in front. Empty meadows with no sign of cattle or horses. There was a barn, three smaller sheds and a henhouse. Possibly an earth cellar in the right-hand corner of the plot, but it was hard to tell. The nearest farm lay five kilometres to the south. Apart from satellites way up in the sky, there was no way of seeing any of Roger Renlund's land. Very practical, if you had something to hide.

Lelle didn't want to dwell on that, but at the same time it was the only comfort he had. He refused to believe that Lina was dead. And he had said to Anette from the very beginning that someone had their daughter. Someone out there in the big wide world knew where she was, and he would find that someone if it was the last thing he did. That first summer he had knocked on the door of every lone man and village eccentric he knew and asked to have a look in their cellar and loft. He had been met with both profanities and invitations for coffee, but what remained with him was the loneliness, the fact that there was such loneliness everywhere. It corroded the region at the edges, spreading like a sickness among those who remained when all the others had moved away. And now he was one of them. One of the lonely people.

'Do you know a village called Hedberg?'

Kippen frowned and pursed his lips, fixing his gaze on the cigarette shelf as if the answer was written there.

'No. Where is it?'

'Up near Arjeplog.'

'Are you going there to look?'

Lelle nodded and tore the cellophane from the cigarette packet. 'If I don't come back, you know what to do.'

'You're not going to trespass on someone's land?'

'I'm going to visit the farm of a convicted rapist and abuser.'

The flabby skin on Kippen's neck trembled as he shook his head, but he said nothing and gave a low whistle instead. Some youngsters came into the shop and Lelle put the cigarette in his mouth and winked at Kippen as he walked to the door.

He parked on an overgrown turning circle he had found on a satellite image. From there he could follow a brook that carved a channel through the back of Roger Renlund's land. He stepped out into thick scrub that came up to his armpits. Dark clouds of flies rose up from the wild flowers as he forced his way through. Roger Renlund's farm lay like a medieval fortress, surrounded by wildly overgrown fields and thorny forest. It would be a nightmare trying to get through that lot.

Lelle tucked his trousers into his boots and pulled up his hood as protection against the mosquitoes. At the tree line he broke off a branch and used it to beat the air. The whining settled all around him, along with his revulsion. The ground was marshy and foul-smelling, and the night sun painted strips of light between the trees where the midges gathered in angry clouds. He felt them biting, despite the hood and his attempts to shake them off. They bit through to his head where his hair was soaked in sweat. The gun was in his waistband and he sensed the smell of fear permeating from his pores. Perhaps it was the smell that attracted the damned mosquitoes.

He didn't know what he was afraid of, whether it was the feeling of being on someone else's land or the fear of what he might or might not find. It didn't matter. He would search for his daughter using all possible means, legal or not. Perhaps he was afraid he was losing his mind. This business of acting alone was seductive; no one saw what he saw or drew the same conclusions. Lelle was in it on his own and he knew it. Perhaps he should start knocking back the diazepam or zopiclone and spend his evenings grieving his lost daughter on social media. That seemed to work for Anette. She didn't break any laws. She didn't run around, armed, on someone else's property in the middle of the night. She didn't drive to dying villages to look for her daughter among the ruins. It was him, and him alone.

When the forest opened up, his T-shirt was sticking to his skin and he could no longer hear the whining of the mosquitoes for the blood rushing in his ears. In the glade he glimpsed a paddock full of grass that hadn't been grazed for many years. He crouched among the moss and flowers and looked towards the main house, two storeys that had been subjected to wind and weather. The night sky was reflected in the sad-looking window panes. There was no sign of life, animal or human. Lelle hunched over and made his way across the paddock. The car was parked beside one of the walls, he could see it now. A snowmobile or motorbike stood under a tarpaulin. He crept past a rusty wheelbarrow filled with dark earth and on to a recently dug potato plot waiting for the new shoots to appear. The ground was wet and cold beneath him. He set his sights on the woodshed, the building closest to him, and listened for the sound of barking a final time before getting to his feet. He began to run, but didn't get far before he had to fall flat again. The squeal of a hinge broke the silence, followed by a dry cough. Lelle tried to lie still, but his heart and lungs heaved against the ground. Dew soaked through his layers of clothing and the cold made him think of the ice he had fallen through as a child. His hands had scraped themselves bloody on the jagged edges and his father, suddenly sober, yelled at him to grab the rope. *Hold on to the rope, boy!*

Through the blades of grass he saw a figure on the veranda steps. Renlund was dressed in a pair of green underpants and his stomach was hanging over the waistband. He put his fingers to his mouth and whistled, and a greying dog bounded out of the trees. Lelle pressed his cheek to the ground and closed his eyes. He heard Renlund say something to the dog and then the hinge squealed again as the door shut behind them. Lelle stayed where he was for a long time, until the cold seeped through to his bones and made his joints and jaws shudder. He began crawling to the woodshed, all the time keeping his eyes on the house and the windows where the sky gleamed. Not until he was out of sight did he stand up and start to run. The door to the woodshed was half open and he slipped in sideways. He peered through the darkness and breathed in the smell of dried wood. Logs were stacked several metres high along one wall, more than enough for three winters. Renlund might be a bastard, but there was nothing to indicate that he was lazy.

Lelle padded through the barn, which was empty of animals and stank of rotten hay. He shone his torch on the stalls and prodded piles of hay with a rake to make sure nothing was concealed underneath. Spider webs and bird droppings covered the walls, testimony that it had been a long time since any livestock had been kept here. He came out to an empty dog pen with food bowls filled with rain and earth. Next to that was a hunting hut with sloping walls and two hares strung up in the doorway, waiting to be skinned. Lelle peered through the scratched window and saw that the hut was filled with tools, fishing rods and knives. A butchery bench ran along one of the short walls. There was nothing unusual or worrying there. He looked back at the house. He really would like to take a look inside. It was a big place for just one man, with many rooms that were never used.

He got as far as halfway across the yard before the first shot rang out, a loud rifle shot that shook the pines above his head. Lelle crouched down and started to run. Over his shoulder he saw Renlund on the veranda steps, still in his underpants, but now with a rifle under his arm. He yelled something at Lelle, but the words didn't reach him. Then there was a second shot and this time he felt the rush of air as the bullet passed him. He threw himself to the ground and crawled on all fours. Soon the dog was barking behind him. He could hear how close it was. The ground swayed beneath him and when the dog's paws landed on his back he fell flat on the ground, covering his head with his hands. He heard the dog give a bark, the kind of bark that meant it had caught its prey. Lelle lay totally still and heard the grass being parted by heavy footsteps. A hoarse voice ordered the dog to be silent. Lelle made an attempt to get up, but the man pressed a foot between his shoulder blades and forced him down again.

Meja drank cold coffee and glared at the forest. The days were endless in the wait for night-time and Carl-Johan, because it was only then he came. An image of the pack of cigarettes she had thrown away kept floating into her mind and she thought that just one couldn't hurt. But she didn't want to smell of smoke if he suddenly appeared, standing there at the edge of the forest.

The restlessness drove her out of the house. The sun was playing hide-and-seek behind the clouds and there was no real warmth in it. She took the dog with her, but it soon abandoned her to follow a promising scent. It nosed its way through the low lingonberry bushes and blended in with the shadows. Meja called, but didn't like hearing the sound of her own voice. The wind seemed to make the forest reach out to her and it gave her goosebumps. Her loathing of it lay like a heavy blanket around her shoulders. She walked towards the barn.

The door was heavy, but it swung open easily on its hinges. Inside the barn the roof was high. Assorted vehicles slumbered under dark tarpaulins and one of the long walls was hung with tools of all kinds. Torbjörn appeared to be especially interested in axes; he had at least a dozen hanging in a row. The shiny cutting edges nestled inside their leather sheaths. Meja ran her fingers over the thick handles and wondered what it would feel like to swing one, but she didn't dare try. Perhaps Torbjörn would show her.

Two cycles were propped in one corner, both old and without gears, but with sturdy rear carrier racks. Meja left them and went into an adjoining room, where various animal hides were stretched across the walls and a heavy iron hook hung from the ceiling. A wooden work bench took pride of place in the middle of the room and when she walked closer she noticed the surface was dark with bloodstains. She realized this was where Torbjörn butchered the animals that filled the freezers in the cellar. The thought made her recoil.

The dog started barking outside and when Meja turned to leave she caught sight of yet another door. It was hanging off its hinges and a pool of daylight shone through from underneath. She walked over and felt the handle. The door opened straight away with a long creak. There inside was a tiny room, really nothing more than an alcove, with a dirty window letting in a beam of daylight. The walls were lined with narrow shelves packed with carved wooden figures in long rows, everything from rabbits to large-breasted women. On the floor among the wood shavings were old drink crates full of magazines.

She could see immediately what kind of magazines they were. Glossy pages of naked women. Close-ups of gaping buttocks and genitals. Images that both fascinated and repulsed her. She thought of Torbjörn, imagined him sitting here, carving figures and leafing through the porn mags in the evenings. The thought was more sad than laughable. She flicked through a few of them until she came to a collection of photographs of a more amateur kind. They fell out like bookmarks. They were pictures of women at the lake beach. Young women in colourful bikinis, diving from rocks and drying themselves with towels, apparently unaware they were being photographed. Meja squinted and tried to make out their faces. A feeling of uneasiness came over her. When the dog barked outside she hurried to put the photographs back, her hands trembling.

Then she rushed out, past the butcher's block and the

axes, grabbing one of the ancient bicycles on the way. She pushed it outside, leapt on to the saddle and began pedalling unsteadily along the cracked asphalt that led to the village.

✳

Roger Renlund still brewed his coffee on a cast-iron wood stove. Lelle sat on the edge of his chair, playing with the brown-striped wax tablecloth that must have been there since the Sixties. The grey dog was stretched out in the doorway like a shaggy prison guard, keeping a sleepy eye on him. Renlund spat his snus into the sink and poured coffee into green plastic mugs. It was thick and black and steamed intensely in the sunshine.

'I apologize for the warning shot,' he said. 'But I wasn't aiming at you. I've had a problem with diesel thieves the past few years and I thought I'd teach them a lesson.'

Lelle's hand was still shaking as he picked up the mug.

'Can't be helped,' he said. 'I shouldn't have been nosing around your property in the middle of the night.'

'So we don't need to contact the police?'

'Hell, no.'

They gulped their coffee in silence for a while and Lelle looked around him. It was clear the house had belonged to the man's parents and the furniture had been handed down through generations. A wooden clock ticked away the seconds and above the pine panelling the striped wallpaper was hung with hunting knives and a bundle of dried cat's foot flowers.

Renlund kneaded tobacco between his fingers and kept his eyes on Lelle.

'I recognize you,' he said. 'I met you the other night. It was your phone I borrowed to call the wife!'

'That's right,' said Lelle.

'I'll be damned.'

Renlund frowned and looked down at the photograph of Lina that was lying between them on the tablecloth.

'So she's your daughter?'

'You had a T-shirt with her picture on. In the car.'

'Yes. We were involved in the search, the old lady and me. Part of the human chains. And we've been on the torch-light parades through the years.'

'Where is she?' he asked.

'She's got a farm up in Baktsjaur. We don't live together.'

'Why not?'

'Because I don't want to sell my family home and she doesn't want to sell hers.'

'Oh, right,' said Lelle. 'And she works in a care home?'

Renlund looked astonished.

'How do you know that?'

'You phoned there the night we met.'

'She insists on working nights,' he said. 'Because that's when they die. And she doesn't want anyone to die alone.'

There was a long silence while Lelle thought about this,

broken only by Renlund gulping his coffee and aiming gobs of spit into a tin bucket on the floor. The dog had rolled on to its back, revealing the white hair on its stomach.

'But I still don't understand what your girl would have been doing here on *my* farm, of all places,' Renlund said.

Lelle took a deep breath. 'I don't know. All I do know is that she's been missing for three years and it's my job to look for her. I heard about your past,' he said, 'and to be honest every sodding person is a potential suspect in my eyes. Until I know what has happened to my daughter I'd even suspect the king himself. So, don't take it personally.'

Renlund scowled and considered this for a while. 'I guess I can understand that. I'd have done the same if I had kids of my own. I'm not proud of the stuff I got up to in my younger days, I can tell you that. But I swear I've had nothing to do with your daughter's disappearance.'

It was full daylight when Lelle stepped out on to the veranda and began to make his way through the under-growth to the car. Renlund's eyes burned into the back of his neck and before he disappeared into the trees Lelle lifted a hand to him. The lone man waved back. He was standing on the veranda steps with the rifle propped against the flaking wall of the house, and the dog was sitting beside him. Lelle ducked and wound his way between the trees and as soon as he was out of sight he began to run.

✳

'You look an absolute wreck!' Anette put her arm around Lelle and held him tight. 'You stink, too.'

'Thanks for those kind words.'

She held him away from her, looking at him with tear-filled eyes. There were new lines on her face that he didn't remember. She looked older, more tired. But unlike her, he said nothing. He hadn't had time to get cleaned up or change his clothes. His body felt battered after the night up at Hedberg.

Anette pulled a tissue from her pocket and dabbed her eyes.

'Three years,' she said. 'Three years without our little girl.'

Lelle could only nod. He knew he wouldn't be able to stop his voice breaking. Instead, he held out his hand to Thomas, who was standing to one side. A mass of people had gathered around them, but all he saw was the grey outline of a crowd. He felt their eyes on him, but couldn't see any faces. He couldn't bring himself to look.

They lit torches and handed them around. The crowd came alive, but the flames helped to block them out. Lelle's shoulders relaxed a little. Anette stood on the steps of the old school and said something in her high voice that Lelle couldn't hear, but its sound was familiar to him.

Other voices followed. Local police officer Åke Ståål gave a brief account of the case that was still open and how the search would continue. One of Lina's friends read a poem and another sang. Lelle kept his eyes on the ground, wishing he was somewhere else, wishing he could get behind the wheel and drive the Silver Road to look for his daughter.

'Lelle?' Anette's voice cut through his thoughts. 'Do you want to say a few words?'

Everyone's eyes were on him and he felt his cheeks burning. The torch crackled in his hand, but he could still hear muffled sobs. He cleared his throat and licked his lips.

'I just want to say thank you to everybody who has come here today. These three years without Lina have been the worst of my life. And it doesn't get any easier. It's time we got her home. I need my daughter.'

His voice broke and his head dropped to his chest. A longer speech was impossible. This was all he had to offer. Someone slapped him on the back and it felt like the slap someone would give a horse. Lelle looked sideways at the pair of shoes and knew it was Ståål, the incompetent old bastard.

They began walking in a long line with their burning torches towards the bus stop where Lina was last seen. A reporter from *Norrlands-Posten* was there, taking pictures. Lelle walked with his head bowed and his coat collar turned up. The air was heavy with damp and the scent of lilacs. Ahead of him was Anette, with Thomas's arm around her shoulders. The rest of the people lacked dimension, as if they were not really alive.

The bus stop came into view at the top of the slope and he could feel his heart beating faster. Waves of dizziness washed over him and he focused on putting one foot in front of the other and filling his lungs with air. The hope that Lina would be standing there, waiting, was always under the surface, even if it never became a reality.

The villagers made him feel uncomfortable. His whole body reacted against them, but he couldn't explain why. A rage burned under his skin and made it impossible for him to look them in the face. Lina's friends and their parents, teachers and acquaintances, neighbours and neighbours' neighbours – all these people who ought to have seen something, ought to know something. Who were possibly involved. The whole of Glimmersträsk was to blame. Until the day Lina came back to him he wouldn't trust a single one of them.

By the time they reached the bus shelter he was so angry he found it hard to keep the torch still. He pictured himself lunging at the crowd, scorching the faces of the inquisitive people closest to him. He could almost hear the screams. He lowered his face to look at the fractured asphalt and started to count the cracks. Anette's voice was coming from somewhere and he was amazed at how clear and controlled it was.

When he dared to raise his eyes he saw they had started giving out the T-shirts, the same as the one Renlund had in his car, with Lina on the front and thick black letters under her name saying: *Have you seen me?* The grey, face-less mass of people reached out for the T-shirts and soon Lina was smiling at him from all directions. Hundreds of Lina-faces surrounded him and were reflected in the scratched glass of the bus shelter. His heart was thumping in his throat, choking him. Lelle looked down again, at the hundreds of pairs of shoes around him. Sensible walking shoes, boots, neon-coloured trainers. Lelle wondered what kind of shoes Lina would have worn if she had been here.

The hordes of people alternately sang and wept. There were voices everywhere. Anette's face was wet with tears, but glowing at the same time with a kind of joy at all the people who had gathered, the sense of community. Lelle saw it and it left a bad taste in his mouth. A feeling that they were wasting time. It was the same feeling he had when he clicked through the Facebook posts and read all the empty comments that didn't lead anywhere. Finally, he waved the torch above his head to draw everyone's attention.

'It's good there are so many of us who want Lina back,' he said and cleared his throat. 'But I believe it's important that we don't sit at home grieving, but get out and actively look for her. Ask questions. Find answers. Lift every stone and have a good look underneath. Put pressure on the police when they're not doing their job properly.'

He looked sideways at Åke Ståål and then back at the crowd that had fallen quiet. The evening sun burned brightly beyond the trees and he was squinting so hard his eyes were almost shut.

'*Someone* out there knows something. It's time for them to come out in the open. Anette and I have waited long enough. We want Lina back. And to those of you who don't know anything, I've only got one thing to say: stop mourning and *start looking*.'

He dipped the torch in a puddle and it went out with an angry hiss. Then he turned his back on them and left.

Meja stood up and pedalled as fast as she could to get away from the forest. It had stopped raining, but black puddles glittered in the cracked asphalt and the water splashed her jeans. Spruce saplings and brushwood grew up from the ditches and reached after her in the slipstream. She kept her mouth shut because of the mosquitoes, thankful for the rush of air that prevented them settling on her.

It felt like an eternity before she caught sight of any kind of habitation, but eventually there were farmsteads, boxy, red-painted houses with generous lawns and the forest behind them. Dogs barked at her from their pens and in lush paddocks stocky horses flicked their tails to keep away the flies. The smell of manure and vegetation lay like a film over everything. She dared to slow down now that there were signs of life, but the unease stayed with her. They had lived in many places through the years, she and Silje, but nothing had felt as alien as this place.

She came to a wider road that took her past a church and its graveyard. Gravestones nestled in the shade of huge weeping birches. An elderly, bald man was raking the grass and raised a hand as she cycled past. Other than that she saw no one. The scattered houses appeared to slumber in the sunlight. Not a single car had passed. Glimmersträsk was beginning to feel more and more like a ghost town.

Then she heard the voices, a growing sound of voices and of feet scraping against the road surface. Meja pulled the bicycle in among the trees when she saw them coming. It looked like a demonstration of some kind. A group of people were marching with burning torches in their hands. Black smoke and a strong smell of fire rose into the light sky and she could feel the heat as they passed. She stood rigid and motionless under the trees, not wanting to be seen. They were young and old, men and women, and they gave off an aura of solemnity. It was certainly no party atmosphere, quite the reverse. Some of them were crying openly and leaning on each other for support. Meja held her breath.

'You'd think she was a fucking rock star the way they carry on.'

The voice made her jump and she let go of the bicycle. It landed softly in the moss. Meja turned her head and saw a figure submerged in the lingonberry bushes, her back against a large rock. It was a girl of about her own age, with pink hair and huge wooden ear studs. She was smoking a

99

skinny roll-up and stared at Meja through heavily painted eyes.

'Who?'

'Lina Gustafsson. That's who they're walking for.'

Meja glanced back at the procession and then reached for her bicycle.

'Is she dead, or what?'

'Presumably. No one knows for sure.'

The girl spat into the moss and regarded Meja sleepily.

'All you have to do to become a saint in this dump is vanish into thin air. Then everyone competes to say how much they love you.'

Meja brushed pine needles off the saddle. She looked at the crowd of people. They were moving like a burning snake up the hill. She wondered where they were heading.

'What's your name?' the girl asked, with her lungs full of smoke.

'Meja. You?'

'I'm called Crow.'

'Crow?'

'Yep.'

A smile flickered on her lips, but didn't stay. Crow held out the roll-up to Meja.

'Want some?'

'I've given up.'

Crow put her head on one side. Her eyes shone blue like the sky.

'You're from down south, right?'

'Mm.'

'What are you doing in Glimmersträsk?'

'Mum and I have just moved here.'

'Why?'

Meja hesitated and felt the blood rush to her cheeks.

'Her bloke lives here.'

'So what's this bloke's name?'

'Torbjörn. Torbjörn Fors.'

Crow gave a raucous laugh, revealing a hidden brace.

'You can't be serious. Your mum's got it together with old Pornbjörn?'

'Pornbjörn?'

'Yeah. He's called that because he's the owner of Norrland's largest collection of porn. That's all he fucking does. Every teenage guy in this village stands outside his window, gagging for a look.'

Meja gripped the handlebars so tight her hands hurt. She felt the humiliation rise like a lump in her throat. Crow smiled triumphantly.

'You sure you don't want a smoke? Looks like you could do with one.'

Meja shuddered and her hair fell over her cheeks. She could hear Crow clicking a lighter. When it wouldn't work she gave up and threw it into the trees. She let out a stream of profanities that sounded comical in the silence. Meja swallowed the lump of shame.

'Why aren't you taking part in that procession?' she asked.

'Because I'm not a fucking hypocrite. I won't pretend to miss someone I didn't even like. I wasn't keen on her before she disappeared, so why should I pretend now?'

'Why didn't you like her?'

Crow stared down at her nails. They were cut short and painted black, and between the knuckles were tattoos. Meja was standing too far away to make out what they said.

'Lina didn't give a toss about taking what didn't belong to her. Make what you like of that.'

Meja nodded as if she understood and started to push the bicycle through the birches and back to the road. The torchlight procession had disappeared over the brow of the hill and only the voices and smell of fire hung on the wind.

'I'll get going now. Nice to meet you.'

Crow saluted, sucked in her cheeks and pouted with her red-painted lips.

'Say hello to Pornbjörn!' she called, as Meja cycled off.

✳

The worst part was not being able to remember everything. The time immediately after Lina's disappearance was fragmented: the police officer in the hall who wouldn't take off his jacket; Anette's fingers clawing at him; the half-open window in her room. All the blank faces staring after him wherever he went.

He had set off almost straight away, possibly even that same night. Driven along the Silver Road until the tank was empty, all the way up to Arjeplog, where twenty-three youngsters were getting ready to plant trees at dawn. They were standing in a circle holding spruce saplings and planting tubes, and he had walked right up to the group, stood in the middle of the circle and looked at each of them in turn to make sure she wasn't among them.

I'm looking for my daughter. She should be here with you, planting trees.

They smelled of mosquito repellent and wet forest and he couldn't remember what anyone said, only that he was made to sit in a black jeep with a coffee thermos in his hand. The guy who was overseeing the planting insisted on him taking a rest. He spoke a Finland-Swedish dialect and let Lelle smoke in the vehicle.

You mustn't scare the kids. They won't come and work here otherwise.

He had promised to get in touch as soon as she turned up. If she turned up.

It was chaos, that first summer. Their muddy shoes in the hall, post that went unopened. Upstairs Anette slept next to her blister packs, so deeply she couldn't be woken. He was grateful for that; at least he didn't have to hear the accusations and the weeping. But it frightened him to see her so detached. The tablets took care of the weeping. All he did was drink. He was given a direct number for the police that he used repeatedly, and heard his own tremulous voice on local radio when he asked the public for tips-offs. Information had poured in from all directions, people who said they had seen Lina in cars and on roadsides, on board a ferry to Denmark and on a beach in Phuket. They had seen her all over the place, but still she was nowhere.

Lelle took a short cut through the forest on his way home, holding the torch close to his body. His feet were unsteady on the moss. The ground leaked water under him, trying to suck him down. He felt his mobile vibrate in his pocket, but ignored it. He couldn't bear to hear Anette's disappointment. His own was bad enough. The thirst was eating away at his throat and he thought of the Laphroaig and promised himself two mouthfuls, two decent mouthfuls, so he could put the bloody procession behind him and start again. He could still feel the villagers' eyes boring into the back of his neck as he strode through the bushes, still feel their silent recrimination driving him on.

He didn't bother taking off his shoes, but strode straight into the sitting room, leaving muddy footprints on the wooden floor. He grabbed the whisky bottle and took a long gulp, which immediately made him gag. He pressed the back of his hand to his mouth and fought against the nausea. It felt as if his throat was on fire, as if he was burning up from the inside. He put the bottle down and swore loudly into the silence. Now he didn't even have the alcohol.

A thud from the floor above caught him by surprise. He looked up at the cracked ceiling, held his breath and listened so intently his muscles ached. There it was again, the dull thud of human footsteps above his head. It sounded as if it was coming from Lina's room.

He was up the stairs in three strides, tripping on the landing and just stopping himself from crashing into the wall. He felt the taste of blood in his mouth, but staggered to Lina's room and pushed the door with his elbow. Inside the window was wide open and the wind was whipping the curtains, making Lina's posters flap eerily. For a few seconds he was rooted in the doorway in a state of shock. The window in Lina's room hadn't been opened for three years. He had made it a thing never to air the room. To keep her there.

He raced to the window and looked down at the terrace. It was possible to slide down the drainpipe and from there it was an easy drop to the lilac bushes. He had caught Lina in the act on more than one occasion when she had tried to get out at night. He scanned the garden: the apple tree with its trunk half-obscured by the neglected lawn, the hedge that kept the neighbours away, and the tangle of under-growth by the trees that marked the boundary of their plot. The wind tore at the plants, giving the impression that everything was moving, and perhaps that was why he saw it. A motionless heap hidden between the lilacs. Without thinking, Lelle hoisted one leg over the windowsill, then the other, and slid clumsily over the tiles until his feet found the guttering. After a momentary hesitation, he plunged over the edge, hanging on to the guttering for a few heart-stopping seconds before dropping to the ground. There was a worrying sound of crushing and snapping as he landed, but he felt no damage to his feet as he headed for the lilacs.

The shape had got up and was starting to run, spiky dark hair against the grey sky and long spindly legs hobbling through the tall grass.

Lelle's heart hammered like a pumping fist against his ribs as he chased after the figure.

'It's no good running! I've already seen you!'

The young man was injured and only got as far as the forest before he fell down and lay still. Seconds later Lelle was on top of him. He gripped the sweat-soaked hair and yanked the pale face up to his own.

'What the fuck do you think you're doing?'

Mikael Varg groaned, dirty streaks on his contorted face.

'Let me go,' he begged. 'Please.'

*

When Meja returned to the house she saw Silje had set up her easel facing the forest. She was stark naked and standing in full view of the kitchen window. Her pallid buttocks caught the sunlight and Meja could see the dark lines of sweat on Torbjörn's forehead.

'Your mum looks like one of those Greek statues.'

Meja hid her face behind her hands. She blew on the coffee Torbjörn had given her and pretended Silje didn't exist.

'I cycled to the village this morning.'

'Did you now?'

'There were hundreds of people in a march with torches, for some girl who went missing.'

Torbjörn took a can of beer from the fridge and held it against his hot cheeks and neck. 'Well, now you know the great village mystery. It was a while ago, but folk can't seem to get over it. No one's forgotten.'

'What do you think happened to her?'

'Lord knows.' Torbjörn pulled the tab of his beer, turned away and looked for something to pour it into. Dirty dishes were stacked up on the counter. Silje's lipstick smiled from the wine glasses. She had already given up the housewife charade and Torbjörn wouldn't complain, not while she walked around naked. He gave up and drank from the can quickly, as if it was water, and didn't try to smother a belch.

'They said she was going to get the bus that morning, that she disappeared while she was waiting. But that's not true.'

'How do you know that?'

'Because I was there! I had a crap Volvo in those days

that kept giving me trouble, so I got the bus every morning. Bloody nuisance. And the police wouldn't leave me alone, asking questions, turning the house and yard upside down, even though I never even saw the poor girl. The bus driver didn't see her, either. I don't think she was ever there.'

He finished his beer, crushed the can and dropped it.

Meja shuddered, despite the heat. 'So they suspected you?'

'They suspected the whole village! I was no exception. And the longer it goes without her turning up, the worse it gets.'

Silje had started singing outside, demanding attention. Through the flimsy curtain Meja watched as she bent over seductively to pick up the bottle of wine hidden in the grass. She filled her glass to the brim and rested the paintbrush on her shoulder as she drank.

Torbjörn's eyes glazed over. Meja thought of the photographs in the shed and wondered if he had taken them.

'Do you think she ran away?' she asked. 'Or that someone's hurt her?'

'It wouldn't surprise me if that father of hers was behind it. Everyone knows about Lelle Gustafsson's fiery temper. He was barred by the hunting team because he was always starting a fight. Maybe he got angry with the girl. Couldn't stop himself and then tried to cover it up when he came to his senses. That's what I think.'

Torbjörn took off his grimy string vest and wiped himself under the arms with it. 'Now it's about time we went out into the sunshine and saw your mother. No point standing here brooding about it.'

*

Mikael Varg sat perspiring in Lelle's kitchen. His injured foot was propped up on a chair opposite him and his ashen face twitched constantly. Lelle couldn't decide whether the boy had been drinking or taken drugs, but the words tumbled out and the pupils of his eyes were constricted and predatory.

'Why did you break into my house?'

'I didn't break in anywhere. It wasn't locked.'

'What were you doing in Lina's room?'

Varg chewed his cuticles and his eyes darted around the room.

'I don't know.'

'You don't know?'

Lelle banged his hand hard on the table, making the crockery jump. 'You might as well start talking, because I don't intend to let you go until I've got some answers.'

Varg grimaced.

'My foot's killing me.'

'I don't give a shit about that. If you want to get out of here alive you'd better start talking. What were you doing in Lina's room?'

'I just wanted to get close to her.'

'You wanted to get close to her, so you broke into my house?'

Silent tears began to trickle down his dirty cheeks. Varg didn't bother wiping them away.

'You're not the only one who misses her, you know. There's not a minute when I don't think about Lina. I knew you'd be on that fucking march, so I thought this was my chance to get close to her again. I only wanted to see her room. See her things. Smell her clothes.'

Lelle raised his hand. 'Let me see if I've got this right. A torchlight procession is arranged for your missing girl-friend *and you choose not to take part*?'

'It's not easy taking part when the whole village is staring at you.'

'You don't expect pity, do you?'

Tears streamed from his eyes, but Varg seemed unaware of them. His T-shirt was wet and grass-stained and clung like an extra skin to his wiry body. His jaw was taut, as if the flesh was pulled too tight. The boy had gone to pieces since he last sat in the kitchen with Lina. He'd had muscles then, and a laugh that filled the whole house. Anette loved that laugh.

Lelle leaned across the table, so close he could smell the fear coming off Varg. 'Empty your pockets.'

The whites of Varg's eyes widened.

'Why? I haven't taken anything.'

'Stand up and empty your pockets, before I twist that other ankle of yours.'

Varg's eyes twitched as he hesitated, and not until Lelle lurched forward to grab him did he hurry to empty his side and back pockets. He placed an iPhone with a cracked screen, a black leather wallet and a penknife on the scratched tabletop.

Lelle took the wallet and looked through it: fifty kronor in coins, bank cards, and two dog-eared photographs of Lina. One of them was of her face. She was looking into the lens with a secretive expression and smiling with her lips closed. In the other she was stretched out on a bed, entirely naked apart from her briefs. Her face was turned away and strands of hair fell over her bare breasts. The air caught in his lungs and instinctively he lashed out, hitting Varg so hard he fell back in his chair.

'What the fuck kind of pictures are these?'

'They're my pictures. I took them.'

'*You took them.* I can bloody well believe you did. What I want to know is whether Lina knew you were taking naked pictures of her? Did she?'

Lelle stood over him and watched as Varg shrank into the chair, hugging himself for protection.

'Of course she knew! We were together. We took pictures of each other. Nothing weird about that.'

Lelle's rage made him grab the picture of Lina. He tore it to shreds with trembling fingers and let them rain down on the table. Then he turned to Varg and cuffed him out of the chair.

'Get out of here, before I kill you!'

✳

Two nights and no sign of Carl-Johan. When Silje and Torbjörn had fallen asleep Meja sat on the veranda, waiting and hoping. Her feet were resting on the dog's rough coat and she was drinking Silje's wine, not to get drunk but to calm the tumult inside her. To keep the loneliness at bay. She lit a cigarette and thought the dog looked at her disapprovingly.

'What does it matter?' she said. 'He's not coming, anyway.'

But in the night he did turn up. It was the dog that heard him first. It got to its feet and ran the length of its chain and wagged its skinny body. She saw his shadow in the line of trees and felt the bubbling in her stomach. She quickly extinguished the cigarette and poured the wine into the flower bed below.

He smiled the smile that made everything in her vibrate.

'Are you sitting here waiting for me?'

'I couldn't sleep.'

He hugged her to him and if he smelled the smoke he didn't say.

'Shall we go down to the lake?'

She nodded. They left the dog on its chain and ran

towards the forest and on to the track where roots made thick ridges across their path. He took her hand and she smiled at his back while she struggled to keep up the pace. The surge of joy inside her was like the rushing in the treetops.

When they reached the lake he led her to a flat rock over-hanging the water.

Small waves on the lake came closer and retreated. The air was cold despite the lightness of the night, and Carl-Johan put his arm around her. He gave off a faint smell of livestock and barns.

'I almost thought you'd forgotten me,' she said.

'Forgotten you?' he laughed. 'Never.'

'I've waited and waited for you to come.'

'We've got so much to do at the farm,' he said. 'I couldn't get away.'

She looked at his hands, at the red skin and the callouses. He seemed too young to have hands like that.

'Then I realized I haven't even got your number,' she said. 'Otherwise I would have texted you.'

'I haven't got a mobile.'

She stared at him. 'Why not?'

'My dad's not keen on new technology.'

The water lapped against the rock. Meja wondered how he survived without a mobile, but didn't like to ask. She thought he looked embarrassed, as if he was ashamed. Maybe his family was poor and couldn't afford mobile phones. She had been in similar situations with Silje through the years, dark periods when all the money went on other things. Silje's alcohol and tablets, mostly.

'Where are your brothers tonight?' she asked instead.

'I made them stay at home.' He smiled. 'I wanted you to myself.'

Meja gasped, looked at the water and saw it pulsating in tune with her feelings. The wind carried with it a chill and the smell of pine needles, but she wasn't cold now. Carl-Johan leaned his cheek on her forehead.

'But Göran would like to know if you've got a sister,' he said.

Meja smiled.

'I haven't got any brothers or sisters. At least, none I'm aware of.'

'It must have been lonely, growing up like that.'

She shrugged.

'And your dad, where's he?'

Meja swallowed and the tingling in her stomach was replaced by anxiety.

'I don't know,' she said. 'He left before I was born. I never knew him.'

'That's so sad.'

'It's hard to miss what you haven't had.'

'You're strong,' said Carl-Johan. 'I can see that. I'd never cope. I'd be nothing without my family.'

He stroked the hair away from her cheeks with **his**

fingertips and looked at her from under his white lashes. Meja stopped breathing. She couldn't hear the water or the whine of the mosquitoes, but she saw him swat them away.

'Shall we swim?'

They swam, even though the water made their joints numb and their teeth chatter in the silence. She could see the blue veins under his skin and the long, thin muscles around his shoulders as he moved in front of her. She struggled to keep up with him. The lake was shallow, but the bottom was soft and loose and gave way under her feet. Carl-Johan turned and beckoned to her, wanting her to follow him out to the middle of the lake where there was a circle of rocks. She was ashamed at being such a poor swimmer, and when she felt a passing shoal of fish brush coldly against her thigh she immediately turned back.

'I'm freezing.'

Carl-Johan had towels with him and Meja wound one round her dripping hair and watched him make a fire. His movements were so smooth and confident, his hands snapping twigs and stripping bark. His knees broke spruce branches with no trouble at all, and his rough hands could touch everything without bleeding. Her own hands and shins were always being scraped by lichen and low bushes, leaving cuts that itched and stung.

'I don't belong here,' she said, as the fire crackled and sent sparks into the sky. 'I feel lost.'

Carl-Johan took her hand and put his lips on an open graze running across the back of it. It gave her goosebumps and she shivered.

'I'll teach you everything I know,' he said. 'And when I'm finished it'll feel like you were born in the wilds.'

His breath brushed against her upper lip and she felt the bubbling in her stomach again. His eyes merged as he moved closer and she looked at his mouth, challenging him to kiss her. When he finally did, she looked at him surreptitiously, checking to see that his eyes were closed. Silje had said you couldn't trust a man who kissed with his eyes open. *If he doesn't close his eyes it's time to pack up and go.*

But Carl-Johan's eyes were closed. Closed tight.

The night was alive, sifting its wet breath through the distorted trees and blowing mist over lakes and rivers, making them dance. It made itself impenetrable where the darkness lurked. Lelle leaned against the car bonnet and filled his lungs with tobacco and moisture. In the gloom the fog lights illuminated no more than a few metres ahead. The Silver Road lay like a death trap beside him, abandoned and waiting. A whole night's search would be lost.

A car pulled up behind his and through the veils of mist he made out garish police colours. Lelle turned his back on it as he heard the door echo through the silence.

'Shit, Lelle, you can't drive in this weather.'

'Does it look like I'm driving?'

Hassan's outline was blurred. He was also changed by the mist, shrunken. A thermos shone in his hand as he approached. He perched beside Lelle and unscrewed the top, poured the steaming liquid, handing it to Lelle. More vapour filled the night.

'Do you want me to get you home?'

'And what am I supposed to do there?'

'Rest. Eat. Take a shower. Watch Netflix. Things normal people do.'

'I can't sit still long enough.'

Lelle gulped a mouthful of liquid and spat it out again just as quickly. 'What the hell is this?'

'It's white tea. From China. Said to be good for the circulation.'

'For fuck's sake.'

Lelle handed the cup back and picked small leaves from his tongue. Hassan chuckled, swallowed a few deep mouthfuls and exaggeratedly smacked his lips. Lelle put a damp cigarette in his mouth and it glowed back to life. He was grateful for the company although he would never admit it.

'Mikael Varg broke into my place last night.'

'Are you serious?'

'I came home and found him in the garden. He'd jumped out of Lina's window. Twisted his ankle.'

'So why didn't you call me?'

'I took care of it.'

Hassan screwed the stopper back in the flask and sighed. 'Dare I ask what you did with him?'

'I didn't offer him tea and cakes, if that's what you're hoping. But I let him go.'

'Did he try to steal anything?'

'Nope.'

Lelle studied the glowing end of his cigarette. He saw Varg's staring eyes, the hollow cheeks, the tears covering his face.

'He had a photograph of Lina in his wallet. One of those naked pictures.'

'From the time they were together?'

'I presume so.'

Hassan inhaled slowly and said nothing. Lelle flicked his cigarette into the ditch and a vague feeling of nausea caught in his throat. He wiped the damp from his face with his sleeve and had the feeling the whole world was crying. That everything was slowly leaking.

'You're a college teacher,' Hassan said. 'You know what kids are like with photographs these days. It's nothing unusual. We see it all the time. Parents report it, pictures are shared and get in the wrong hands. Today's kids like to experiment, take risks.'

'I know. But I don't trust Varg. The guy's fallen apart worse than I have in the years since Lina disappeared.'

'Perhaps he misses her?'

'Maybe. Or else his conscience is giving him trouble.'

Hassan stood up and Lelle felt the car rise under him.

'Do you want me to have a word with him?'

'No, leave him be. He'll slip up sooner or later.'

*

'Can't you go and put some decent clothes on!' Meja said to Silje, who was walking around the sitting room in her underclothes.

Bewildered, Silje looked down at herself, at the baggy knickers and bra splashed with red acrylic paint.

'You know what I'm like when I'm painting,' she said. 'I only see the colours!'

She disappeared into the bedroom and when she came out again she had put on a purple silk kimono and pulled her hair back in a messy knot. Her throat was flushed and she had that fixed expression that meant her behaviour was hard to predict.

They heard the gravel under the tyres long before they saw the car. Carl-Johan's old Volvo was long and angular, with rusty wheel arches. Silje leaned over Meja's shoulder, so close Meja could smell her breath, yeasty from the wine she had drunk.

'He drives, does he? How old is he?'

'Nineteen.'

'Birger's lad has probably been driving since he was twelve,' said Torbjörn 'That's nothing unusual for villages around here.'

Silje straightened her kimono.

'Good-looking guy!' she said, as Carl-Johan got out of the car. 'I never knew you were so superficial, Meja!'

He handed her a bunch of ox-eye daisies that had already begun to wilt, and she gave him an awkward hug in the hall. His hair was still damp and smelled of shampoo. His shirt was buttoned all the way up and stubble showed above the collar. He was no boy. Meja saw it in Silje's reaction when they stepped into the kitchen, saw she was impressed. Brown spittle ran down Torbjörn's chin as he greeted him, asked how Birger was and introduced Silje as his new woman. Silje tipped her head back and laughed, revealing the shiny fillings. She had been drinking, but her eyes were clear and they scrutinized Carl-Johan unashamedly, from the tip of his toes all the way up to his hair.

'You'll want some coffee?'

'No. We're going to my room.'

His palm was cold and damp as she pulled him up the stairs and she let it go as soon as they had reached her room.

'You'll have to excuse my mother. She's a bit pissed.'

'She seems nice.'

Carl-Johan had to duck under the beams. He looked around as if he was searching for something, running his ice-blue eyes over the empty walls and stopping when he came to her backpack. It was open, revealing everything she owned. Meja stood still, feeling ashamed.

'So this is where you live?'

'It's only temporary. I'm not staying.'

'You're not?'

She shook her head. 'I'm eighteen next spring. I'm going back down south then.'

Carl-Johan reached out his hand and drew her to him. 'I don't want you to go. We've only just met.'

He stroked the hair from her face and kissed her below the ear. Then he ran his fingertips over her collarbone and murmured something about how she mustn't leave until she had seen everything. Then he found her lips and soon she was lying under him on the creaking bed. He was heavy and eager and his hands found their way under her top. Meja pushed him away and began unbuttoning his shirt. His chest was heaving. She wondered how many girls he'd had sex with, but didn't want to ask. His shirt slid to the floor, along with her T-shirt. They were all lips and warm skin, and Meja's head rang. Her fingers gripped his shoulders and she didn't want to let him go. It was only when they heard the sound of Silje's resounding laughter that they paused. Carl-Johan's face was flushed.

'Has Torbjörn said anything about me? About my family?'

Meja hesitated. Her lips felt strange, swollen. 'Just that you're some kind of hippies.'

'Hippies?'

'Yeah, you know. Living close to nature. Like people used to do.'

She could see all his teeth when he laughed. One hand cupped her breast, directly over her beating heart.

'Shall we go back to mine? My parents want to meet you.'

'Have you told them about me?'

'Of course.'

'What did you say?'

'Nothing special. Just that you're the best person I've ever met.'

Her ears filled with a wild rushing sound, as if the forest was living inside her head. Carl-Johan pressed his forehead to hers and his eyes smiled.

'What do you think? Shall we go?'

Meja's tongue wouldn't obey. Her heart was so full of joy she could only nod.

✳

For half the night he had splashed through the marshes once the mist had lifted. The whole car stank on the way home, from the red mud and straggly moss on his boots and trouser legs. The first thing Lelle did was lean against the veranda and ease off his boots.

When he stood up he noticed the front door was ajar. He could make out the shoe rack in the dim light inside and the rag rug in the hall. His heart raced. He climbed the steps in his socks, listened and peered through the crack in the door. He put his hand on the gun in his waistband. There was no damage to the door, nothing to show it had been forced open. He edged in sideways. There was only a faint squeak from the hinges. Had he forgotten to lock it? That lousy memory of his, he just couldn't trust it. A few steps in and he picked up a vague smell of perfume that definitely did not belong here. A woman's smell.

He crept through the hall and past the kitchen, then padded over the parquet flooring, his hand still on the gun. He tried to listen, but all he could hear was the blood pounding in his ears and his own breathing. The smell of perfume was stronger here. He rounded the corner and saw the light in the office was on. A strip of light seeped under the door. It took only a few strides for him to reach it, put one hand on the handle and lift his weapon. He flung the door open, aimed the gun directly in front of him and saw the moving shadow on the wall and the figure inside. There was a terrified shriek and then two white palms in the air.

'For God's sake, Lelle!'

'What the hell are you doing here?'

He lowered the gun and looked at Anette. She had used her key, of course. The key he had asked her to return. She looked exhausted with her drooping face and her hair scraped back. She was standing by the map of northern Sweden, which was spread over the wall and festooned with map pins and Post-it notes. Anette flung out an arm.

'What are you doing, running around with a gun? Are you mad?'

'I thought someone had broken in.'

'I rang the bell, but you didn't open.'

'Oh, so you think you can just walk right in? You don't live here any more, Anette. I want that key back.'

She lifted her head and looked at him. Perhaps she was holding the key in her hand, because she clenched her fists and buried them in her armpits. She ran her eyes over his sweat-stained T-shirt and down to the ragged socks.

'Where have you been? You look terrible.'

'I've been looking for our daughter. And you don't look so wonderful yourself.'

Lelle secured the gun and put it down on a bookshelf. His anger made him afraid of it. Anette looked at him in silence for a while. Her eyes were red, as if she had been crying. She turned to face the map and the pinheads scattered across the thin paper.

'What's this?'

'What does it look like? It's a map.'

'And the pins?'

'They mark the places I've searched.'

Anette raised a fist to her mouth. She had stopped breathing, but she wasn't crying. She stood motionless and studied the map for a long time. Then slowly she turned her head and looked at him.

'I'm here to say that you can stop looking now,' she said. 'Lina doesn't exist. She's dead.'

✳

Meja dug in her backpack for something to put on. She was ashamed of how few clothes she had. A couple of washed-out pairs of jeans and four faded T-shirts. Odd socks. For as long as she could remember she had been teased about wearing the same clothes every day, looking wrong, dirty.

Carl-Johan sat on the bed, his eyes shining.

'You're fine just as you are,' he said. 'You don't need to make an effort.'

Silje and Torbjörn had moved to the bedroom by the time they came downstairs. The dog sat outside the door, forlornly scratching it with its paw. It threw a reproachful look at Meja and Carl-Johan as they passed. The TV was on, but they could still hear the coaxing on the other side of the door. Meja couldn't get into the hall fast enough.

'Aren't you going to tell them we're leaving?'

'They won't notice anyway.'

The sign to Svartliden pointed straight into the forest and the road consisted of nothing more than a couple of deep wheel tracks separated by swaying grass. The spruces were so close that their branches scraped the wing mirrors. It seemed unlikely that a road like this would lead anywhere.

The rain came from nowhere and obliterated the forest. Carl-Johan gave a whistle as it rattled against the roof of the car. He had one hand on the wheel, nonchalantly, as if the car was steering itself. From time to time he glanced at Meja and smiled, as if trying to convince himself she was still sitting there. Meja held her head erect and tried not to show the anxiety she felt. She always felt small when she went to other people's homes. Real homes were alien worlds where she didn't know the rules. She was used to mattresses on the floor, bathrooms without toilet paper and kitchens that echoed. She and Silje had never had a proper home, merely versions of something that didn't even come close. For Carl-Johan it was different. He seemed proud of his background.

They reached a tall gate, made of metal bars. *Welcome to Svartliden* was painted at the top. Meja sank further into her seat as Carl-Johan stepped out of the car and opened it.

'What a gate,' she said.

'Me and my brothers made it. Everything you see on this farm has been made by our family.'

The forest opened up to reveal a large meadow where a group of cows was grazing. A gravel drive led to a turning circle in front of a huge house, standing like a wooden castle where the forest began, with barns and outbuildings on either side. Meja's stomach lurched. To think people lived like this.

Carl-Johan pointed out the stables and the dog pens, where the shaggy animals had their front paws on the bars and were barking furiously at them. Beside the pens was a potato plot as big as a tennis court.

'You can't see it because of the forest, but the lake is over there.'

'It's lovely.'

Meja stayed in the car. She put her hands on her stomach and tried breathing slowly to calm herself down. She had always hated meeting other people's parents, hated the way they weighed her up, judged her. Especially the mothers, who could spot the failings.

What do your parents do?

Mum's an artist.

An artist? Oh, I see. What kind of artist?

She paints pictures.

Would we have heard of her?

Don't think so.

And your father, what does he do?

Don't know.

You don't know what your father does?

He doesn't live with us.

Oh.

There was nothing more to be said. At worst they already knew who Silje was, and then they didn't ask any questions at all.

✳

Lelle stared at the floor to avoid looking at Anette's contorted face, but he could hear her whimpering and sniffing.

'For the first two years I felt her, I *felt* she was alive. My heart lit up when I thought of her. You know, a kind of warmth. But it's not there any more. The light has gone out.'

'I don't know what you're talking about.'

Anette took a couple of steps forward, threw her arms around him and rested her cheek on his arm. 'She's dead, Lelle. Our daughter is dead. I've felt it all winter. Something inside me has broken. I can't explain it, but that's how it is – our daughter is dead.'

'I'm not listening to this bullshit.'

He tried to back out of her grasp, but she clung on hard, pressing her wet face against his T-shirt and groping for his skin. She clasped and clawed and in the end he gave up and let her hold him, wrapped his own arms around her, first loosely, but then tighter. They clung to each other as if their life depended on it, and he couldn't recall them ever holding each other this way. As if they were being destroyed from within.

When Anette lifted her face to his he kissed her without thinking. She tasted of salty tears and he kissed her hard and pressed his groin into hers in a desperate attempt to get closer. He had to get closer. Anette began pulling at his clothes, fumbling and tugging at his flies, before dragging him down on top of her and helping him to force his way inside her. She wrapped her legs around his waist as if to lock him to her. He thrust hard, harder than he wanted to, and he could see the tears dropping from his face on to hers. Her nails dug into his skin and it stung, and he realized it was the stinging he wanted. The actual pain.

Afterwards they lay side by side, sharing a cigarette. Sunlight flooded through the blinds and fell in stripes across their naked bodies. Anette prodded his ribs.

'You've lost weight.'

'No need to worry about me.'

'You're skinny and dirty and you don't get enough sleep. You're wearing yourself out.'

She stood up and pulled on her clothes. He studied the freckly skin above her breasts and thought how much he would like to rest his head there, just above her heart. His buttocks stung from her nails. He wondered what it meant, this making love to her. Whether she would go home and tell Thomas, or whether it was just one of those things that happened. He wanted her to stay, but at the same time he knew there was no room for her. A heavy, suffocating weariness had come over him and he thought he could sleep just as he was, naked on the floor. But Anette had disappeared into the kitchen and he heard the sound of breaking eggs and the rattle of pans, the puff of the percolator and voices on the radio. Anette called to him through the coffee aroma to come and eat.

When he went into the kitchen he saw she had pulled up the blinds and was standing in the sunshine, and for a moment everything was exactly as it should be. Lina in bed upstairs, Anette about to call her down. The sun was shining in so convincingly that there was no room for nightmares. But when Anette poured the coffee he saw the sad lines around her mouth and knew it was all an illusion. She sat down opposite him, in the same place she sat when she lived here, but now her back was straighter and she looked uncomfortable. Two heaps of scrambled eggs lay between them. Lelle was so hungry that he felt sick as he stuck his fork into the food. Anette watched him through the steam from her mug.

'Don't get angry now, but I meant what I said. I'm certain Lina has gone.'

'It makes no difference. I still won't give up until I've found her.'

In Carl-Johan's home she was met by light wood and warm colours, and a rich aroma of stewed meat and herbs. A woman in an apron and with rough, red hands came out from the kitchen and greeted them. She was darker and slimmer than Carl-Johan, but had the same fine features. She smiled and pulled at the silver-grey plait hanging over her shoulder.

'You must be Meja. I'm really pleased to meet you. My name's Anita.'

She led them into the kitchen where an older man was sitting at the table, cleaning a gun of some kind. The various parts were spread out in front of him and his eyes were slits when he looked up at Meja. He inspected her from top to toe and all the way out to her fingertips, as if he was taking stock of her. Meja's skin prickled and it felt as if her whole body was on fire.

'And who have we here?' he asked, pointing at her with the dirty rag he was holding.

'This is Meja,' Carl-Johan said. 'My girlfriend.'

'Meja, eh? I've heard a lot about you.'

Birger stood up and when he opened his mouth she could see dark gaps between his teeth. He looked old – too old to have a son of Carl-Johan's age – but he was broad and robust despite his age, and his handshake was strong when he reached out to greet her.

There was milk and rye-bread rolls, and home-made blueberry jam that stained their lips. Birger talked about the farm and the land, the ancient forest, the marshlands and Svartliden Lake. The berries, mushrooms and fish. They could feed an entire village, he said, and things would only get better. Anita stood with her back to them, peeling root vegetables. Her shoulders jerked with the effort. She didn't say much, but neither did Carl-Johan. He only sat with his arm tight around Meja, his eyes shining. The light fell on his throat, illuminating the thin blue veins near the surface. She thought she could see his pulse beating underneath.

'Carl-Johan tells me you're from further south,' Birger said.

'I was born in Stockholm, but we've lived pretty much all over the place.'

'I moved about a lot as well, when I was young,' Birger said. 'My parents couldn't look after me, so I was sent from one foster family to the next. Never got to put down roots. It's a tough way to grow up, gives you a protective shell. That's why I want to give my sons the things I never had. Somewhere settled. Security.'

Meja liked his voice, the way it vibrated through the room. The laughter lines that gave the impression that he enjoyed life.

Anita pushed the plate of rolls towards Meja.

'Don't hold back. Eat some more.'

The kitchen smelled of food and cleaning products. The surfaces gleamed. There were no ashtrays or empty bottles. An antique clock ticked in the corner. The stove had black iron doors and on the rag rug in front of it a cat was lying on its back, peering at them. There was a calmness here and Meja felt her muscles relax.

'You must show her the animals,' said Anita, when they had finished eating. 'We've got newborn calves and kids.'

The evening sun blazed over the barn and the meadow where the cows were grazing. Carl-Johan's fingers felt rough in hers. She could tell he worked with his hands. He led her through the wild flowers and the mosquitoes, and introduced her to the animals as if they were humans. *Agda, Indra, Tindra and Knut. And Algot, but you don't mess with him.* Her hands stroked sun-warmed skin and fed hay to soft mouths. Tiny kids drew circles on the ground with their unsteady legs, and Carl-Johan picked them up in his arms as if they were cuddly toys.

'This is paradise,' said Meja, as they sat with their backs to the barn wall.

It was night, but nothing seemed to be sleeping. Carl-Johan pulled a piece of hay from her hair and she wondered how it would feel to sleep next to him. To wake up in a place like this.

A door groaned in the silence and soon they saw a gangly figure walking towards the clearing. It was Göran, the oldest brother. He was holding a fishing rod and raised it when he saw them. Meja and Carl-Johan waved back.

'He can't sleep when it's this light, so he catches fish for us, for breakfast.'

'Fish for breakfast?'

'It tastes amazing.'

Carl-Johan stood up and brushed as much grass from his jeans as he could, before holding out his hand to her.

'Stay the night here and you'll find out.'

Lelle woke on the sofa in the sitting room. Laughter from the neighbour's barn floated into the room. According to the clock it was 6.30 and his body ached as he stood up and headed for the kitchen. He swore loudly when he realized he had wasted a whole night sleeping. Not until he saw the frying pan in the sink did he remember that Anette had been there. He could still hear her voice telling him Lina was dead, and he shook himself as if to shake off the words.

Anette had always had a kind of sixth sense.

He rinsed his face and mouth with cold water. Through the window he saw the empty hammock and heard the chains rustling in the wind. Anette lay there an eternity ago, spinning her ring from a chain over her distended stomach.

We're going to have a girl, Lelle.

How can you be so sure?

I just know.

He dried his face on one of the tea towels and looked towards the office doorway. Book spines stared back at him out of the gloom. Had they really made love?

He unlocked the front door and hurried to the postbox to get the morning paper. On top of the newspaper lay a shiny key. Anette's key. Ever since she left him she had refused to return the key, as if she couldn't really let him go. In actual fact it was the house she couldn't relinquish, the house where Lina grew up. But here it was, shining as if nothing special had happened.

Back in the kitchen he could hear Lina jeering at him because he still read a newspaper. *Nobody reads newspapers these days.* He could visualize her there, in her place at the table, could almost hear that sarcastic voice she had adopted. He dropped the inky pages on to the worn tabletop with a slap, as if she were sitting there, as if he wanted to tease her in return. *Here you have a real newspaper, not a blasted screen.* But the only thing he stirred

up was the dust, and it took a while before he saw the headline: 17-YEAR-OLD GIRL MISSING – POLICE NOT RULING
OUT CRIME. *The police and the public are searching for
a 17-year-old girl who disappeared from the Kraja camp
grounds in Arjeplog in the early hours of Sunday morning.
The girl was camping with a friend in this popular location
close to Motorway 95. According to her friend she left the
tent early in the morning and never returned. The friend
called the police who have made a thorough search of the
area with the help of volunteers and the Home Guard. 'We
cannot eliminate a crime at this stage and we are therefore
keen for members of the public to come forward with any
information,' said Mats Niemi of Arjeplog Police. The girl
has blonde hair, blue eyes and is 156 cm tall. At the time of
the disappearance she was wearing a black vest top, black
jeans and white Nike trainers.*

Lelle read the lines over and over again, but the words
kept merging into one. The coffee burned in his throat
as he got up and started pacing up and down the floor.
Through the window he saw the neighbours' children, but
their voices didn't reach him. His stomach abruptly con-
tracted and he threw his head over the sink, vomiting up
hot coffee and sour bile. He felt the sweat slide down his
back and his arms begin to shake, and when he sank to the
floor he rammed his fists into his eyes and let out a howl.

*

His right cheek was resting against the cool wooden floor and his mobile was digging into him. Lelle fumbled in his pocket and put the screen to his ear, listened to his heart, beating faster and faster. Finally, Hassan's voice: 'Lelle, what's up?'

'Have you heard?'

'Heard what?'

'About the missing seventeen year old in Arjeplog.'

There was a long sigh above the static of the police radio. 'Lelle, it's way too early to draw any conclusions.'

'Is it?'

'The search is still very much underway.'

'I have a feeling they won't find her,' Lelle heard his voice crack. 'I'm afraid it will be the same as Lina.'

'I can understand that,' said Hassan. 'But currently we have no grounds to suspect...'

'They were the same height!' Lelle interrupted. 'To the millimetre!'

He heard how he sounded, but couldn't stop himself.

'This case has a completely different set of circumstances,' Hassan said. 'Everything points to her boyfriend.'

Lelle gave a frustrated laugh. There was a bitter taste on his tongue.

'When Lina disappeared you accused *me* of all people, and where did that lead?'

'Just calm down, Lelle.'

'I *am* calm! I only want to make sure the police are doing

their damned job. I don't know whether you've noticed, but the girl's description is practically identical to Lina's. And both of them disappeared near the Silver Road. Do you think that sounds like chance?'

'It's too early to say and I don't want to speculate. She's barely been gone two days. There's still a good chance we'll find her.'

Lelle put his hand to his face and noticed his cheeks were wet. 'You won't find her.'

'I really hope you're wrong.'

'So do I.'

Meja was alone when she woke up with the smell of Carl-Johan still on the sheets. The clock radio on the bedside table said 6.30. She wondered if he always got up this early. Dark wooden shutters kept the light out and she squinted in the darkness to find her clothes and her mobile. The battery was dead. Posters of fighter aircraft of various types covered the walls. Meja put on her jeans and T-shirt. An old typewriter sat on a desk by the window. She stroked the black keys with her finger, stopping at the letter C.

'You're awake.'

Carl-Johan stood in the doorway. The light was behind him and she couldn't see his face, apart from his smile. He came into the room and held her tightly. The smell of hay and animals clung to his clothes and his hair was dripping.

'Did you sleep OK?'

'It's so lovely and dark in here.'

Carl-Johan walked over to one of the windows and opened the shutters to let in the daylight. Meja squinted.

Carl-Johan held her hands in his.

'Are you hungry? Would you like some breakfast?'

They were all sitting in the kitchen, Birger, Anita and the two brothers. They studied her inquisitively as she sat down. She combed her hair with her fingers and looked at the food on the table. There was freshly baked bread that steamed when it was sliced, three kinds of cheese, ham, and boiled eggs with speckled shells. Milk foamed in a jug.

'All our own produce,' said Birger. 'You can't get food fresher than this.'

Meja felt the hunger pangs in her stomach.

'Carl-Johan said you usually eat fish for breakfast.'

'And so we do. Göran is our night fisherman.'

Göran leaned over the table, resting his arms on the dark surface.

'The fish weren't biting last night.'

Pär was sitting beside him, his cheeks bulging with food. He grinned at Carl-Johan. 'Only Carl-Johan got lucky last night.'

Crumbs sprayed across the table as he laughed, and Carl-Johan pretended to attack him with the butter knife. Anita protested. Her hair fell like snow over her shoulders and she seemed to find it hard to sit still. She went from the table to the stove, poured out coffee, rinsed plates. Every time her eyes fell on Meja she beamed. The sun and wind had left their mark on her face and made her beautiful. Meja thought she would like to look like that when she was old. Weathered and coloured by life itself.

'Your mother knows you're here, doesn't she?'

'I think so. My battery's dead, so I can't ring.'

'I've got no time for mobile phones,' Birger said. 'They are only a way for the government and the powers that be to keep an eye on us.'

Meja stirred her coffee and felt Carl-Johan's fingers on her thigh, tickling her.

'It's pretty smart, to be honest,' Birger continued. 'Youngsters are dependent on being constantly connected to the world, and that way the folk in charge get total control. They can see you, hear you, film you. They know exactly where you are at all times and can track your movements.'

Birger's eyes reminded her of water as he looked at her. Two pools in ice that never thawed. Meja's T-shirt felt sticky in her armpits and the fresh bread turned leathery in her mouth.

'Who do you mean?' she asked.

Göran and Pär snorted, but Birger had stopped smiling.

'That's just the problem,' he said. 'They know all about you, but we don't know a damned thing about them.'

*

Carl-Johan gathered up her hair in his hand as he kissed her. The gear lever vibrated wildly between them and over his shoulder she caught sight of Torbjörn through the rain, which was lashing the dark planks. Carl-Johan clutched her wrists as he pushed her away from him.

'Don't look so sad. We'll see each other this evening.'

'Promise?'

'I promise.'

She walked slowly through the downpour, but stopped on the muddy drive to watch as he swung out and disappeared among the trees. She was dripping wet when she finally walked into the hall.

The dog did pirouettes and beat its tail against her sodden jeans. Torbjörn bellowed at it to lie down and handed a towel to Meja.

'Where have you been? We were about to call the police.'

'I was in Svartliden, with Carl-Johan.'

Meja wound the towel around her hair and barged past him, searching for Silje. She was sitting in the kitchen, sketching. Her hair was a different colour. Raven-black strands fell over her shoulders and made her look even more unhealthy. Her skinny arms were drowning in Torbjörn's flannel shirt. She didn't lift her eyes from the sheet of paper in front of her.

'Couldn't you have phoned? All this money we spend on your mobile and you don't even use it.'

'The battery died.'

'Torbjörn's been going insane. You should have seen him. He's been driving round half the night, looking for you.'

Meja shot a look at Torbjörn. His unwashed hair was all over the place and he had crimson cuts on his arms as if he had scratched himself.

'Another girl disappeared the other night,' he said. 'Too right I was worried.'

Meja waved a hand at the dirty dishes and the black refuse sack on the floor containing empty cans and bottles. She grimaced at the stink of beer and cigarette butts and thought of the kitchen at Svartliden, with its shining surfaces and fresh smell. The thought gave her strength. She turned to Torbjörn and fixed her eyes on him.

'I don't think it's me you should be worrying about.'

That evening he saw her face on the news. Hanna Larsson. A pretty blonde girl with dark eye make-up and a shy smile. A picture of a blue tent in front of a silvery lake. So like Lina he lost his breath. The old ache inside his ribs returned, making him bend over and press his clenched fists to the pain. Anette had nagged him to let the doctor have a look, but he knew there was no cure. The grief itself had taken root in there.

When he looked up again he saw Hanna Larsson's parents on the screen. Shock and dread lay like a pale mask over their faces. The father begged in a broken voice that was so familiar it made the pain explode in Lelle's chest. He pleaded to all the lucky devils who would never have to feel the utter helplessness of losing a child. Someone no one had seen and knew nothing about, yet still he pleaded. Lelle looked at the man's lips, the unbuttoned shirt collar and the unshaven cheeks, the desperation carved into his face. And the mother, who was beyond speaking. When the ad break came his entire body was shaking.

He could feel her gaze from the mantelpiece. Lina was smiling in the picture, but it was a challenging smile. *Don't just sit there, Dad. Do something!* He paced the floor, trying to breathe, despite all the evil. In the hall he put on heavy boots and his Fjällräven jacket with the enormous hood that kept out the mosquitoes and left an opening for the eyes. He patted his chest to make sure his cigarettes and lighter were in the pocket. He didn't bother to lock the door. Through the window he saw the evening sun burning high above the treetops and he felt the old familiar tingling in his fingertips. A heavy aroma of mown grass and barbecued meat came from his neighbours' garden. Beyond the blackcurrant bushes he could see the children jumping on a trampoline, their downy hair flying up into the air. What wouldn't he give to see that again?

Poor devil.

How do you go on?

If only they had found a body.

He didn't have time to look for anyone else's child. These light nights were too few to waste. All too soon the light would fade and in the darkness everything would rot and freeze and be hidden under layers of blind snow. The summer was a precious time, none of it must be wasted. Even so, the wheel and the pedals steered him northwards and inland, towards the place where the second girl had disappeared.

*

At the Kraja campsite the roadside was lined with vehicles. He had to park at least a kilometre away. He pulled up his hood and felt his heart contract at the sounds of people calling, dogs barking and static coming from police patrol cars. The place was crawling with people. They blinded him with their hi-vis clothing and reflective tape. Lelle made his way to the camping area where the police had put up their cordons. Blue and white barrier tape surrounded the solitary sagging tent in the centre of all the activity. His stomach began to churn. A man was taking pictures of the tent on his mobile and a young police officer went over and told him to leave. Lelle pushed on, taking a detour around the crime scene until he found a woman with short hair and a sharp voice who directed him to the human search line. It had just set off and if he hurried he could join in. She might have asked for his name, but he couldn't be sure because he had blocked off his ears.

The area was a tangle of undergrowth and thick vegetation, and he had to lift his feet high as if he were walking through snow. On his right was an older woman who wheezed as she breathed, but moved as easily as a lynx through the terrain. On his left was a man who couldn't stop talking about his time with the Army Rangers K4 battalion and the mosquitoes that attacked his arse when he took a shit in the forest. He would never forget those days and everyone should have that kind of training. Lelle muttered indifferently in reply, his face to the ground, and listened to all the other sounds: the din of the rapids and the rotor blades of the Home Guard's helicopters in the distance. The forest swarmed with life and the atmosphere was heavy with fear and hope and everything else people were exhaling. Lelle himself was empty. He couldn't bring himself to feel anything other than the tension and the lack of sleep that pounded in his body. This was exactly the way they had looked for Lina at the start, before it became him on his own. He had been so angry with them. The people. So intensely angry. Angry at their awkwardness, their lack of eye contact, their need to pat him as if he were an animal. Angry because they knew nothing, because they couldn't help him, because they went home to their own children after a day's searching and resumed their lives. It was a rage that had never left him. He would never see people in the same light again.

At dawn, when the search was called off, he could feel

blood sticking to his socks from the blisters. No trace of the missing girl and the faces of the search leaders were grim. His body felt fragile and drained as he made his way back to the car through the light mist that had settled between the trees. Blurred figures moved among them. The forest was still full of people, but a tense quietness hung in the air. The shouts, whistles and barking had died down and been replaced by hanging heads. The silence was so familiar he felt it would tear him apart.

He was close to stumbling over some barrier tape that had come loose from a tree when he spotted him. The father. His grey hair had been flat on his head during the TV interview, but now it stuck out in all directions. Despite that, it was impossible not to recognize him.

Lelle wanted to lower his head and walk on, but he couldn't. Instead he walked directly through the low berry bushes and stood in front of the man, almost as if he were the one he had been looking for. They looked at each other as Lelle struggled to find the words. He heard himself say his own name and cough to clear the anguish from his throat.

'My daughter disappeared three years ago. If anyone has the faintest idea what you're going through, it's me.'

Hanna Larsson's father blinked mutely. His eyes were white with fear. Lelle saw it and was ashamed.

'Anyway, I'm on Eniro, if you want to talk.'

That was as much as he could say. He realized that his

presence scared the man, and that he recognized him. Maybe he had seen Lelle on the TV news at that time, while hope was still alive. But time had passed, and three years didn't inspire hope. Lelle's experience was a nightmare that no one wanted to recognize in case it was contagious.

Back in the car he leaned his head against the steering wheel and sobbed silently, without tears. He was ashamed. Ashamed because under the despair were the beginnings of renewed hope. Hope that this latest disappearance would change everything.

*

'Get dressed, why don't you?'

Silje lay on the sunlounger. The white triangle where she had shaved off her pubic hair glowed in the night sun. A wine glass was balanced on a clump of grass beside her, alongside a growing pile of dog-ends from the cigarettes she had stubbed out on the ground.

'There's something about the air here that makes clothes seem superfluous.'

Her voice had that clear ring to it that signified sleepless nights and sudden impulses that had to be obeyed. The black hair dye was only a beginning. Next time it could be more destructive. Meja thought of Dr Roos, wondered whether he could write a prescription, even though they had moved, or whether Silje should look for a new doctor. There were barely any hospitals up here, she thought, let alone psychiatric care. She held one of Silje's cigarettes under her nose and took a deep breath of the tobacco smell.

'I've stopped smoking.'

'Whatever for?'

'Because it's disgusting and because I promised Carl-Johan.'

Silje lit up and blew smoke deliberately in Meja's direction.

'Is he really called Carl-Johan?' she sneered. 'Hasn't he got a nickname, something easier to say?'

'What's wrong with Carl-Johan?'

'It sounds a bit pretentious, don't you think?'

'I think it sounds nice.'

'You shouldn't be doing everything to please him. Men need opposition, otherwise they get tired of you.'

'I don't need your advice.'

Silje poured out more red wine. Her hand trembled and she spilled some of it on to the grass. She leaned forward and stroked Meja's hair with her free hand and smiled at her through the spirals of smoke.

'My wise little Meja. You don't need my advice and you don't need a man, either. You'll manage perfectly well on your own, I've always said that.'

Meja dodged out of the way of Silje's show of affection. Red wine always made her touchy-feely.

'Carl-Johan isn't like other guys. He really likes me. Genuinely.'

'Are you sleeping together?'

Meja broke the unlit cigarette in two and the tobacco spilled on to her jeans.

'That's got nothing to do with you.'

'I know you find this hard to believe, but I am actually your mother.'

They heard the car long before they saw it. Meja reached for the blanket on the grass and threw it over Silje. When Carl-Johan's Volvo pulled up she was already on her feet, ready to leave.

'Where are you going?'

'I'm spending Midsummer with Carl-Johan at Svart-liden.'

Silje flicked ash into the grass and stretched out her arms. 'If you're going to be away all weekend, I need a hug.'

Reluctantly, Meja turned back. She felt her muscles stiffen in Silje's embrace and breathed in tobacco and hair dye. Silje pushed her away, lifted her sunglasses and their eyes met.

'You're not like me, Meja. Remember that. You don't need a man to survive.'

✳

He went back to Arjeplog the following evening. The tent had gone and they'd put up a Midsummer pole. Lelle steered clear of the people and disappeared among the bushes, lost in his solitary searching. He didn't give in until the mist floated up from the lake and the world vanished from sight.

Perhaps it was the tiredness, the cigarette smoke or the sun blinding him, but when he drove past Långträsk marshes he didn't see the reindeer. At least, not until it was too late. They were scattered about in the sunlight with their shedding coats and ribs heaving against the blue skin underneath. Instinctively he turned the wheel and skidded into the middle of the road, but he couldn't avoid a collision. He felt a jolt and heard the dull thud when one of the thin bodies hit the bonnet. The car screeched to a standstill and he saw the animals disperse and vanish over the marshes. His heart was racing. The half-smoked cigarette had slipped from his hand and was smouldering on the window frame. He reached for it with shaking fingers and climbed out of the car.

A dark shape lay on the asphalt. A yearling, judging from the size. Lelle swore out loud when he saw it was still breathing. Its ribcage was quivering and in the white tufts that remained of its winter coat he could see streaks of blood. Lelle fetched his pistol from the glove compartment and hurried back to the animal. The whites of its eyes gleamed up at him as he pressed the muzzle to its forehead and pulled the trigger. A few tremors ran through the animal's legs as its life ebbed away, then there was peace. Lelle put the gun in his belt, bent down and took a firm grasp on its hind legs just above the hooves. With some difficulty he dragged the carcase over the road and heaved it into the ditch. It left a wide brushstroke of blood across the asphalt. Lelle wiped his hands on his jeans and tried to get his breath back. He knelt beside the car to make sure no damage had been done. As long as it was fit to drive, he wasn't worried. Just as long as he could carry on looking for Lina. The sun was rapidly climbing in the sky and the birds were singing as if nothing had happened. When he sat behind the wheel again a cold shudder ran through his body and he cried without making a sound.

The forest and fields were painted blue in the midsummer night and black swarms of mosquitoes danced above the wild flowers. There was constant biting and stinging. Earlier that day they had slaughtered a pig. Meja didn't watch, but she heard the death cries echoing in her head for a long time afterwards. Over by the stables there was a dark, spreading pool of blood where flies had gathered. And then there was the pig itself, hanging on a spit over an open fire. There wasn't much meat left. The Midsummer pole cast a long shadow over the ground, and the wild-flower wreathes Anita had made to hang on the pole were dangling in the wind. Birger had led the dances round the pole until their legs ached. Not a single drop of alcohol had been on offer all evening. Meja lay with her head resting on Carl-Johan's chest and she could feel his heart beating.

'I don't think I've laughed so much in my entire life.'

'Neither have I.'

The fire shot flames into the sky and did its best to keep the mosquitoes away. Birger and Anita had said goodnight long since, but the lateness of the night meant nothing to the youngsters. Pär had suddenly become talkative in the early hours and he was filling the beautiful night with a string of weird tales about the end times, as he called it. Meja pretended not to hear and chatted quietly with Carl-Johan, drawing invisible circles on his skin with her fingertips, counting the moles on his arms and tickling his earlobes with a blade of grass, which made him laugh and bundle her up in his arms.

'It'll start with nuclear weapons,' said Pär. 'The mother of all bombs will kill half the world's population. After that only the people who are strong and prepared will survive. Then we can start over from the beginning. Learn from our mistakes.' He prodded the charred wood, his face glowing like the fire. 'Either that or nature will cause our downfall. If we don't get there first, then it will be nature that protests. Maybe Yellowstone, maybe somewhere else. The survivors will find out. But however it starts, there will be war. The bloodiest war in the history of mankind.'

He made it sound like something he was looking forward to. His voice quivered with a kind of suppressed tension. Several times he nudged Göran, who was sitting like a silent shadow beside him. Göran didn't appear to be

151

listening. He was hardly present as he sat staring into the fire. From time to time he scratched his chest and his arms viciously, as if he could hardly bear his own skin.

Pär drew a black cross on the ground with a charred barbecue skewer.

'I don't agree with the old man,' he said. 'All his talk about killer viruses and sickness. Yeah, stuff like that will happen, but not enough to bring an end to all humanity. A virus is simply a way of keeping the population down. Total downfall needs all-out war.'

Meja felt brave in Carl-Johan's arms. She looked up at Pär and challenged him. 'Do you really believe in all that?'

'All what?'

'That there's going to be a war.'

'Of course there will be a war. Look at the history of mankind. We have always fought. The problem now is that we've got weapons that can destroy the whole world. No one will escape.'

He stroked his stubbly chin and looked at Meja confrontationally through the flames.

'How long would you last if society collapsed?' he asked.

'What do you mean?'

'Without electricity, running water, supermarkets. How long would you survive?'

Meja looked down at Carl-Johan's hand in hers and stroked the rough callouses. 'No idea.'

'Do you know how long we would survive out here at Svartliden?'

She shook her head.

Pär held up one hand and spread his fingers wide. 'Five years. At least. Maybe forever.' He turned to Carl-Johan. 'Are you going to show her?'

Carl-Johan had his nose in Meja's hair.

'Show me what?' she said.

'Tomorrow,' he murmured. 'We'll do it tomorrow.'

'That's enough of this bollocks,' Göran said suddenly and stood up. He grabbed a bucket, filled it with water and flung it on the fire. He extinguished the last embers with his foot. A few of the sores he had torn open with his scratching were bleeding, but if he was aware of that he didn't show it. He fumbled with his flies and walked in among the trees. Pär dropped his skewer into the ashes.

'Only those who are prepared will survive,' he said and looked at Meja. 'The rest can only hope for mercy.'

They lay beside each other in the dark and the quietness, free of the midnight sun and the mosquitoes and with only the sound of Carl-Johan's breathing in the room, deep and throaty in sleep. His arm lay warm and heavy over her hip, but she didn't want to move it. She wanted to keep the loneliness at bay. She thought of her old city life, the high-rise flats she and Silje had lived in. The lifts that sighed between floors and the smell of cooking that never came from their flat. The hum of voices from people who lived their lives so close together. Close but never touching. On the nights Silje didn't come home, the voices were all she had.

She was woken by her mobile vibrating beside her. Carl-Johan had slid away from her, but she felt his warmth against her back. She peered at the display and saw it was Silje. She considered not answering, but then felt her pulse start racing. It wasn't even eight o'clock. Silje was never awake this early. Something must have happened.

'Hello?'

'Meja, you've got to come home.'

'What's happened?'

Silje's breathing hissed in her ear. 'It's Torbjörn. Please, Meja, I don't want to be alone with him a minute longer. You've got to come home as soon as you can.'

The poor signal cut short her words. It sounded as if she was holding the phone right up to her lips as she spoke, as if she didn't want to be overheard.

Lelle was standing in his underpants frying potato dumplings when the police car pulled up in the drive. He hurried into the bedroom to put on a pair of jeans and a T-shirt, leaving the spatula greasy-side down on the bedside table. The legs of his jeans were still wet and stained after his night's search, but he didn't notice. Through the gaps in the blind he watched the police officer walk up the gravel path, his uniform jacket tight over his shoulders. Thick black hair showed from under his cap.

'What the hell is it now?' he whispered to himself. As usual the familiar hope surfaced and the blood raced through his veins. Perhaps they had found her. Perhaps it was over now. Or else it had only just begun. He flung open the door with such force that Hassan staggered back.

'What's going on?'

Hassan held up his hands in their leather gloves. 'It's not about Lina. Not this time.'

The disappointment – or was it the relief? – made him slump heavily against the doorframe.

'So what is it about, then?'

'Are you going to let me in?'

Lelle stepped aside and as he did so he felt Hassan's eyes on him.

'You really need to do something about your hair, mate.'

Lelle lifted his hand to his head. The hair felt stiff, oily and a mess.

'When did you last have a shower?'

'We can't all be as well-groomed as you.'

Hassan looked at him reflectively. 'I can smell food.'

'I'm frying potato dumplings. Want some?'

'You know very well I don't eat pork.'

'You eat potatoes, don't you?'

'There's pork inside them, isn't there?'

'You can pick it out. A little pork won't kill you.'

Hassan removed his dark police jacket and was about to hang it over the back of a chair when Lelle shouted: 'Not that chair! We don't use that chair. It's Lina's.'

Hassan jerked the jacket away from the chair without a word and chose another one. His eyes looked concerned, but he said nothing. He sat down, rested his hands on the table and looked at Lelle. It was as if he could see every thought that churned in his head.

Lelle piled the dumplings in shiny heaps on two plates and spooned out the lingonberry jam. Hassan looked sceptical.

'Can you tell me what this is all about?'

'I really just wanted to drop by.'

'Drop by. In work time?'

Hassan stuck his fork into a piece of gleaming dumpling and contemplated it before putting it in his mouth. 'I know this has been a difficult time for you,' he said, between bites. 'But I just want to reassure myself that everything is OK with you.'

'You can cut the crap,' Lelle said.

Hassan grimaced as he swallowed. He put his fork down and looked at Lelle. 'OK, let's cut the crap. Where were you on the night between Saturday and Sunday?'

'Driving.'

'Whereabouts?'

'Up and down the 95.'

'Were you by any chance in the vicinity of Arjeplog?'

'I drive through Arjeplog every night.'

'What time were you there?'

Lelle shrugged. 'I guess between three and four a.m. Maybe a little later.'

'Did you stop at the Kraja campsite?'

'Not that I can recall. Not on Sunday.'

'For God's sake, Lelle.'

Lelle drew circles in the lingonberry jam. It might be because they had suspected him earlier, but he didn't feel any fear now, just more weariness. He had been the last person to see Lina at the bus stop before she went missing and now he had been in the area when Hanna Larsson disappeared. Naturally that could be misinterpreted.

'You told me the other day that we are never going to find her,' said Hassan. 'What did you mean by that?'

Lelle pushed his plate away from him. 'It's just a feeling. She is so like Lina it can't be chance. There has to be a connection.'

'Three years is a long time for there to be a connection.'

Lelle picked his teeth with his fingernail. He wasn't going to let himself be put off. 'How much do the police really know about Hanna Larsson?'

'Nothing I can discuss with you.'

'In other words you know fuck all.'

'I'd watch out if I were you, Lelle,' Hassan said in a voice Lelle didn't recognize.

'And the boyfriend, what have you done with him?'

'The last I heard he was released. While Hanna is still missing we haven't got a lot to go on. You know that.'

'But you don't seriously think I've got anything to do with this?'

Hassan ran his hand over his face and rubbed his tired cheeks. 'I'd like to take a look at your car.'

'Help yourself. The key's hanging in the hall.'

Hassan carried his plate and cutlery to the sink, scraped off what was left of the dumplings and rinsed the plate before putting it in the dish rack. Lelle regarded the thick neck and bulky arms. The same arms that had lifted him from the floor when he had been lying in his own vomit, and carried him upstairs and put a bucket by his bedside. It was Hassan who had stayed with him all night even though that went above and beyond the duties of a local police officer. Who had emptied the plastic container full of hooch, and broken every single bottle in the drinks cupboard after Anette left. His eyes began to sting at the thought of it.

'Do you know there are war veterans living in the forests round here?'

Hassan turned off the tap. 'Did you say war veterans?'

'Yes. I came across an ex-UN soldier in a forest one night when I was looking for Lina. He had set up home in a deserted farmhouse. You should have seen him. Long hair, filthy, like some kind of wild creature.'

Hassan dried his hands on the kitchen towel and he

looked at Lelle sadly. 'Don't you think it's time you took a break from all of this?'

'A break?' Lelle's voice echoed round the room. 'My daughter has been missing for three years – three years without a single trace. How the hell can I take a break?'

'You're running yourself into the ground.'

Lelle dismissed this with a wave of his hand, but the stinging in his eyes grew worse. 'Do you want coffee?'

'No time, but thanks for the chow.'

Hassan disappeared into the hall and Lelle heard the rattle of keys as he took the keyring from its hook. He watched through the sitting-room window as Hassan pulled on a pair of blue disposable gloves and walked towards the Volvo. The door was unlocked. He saw Hassan reach in with both arms and search through the rubbish, sending old cigarette ash whirling around his head.

He turned around and threw a fleeting glance at Lina, still smiling from the mantelpiece.

'Can you believe your ears?' he said out loud. 'They're going to put the blame on me again.'

He was sitting in the kitchen listening to the coffee brewing when Hassan came back in. He stood in the doorway and held up a stained piece of cloth. Lelle peered at it and saw it was the top he had been wearing last evening.

'The whole front seat is covered in blood. What the hell's going on, Lelle?'

*

'You don't have to come in with me.'

'Don't be silly, of course I'm coming with you.'

Carl-Johan pushed his arm under the driving seat and pulled out a knife.

'What are you doing?'

'What do you know about Torbjörn, exactly? How long have you known him?'

Meja swallowed. There was a sour taste in her mouth. 'I don't know. Silje found him on the internet.'

Carl-Johan grimaced and he looked towards the house. 'I want you to keep behind me.'

He pushed the knife up his sleeve before climbing out of the car. Meja had words of protest on the tip of her tongue, but couldn't make a sound. All she could hear was the thudding of her heart. She followed him hesitantly. Dew glittered on the uncut grass and soaked into their shoes. Carl-Johan stood on the veranda and knocked. He held an arm in front of Meja to keep her back.

Torbjörn opened the door. He was holding a blood-soaked kitchen towel to the side of his head. His eyes darted about and finally fixed on Meja.

'The woman's raving mad! There's no talking to her.'

Carl-Johan pushed past him and called out Silje's name. Meja hurried after him and caught a glimpse of the knife in his hand. Silje was sitting on the kitchen floor in a pool of glossy magazines. Her hair clung in sweaty strands round her skinny throat and her mascara had run in black lines down her sunken cheeks. She held up a couple of shiny pages to Carl-Johan and Meja. On them were images of swollen-breasted women with parted legs and bare, jutting backsides.

'A whole cellar full of this garbage,' Silje said. 'Young girls, hardly eighteen years old. It's enough to make you want to throw up!'

Meja felt the vinyl flooring give under her feet. The shame burned in her cheeks.

Carl-Johan closed the knife and dropped it into his pocket. His neck was as red as if he had been sunburned. Behind them they heard Torbjörn's gruff voice.

'I've been a bachelor for over forty years. Those magazines were all I had. I meant to get rid of them, but somehow never got round to it. I'm not proud of myself.'

'A whole outhouse full!' said Silje. 'And he tells me he's going out there to do some carving. Carving!' Her laughter turned into rasping sobs. She hid her face in her hands, sobbing and convulsing as if she were about to collapse. They stood and watched, helplessly, too embarrassed to do anything. Eventually Carl-Johan turned to Torbjörn and said: 'I can help you burn the stuff.'

It took all morning. They lit a bonfire on the slope by the stable block and emptied wheelbarrows full of magazines and old VHS tapes on to the flames. Sordid black smoke rose up into the innocent summer sky. Meja packed her bag and waited. She went and stood in the bathroom and looked herself in the eyes. Her fingers ached as she gripped the rust-stained porcelain. The shame had etched itself into her cheeks and her face was flushed. Then she went to the kitchen and drank coffee until her hands shook. She saw the two men sweating outside as they shovelled porn with long-handled spades as if it were cow dung. Carl-Johan's muscles reflected the sun as he ran up and down with the wheelbarrow. She wondered how she would ever be able to look him in the face again.

Silje was engrossed with her pencil, sketching with surprisingly steady hands the fire that was burning outside. Meja rolled the words around in her mouth for a long time until she found her vocal cords.

'You've gone too far this time.'

'I hit him with a log. That's why he's bleeding.'

'You call me and ask me to come home because your bloke's got a collection of porn in the outhouse. Do you get how sick that is?'

'I didn't know what to do. I had a shock! He says he's going to do some carpentry and when I go out there it's like walking into a jungle of filth! Floor to ceiling with young girls – your age, Meja. I was so stunned I screamed out loud. You should have heard me scream.'

'Well perhaps you should have thought about that before you moved in here. Done some research. Then you would have known the whole village calls him Pornbjörn.'

'You're having me on.' Silje hid her face behind the sketchbook for a long time, as if she were going to start crying again. But then Meja heard the laughter.

'It isn't funny. You embarrass me. You embarrass us. Why can't you act like a normal person?'

Silje lowered the paper and dried the tears of laughter with the back of her hand. 'I knew there was something wrong with him, that was clear straight away. He isn't like other men when it comes to the sexual side of things, I could tell that...'

'I don't want to hear this!' Meja reached for her backpack and went out on to the veranda. It sounded as if the entire decrepit place would collapse when she slammed the door behind her.

She walked straight up to Carl-Johan, pushed aside the wheelbarrow and locked her fingers around his wrist. She heard the words come from her mouth: 'Take me away from here. Now.'

✳

At Svartliden the Midsummer pig was still on the spit, smiling up at the white sky. The smell of burned flesh floated in the mist that had forced its way between the trees and settled in an ethereal cloud over the gravel drive. Carl-Johan and Meja sat in the car with the windows down, breathing in the dense air. Carl-Johan had replaced the knife under the driver's seat.

'I don't think we should have left your mum like that,' he said, abruptly.

'She's known worse, believe me. All she wants is attention.'

He sighed deeply. 'Did you see that collection of crap he had? The guy must have bought every single porn mag in the country.'

The laughter felt liberating and shifted the lump of shame from her throat.

'Don't tell anyone, will you?' Meja asked, when they had stopped laughing. 'Not your parents or Göran or Pär. It makes me feel so embarrassed.'

'I promise.'

He made circles on her knuckles with the tops of his fingers, sending small shudders through her body and giving her goosebumps. At the forest edge Anita moved in and out of the mist. Her white hair had taken on a supernatural lustre in the watery light. Her shoulders were stooped and she wasn't looking in their direction. Meja felt a flutter of anxiety.

'Do you think Birger and Anita will mind if I stay here for a while?'

'No, they'll be only too happy.'

Despite this, he stayed where he was in the car. Meja could see his heart beating under his T-shirt.

'Maybe *you* don't want me to stay?'

'Of course I do! But it's a big step. I want you to know

what you're letting yourself in for. My family isn't like other people's.'

'What do you mean?'

'We work hard.'

Meja reached out and pushed his fair hair from his face. She could feel the heat rising from his pores and thought that she had never met anyone so alive, so full of vitality.

'It doesn't matter how hard I've got to work. Nothing can be worse than life with Silje.'

They found Birger in the barn. He looked youthful in his dark blue dungarees, his body like a young man's and his greying hair hidden under a cap. The slurry and the flies didn't appear to worry him. He put down the rake when he saw them coming.

'I'd give you a hug, Meja, if I wasn't so blasted dirty.'

Meja grinned, suddenly self-conscious. It was stifling in the dim barn. She wasn't used to the smell of animals or the warmth from the bodies jostling in the straw or the flicking tails at war with the flies.

Carl-Johan also seemed uncertain. His voice was low and hesitant as he faced his father. 'Is it OK if Meja stays with us for a bit? It's not been easy for her at home.'

His blue ice-water eyes shone in his weather-beaten face, but Birger's smile faded. He stood erect and stared directly at Meja. She looked down at the uneven floor of the barn, the clods of mud and the hay, the urine trickling out from the stalls. Her heart lurched and she regretted her suggestion. Nobody wanted her under their roof. She should have learnt by now that it was written all over her how damaged she was. That she wasn't good enough.

Birger's voice was like velvet against her racing pulse. 'Well, of course Meja can stay with us. As long as it's OK with her mother.'

The relief made her feel giddy. Carl-Johan threw an arm round her and pulled her to him.

She could hear them laughing, and perhaps she was laughing too.

They left Birger among the animals and hurried out into the light. The sun was directly in their eyes. Carl-Johan drew her into the shadows and kissed her until she couldn't breathe. He lifted her up against the sun-warmed wall and pressed himself to her as if he were trying to melt into her.

Göran's voice came from nowhere and they sprang apart.

'Get a room, why don't you?'

'What the hell are you creeping about for?'

Göran smirked and wiped his hands on his overalls. His trouser legs were carelessly stuffed into his boots and he was sweating profusely.

'Has something happened?' he asked. 'You seem pretty excited.'

'Meja's moving in,' Carl-Johan said.

Göran took a step back and lurched on the uneven ground. He turned to Meja. 'Is that right? Are you going to live here?'

'For a while, at least.'

The face above the blue overalls changed colour. Göran looked up at the house, then back at Carl-Johan.

'Some people have all the luck,' he said, and spat on the grass.

∗

It was almost midnight and Lelle was finding it hard to sit still. He wandered from room to room, an unlit cigarette first in his fingers, then in his mouth, then behind his ear. Hassan had called a colleague and they had confiscated his car. The forensics team at Skellefteå police were going to take a look at it, even though Lelle had repeatedly explained.

I collided with a reindeer calf up near Långträsk marshes.

Do I look like a German shepherd? Do you think I can tell the difference between human and reindeer blood?

I need the car!

Think yourself lucky we're not taking you in as well.

Perhaps he had been an idiot to think Hassan was his friend, that he could be trusted. You could never let your guard down, because in the end you were left standing there defenceless and stupid. If he had learned anything at all these three nightmarish years it was that the world is a lousy, unreliable place and the Norrland interior was no exception. You couldn't rely on people. End of.

At ten past twelve he couldn't stand it any longer. He put on his jacket and shoes and walked out into the luminous night. The birds were roosting and the only sound was of his boots on the gravel. The air was still and heavy with the scent of vegetation. He cut through the pine forest where Lina had built a camp when she was younger. A few mouldy planks were still nailed to the tree trunks, but the remainder had fallen down and been covered in moss and weeds. He tried not to look.

He came out on Ängsvägen and carried on towards Storgatan and the wretched bus stop. His feet were doing the steering, the rest of his body was on autopilot. Including his thoughts. He lit a cigarette and looked at the night sky sparkling in the puddles. Still smoking, he walked over and sat in the solitary shelter. There was a half-empty can of Carlsberg on the seat and he thought a beer would go down well at a time like this. Just as he felt the need for alcohol run through his body he heard voices. He lifted the cigarette to his mouth and inhaled deeply, and out of the corner of his eye he watched as two young men approached. One was carrying a skateboard and the other limped as he walked. At the corner they went their separate ways with a fist bump. The lad with the skateboard set off down Storgatan, the small wheels clacking against the asphalt. The other hobbled in Lelle's direction. He had dark hair down past his ears, and black tattoos coiled round his thin arms and up over his neck.

He was black around the eyes, too, as if he was wearing make-up. Lelle sat upright and felt his fingers stiffen as the lad slowed down.

'You don't happen to have a spare cig, do you?' he asked.

'Sure.' Lelle handed over the packet and the boy hobbled into the bus shelter. He had tattoos on his knuckles as well, a four-leafed clover on his left hand and some letters on his right.

'What have you done to your foot?' asked Lelle.

'Skateboard mess-up.'

'Oh, right.'

Lelle stubbed out his cigarette and felt the boy's eyes on him. They were oddly light inside the dark shadows.

'Aren't you Lina Gustafsson's dad?'

Lelle's heart leapt. 'Yes, I am. Do you know her?'

'No, but everyone knows who she is.'

Lelle nodded. He was pleased to hear him speak of Lina in the present tense. 'What's your name?'

'Jesper,' said the boy. 'Jesper Skoog.'

'Don't you go to Tallbacka?'

'I left last year. I was in the class below Lina's.'

Lelle couldn't recall seeing the boy before, but then he didn't notice people now the way he used to.

'Didn't I teach you maths?'

'You would have done, but you were mostly off sick.'

Lelle studied the youth. His restless limbs, his feet constantly scraping the ground.

'So you never hung out with Lina?'

'I doubt she even knew who I was.'

'Really?'

Jesper took a last drag and flicked away the cigarette. He had a tongue piercing that he clicked against his front teeth.

'She only had eyes for Micke Varg.'

'You're right.'

'They were totally obsessed with each other.'

'Obsessed?'

'Yeah, everyone thought so.'

Lelle considered this for a while. The night was silent around them. The only sound was the silver tongue ring clicking against enamel. It couldn't be good for the teeth to keep doing that. Lelle held out the cigarette packet and offered Jesper another one. For the first time in ages it felt good to talk about Lina with someone else.

'You're probably wondering why I'm sitting here in the middle of the night,' Lelle said.

'Isn't this where she vanished?'

'That's right.'

'So you're sitting here waiting for her to come back.' It was more a statement than a question.

'Yes, I suppose I am.'

Jesper smoked fast and inhaled deeply. The night sun picked out silvery streaks in his black hair and under his dark eyelashes the boyish eyes looked uncertain.

'Everyone liked Lina,' he said. 'But nobody liked Varg.'

'No one told me that.'

The boy inhaled and there was more clicking against his teeth.

'He behaved like a total arse to us kids. Really looked down on us.' Jesper spat. 'He was so full of himself.'

'Oh, he was full of himself all right,' Lelle said.

'She was good for him. Everyone thought so.'

'I wasn't aware of that.'

Jesper dropped the cigarette in a puddle and Lelle watched the glow die. 'There are some who say he did it. That he's admitted it.'

'Admitted what?'

'Killing Lina.'

The words echoed in Lelle's head. 'Who says that?'

'Some guys I know, from Lajkasjärvi. Brothers. They used to sell alcohol to him and his scummy mates. They say he admitted it when he was drunk.'

'That has to be a lie. Micke Varg has an alibi, according to the police.'

Jesper clicked his tongue stud. 'I'm only saying what I heard.'

'Lina isn't dead,' Lelle said, feeling his hands perspire against his jeans. 'No one has killed her, because *she isn't dead.*'

Jesper's eyes darted over the ground. Lelle felt his irritation grow.

'What are they called, these brothers?'

'Jonas and Jonah. Ringberg.'

'Jonas and Jonah?'

'Twins.'

Lelle got out his mobile and entered their names. He tried to recall how far it was to Lajkasjärvi.

'Do you know how I can get hold of these brothers?'

'They usually hang out on Glimmers Hill at the weekend. They sell booze to kids up there.'

Lelle tapped in the information, struggling to stop his hands shaking.

'I'm off home now,' Jesper said. 'Are you going to sit here all night?'

'Maybe.'

'Want a beer?'

Lelle gulped and noticed the thirst along with his frayed nerves.

'I wouldn't say no.'

Jesper shrugged off his faded blue Fjällräven backpack and slid out a bottle of Corona that he handed to Lelle.

'Summer beer,' he said. 'Really you should have a wedge of lime with it.'

'It'll be fine as it is.'

Jesper shook his hair back and started to limp towards the village centre. When he was almost at the underpass he turned, and Lelle saw him take a deep breath.

'I really hope she comes back!' he shouted.

Lelle raised a hand and the words hung in the air. He sipped his beer.

'So do I.'

*

Lelle downed the beer, but there was no feeling of intoxication. The sun's rays were beating down on the small bus shelter, but the warmth didn't reach him. His whole body trembled. How come he hadn't heard of the Ringberg brothers until now? And if rumours were going around that Mikael Varg had admitted his guilt, shouldn't the police know about them?

He threw the empty beer bottle into the waste bin and started running. He ran through Glimmersträsk shopping centre, deserted and slumbering in the dawn, ignoring the water that splashed up from the puddles and left dark streaks on his jeans. With Storgatan behind him he took a short cut over the football pitch, where the sprinklers were painting rainbows in the air.

His throat was burning when he reached the white house on the brow of the hill. A police car was parked on the drive and small clumps of violets shone in the flower beds. The sound of his feet on the gravel pounded in time with the beats of his heart and he bent double on the veranda to get his breath back. He leaned on the doorbell and when no one opened he began banging wildly on the door with his clenched fists. The sound echoed back from the edge of the forest.

When the door opened he stumbled headlong into Hassan's naked chest. Hassan was in his underpants and his hair was sticking up.

'What's this all about?'

'The Ringberg brothers,' panted Lelle. 'Jonas and Jonah. Do you know who they are?'

Hassan squinted in the night sunlight as if it hurt his eyes. 'What the hell, Lelle? Have you been drinking? You stink of beer!'

'One bottle. But forget that and listen to me. I was sitting in the bus shelter and got talking to a lad called Jesper. He told me the Ringberg brothers are going around saying Mikael Varg has admitted killing Lina.'

The words left a bad taste in his mouth and he turned and spat on the gravel.

Hassan scratched his chest hair and seemed too sleepy to understand the significance of what Lelle was saying. 'Do you have any idea what the time is?'

'Do you know the Ringberg brothers?'

'Every social worker and cop north of Sundsvall knows those two. Small-time crooks who like peddling moonshine around here. Some burglary and minor theft. They've gone from one care home and foster family to the next since they could walk, basically.'

'They say Mikael Varg has admitted the crime.'

Hassan sighed. 'The Ringberg brothers are about as reliable as the weather. I wouldn't trust anything they said.'

'So you've heard they're accusing Varg?'

'Listen to me, Lelle. We've heard endless rumours concerning Lina's disappearance over the years. You know that as well as I do. We went through the Varg property with a fine-tooth comb early on in the investigation, with forensics, dogs, the lot. We even went to their holiday cottage in Vittangi to have a look. We've heard the claims about an admission of guilt and we've interrogated Varg for hours about it. Over forty interviews with him and we got nowhere. He's admitted sod all, and without a body or any forensic proof we can't nail him.'

'Sounds to me like you need a new interrogator.'

Hassan rested his head against the doorframe and shut his eyes. 'You're on bloody thin ice, Lelle. I know you're suffering, but I've had it up to here with you and your accusations.'

Lelle took a step backwards. The tiredness and excitement had gone to his legs and made the ground sway beneath him. He looked over his shoulder at the patrol car gleaming in the sunlight, and the damned clumps of violets under his feet.

'I need the car,' he said. 'I want to drive up to Lajkas and have a chat with those brothers.'

'Your car is at the station.' Hassan fixed his gaze on Lelle. 'And if I hear that you have gone up to Lajkas I'll make sure it's impounded for the rest of the summer.'

Lelle leaned against the veranda railing and tried to

steady his trembling legs. Hassan held the door wide open.

'Come in and get some sleep. We'll talk about this later.'

＊

'I don't want you to be alone with Göran.'

Carl-Johan's hair brushed against her neck. Meja turned over in bed to see his eyes. 'Why not?'

'Because you're my girl,' he said. 'And Göran always wants what I've got.'

Meja pushed him away.

'You talk as if I was some kind of possession.'

'I didn't mean it like that. But you see the way he looks at you?'

Meja put a finger on his lips.

'He can look as much as he likes,' she said. 'You don't have to worry about a thing.'

He pulled her close and his breath warmed her throat. 'Keep away from him. Promise?'

At dawn he left her. Meja could feel the warmth where his arm had been. The air was clammy in the room, but he had insisted on holding her all night. She had dreamed about the forest, that she was running along a track and the trees leaned out to grab her. Long strands of hair were left hanging from the pines.

She reached for her phone and saw a text from Silje.

All the filth has gone. I've forgiven T. He wants you to come home so he can apologize.

Meja got up and opened the shutters to let in the light. It took a while for her eyes to adjust and for the paradise to take shape. It was like a film, with the cows grazing in the meadow and flowers climbing the barn walls. Hens were pecking in the gravel and she thought she saw Carl-Johan by the woodshed. He had told her they were behind with the logs this year and she had nodded as if she understood. She was used to this feeling of being lost, used to ending up in new places with new people, not knowing what was expected of her. Her life was all about watching and playing along.

Down in the kitchen Anita was hurrying between the oven and the wood stove. A blood-red scarf was holding back her white hair and when she saw Meja she stopped and gave her a swift hug, careful to keep her floury hands out of the way. Several loaves were rising under a tea towel and the room smelled of boiling jam. Meja felt her hunger begin to gouge a hole in her stomach.

'Birger wants to talk to you.'

'Me?'

'He's out in the dog pens.'

Meja had always liked dogs, but this Norrland breed seemed wilder, more wolf-like, as they sat in their pens and howled. There were seven of them, all with thick grey coats and pale blue eyes that followed every move she made. Carl-Johan had said they were working dogs and not pets. If she wanted something to pat she should go and find the goats.

Birger was holding two buckets when she found him.

His neck muscles were bulging out like ropes.

'Morning, Meja. Did you sleep well?'

'Yes, thanks.'

'I'm glad.'

The skin on his face had begun to sag and his chin quivered as he spoke. He put the buckets down and rested his hands gently on her shoulders, as if he was afraid she would be crushed if he pressed too hard.

'We are so very pleased to have you here.'

Meja looked down at his work boots planted firmly on the damp ground. A strong, rotten smell came from the buckets.

'I'm the one who's glad.'

He took his hands away at last, picked up the buckets and went into the dog pens. He shovelled fish entrails into a long line of bowls, while the dogs jostled around him impatiently. Meja stayed on the outside of the bars, breathing through her mouth to escape the stench of fish. She tried not to look at the slimy pink strands the dogs were gulping down.

'As you have probably noticed by now we work hard here at Svartliden to support ourselves. If you are going to live with us, you'll have to do your share.'

Meja gripped the bars. 'I've always lived in cities. I don't know anything about farming and stuff.'

'Don't worry about that. Naturally, we'll teach you everything. You won't get a better training.'

Birger tipped the last of the fish guts on to the ground and two of the dogs fought over the remains. He swung the buckets at them in irritation.

'I thought you could start in the henhouse, have responsibility for collecting the eggs and keeping it clean and tidy. Anita can show you how to do it. How does that sound?'

'It sounds good.'

'So we're agreed.'

He smiled, revealing the gappy teeth that made her think of piano keys. She heard her stomach scream for breakfast and pressed her hands against it to disguise the sound. Behind the bars the dogs had begun to whine over the empty bowls.

'One more thing. You probably won't like this, but I want you to get rid of your so-called smartphone.'

Meja felt the iPhone burning a hole in her pocket. 'Why?'

'Because those phones are nothing more than surveillance tools. We have made a joint decision here at Svartliden to guard our integrity as much as possible, and to do that I'm afraid we must get rid of some new technology.'

Meja took her mobile from her pocket and held it tight.

Birger pushed his fingers under his spectacle frames, wiped his eyes and looked at her with sympathy. 'I know it's hard. Your generation has grown up with this need to be connected at all times. My sons have struggled with the same forces. But we have taken this decision to protect our own security.'

179

'But it's the only way Silje can get in touch with me.'

'We've got a landline. Give her our number and she can call whenever she likes.' He waded through the pack of dogs and locked the gate securely after him.

'Have a think about it. Unfortunately, I can't allow you to do something my sons are not allowed to do. We've all got to follow the same rules.'

Meja weighed the phone in her hand and thought about it. She felt a tingling in her spine. 'I'll just send one last text to Silje.'

She was so eager her fingers stumbled over the keys. Only two sentences. Then she pressed send and gave the phone to Birger. She felt the lightness in her hand as he took it, as if a weight had been lifted, and a feeling of hope inside. Without her mobile Silje couldn't get at her. Now she was free.

Lelle woke at dawn as the light filtered across Hassan's recently sanded oak floorboards. His neck was stiff after hours on the arm of the sofa, but at least he hadn't dribbled all over the fancy cushions. He could hear piano music, and eggs being cracked into a pan in the kitchen. He made his way there, feeling the old shame on his cheeks from that first drunken winter.

Hassan's kitchen was modern and snow white, with angular, anonymous lines. The kind of kitchen where everything that isn't smart or stylish seems out of place. Himself included, perhaps. He stopped in the doorway and Hassan whirled round when he heard him.

'Ah, here he is. Did you get any sleep?'

'An hour or so.'

'Sit down and have some food.'

'Thanks, but I've got to be going.'

Hassan put down the spatula and looked at him. 'I hope you're not planning on doing anything stupid.'

'What do you mean?'

'No one messes with the Ringberg brothers.'

'No one messes with me these days.'

Hassan added salt and pepper to the scrambled eggs and began eating straight from the pan. 'Do you truly believe Mikael Varg is behind this? Do you really think the lad is smart enough to keep us fooled for three years?'

'I don't believe anything. I've stopped believing. The only thing I know is that I've got to investigate every nest of vipers I come across, however much it disgusts me.'

'The Ringberg brothers are not just any nest of vipers. They are one piece of shit, believe me. They'd stop at nothing.'

Lelle scratched the bristles on his face. 'Sounds like they need putting in their place, once and for all.'

'Will you promise me to leave the Ringbergs alone?'

Lelle squinted up at the spotlights in the ceiling. 'Let me know when I can collect the car.'

181

*

Four eggs a day, sometimes five. Meja made repeated trips to the henhouse and for the first few times she was afraid they would set on her. There was something about their blinking eyes and jerking necks that frightened her. In the beginning all she did was stick in her hand long enough to feel for the eggs and lift them out, but soon she began to stay longer, getting to know their ways. They crapped a lot and it was hard to keep the henhouse clean. One of the chickens was always being pecked by the others. Even the cockerel would walk over and peck her whenever he had the chance. One morning when Meja stepped into the dim shed the bullied chicken was huddled in a corner and had hardly any feathers left. The sawdust was covered in blood-stains.

Anita gave her a tub of pine tar ointment. 'Rub this over the bullied chicken and they'll leave her be. Don't waste any tears over it.'

Carl-Johan worked hard at the logs with a saw and an axe, while Meja sat in the long grass and watched. She was fascinated by his body, shining with sweat. His arms and shoulders swelled with every effort. It excited her. She didn't care if he smelled when he came to her or when his sweat-drenched hair left marks on her clothes as he heaved himself on top of her. During breaks they hid in the grass, exploring each other's bodies with hands rough and scarred by work. Neither the dirt nor the exhaustion could stop them, they found each other anyway – brief, intensive moments, until someone called them back to work, but never long enough to extinguish the fire.

At mealtimes they all sat together, even though the others disappeared to the periphery. Birger and Pär liked to talk about the end time. In the evenings they listened to podcasts, mostly Americans talking about survival and how people should prepare themselves for various crises, anything from stocking up on necessities to how to carry out simple operations. There was also a lot of talk about imminent catastrophes. Birger and Pär were keen to discuss their theories: conspiracies between the United States and Russia, biological warfare and programmes peddling fake news. At times they were so worked up they thumped the table and made the plates jump. Meja couldn't understand the gravity of it. Her senses were all the time focused on Carl-Johan. His bare knees against hers, his fingers under the leg of her shorts, the smile that always played on his lips and made her smile too.

'What are you two sitting there smirking about?' Birger demanded.

Meja wished they could be alone so she didn't have to face the questions. Birger liked turning the spotlight on her, while Pär and Göran looked on, sneering.

'We stand on the threshold of world collapse and Sweden has slashed the size of the Home Guard. What have you got to say about that, Meja?'

'About what?'

'Why do you think we've cut the size of our defence force?'

'Because it costs too much?'

Pär laughed, spitting pieces of food across the table.

'That's what they want us to believe,' Birger said, good-naturedly. 'In reality they want us to go under, to stand here helpless when all hell breaks loose.'

'Leave her alone,' Carl-Johan said. 'There's no need to frighten her.'

'I only want her to be aware, to open her eyes. The world is no playground, sadly.'

Sometimes at night as they lay wrapped around each other, worn out and satisfied, she would ask him if he really agreed with everything Birger and his brothers said.

'People don't want to believe the worst about the world or each other,' he said. 'We don't want to face the inevitable. Our natural instinct is to bury our heads in the sand until it's too late. But Dad has taught me to think like a survivor. Always be prepared, always be one step ahead.'

'But isn't it depressing, always thinking the worst about everything?'

'It would be more depressing to lose everything over-night – everyone you love, the things you've worked for – simply because you didn't have the guts to look reality in the face.'

'But do you actually believe it will end that badly? A war, in Sweden?'

Carl-Johan slid his arm around her waist and propped his chin on her collarbone. His voice was gravelly with tiredness.

'Yes, I do. The signs are all around us. But it won't matter. The most important thing is that we are prepared, whatever happens. No one can get at us. Especially you, Meja. I will protect you with my life.'

In her dreams she was the bullied chicken. She was sitting in Anita's sunny kitchen when they started tearing at her, Birger and the others. Tearing and lunging with sharp beaks, until only a heap of rough skin remained.

It was Saturday evening and the sky hung low over the treetops. Dark clouds, threatening to burst open. Lelle put on his boots and pulled up his hood. He weighed the gun in his hand for a while, before eventually leaving it where it was. It was safest that way. He was without a car, but it wasn't that far to Glimmers Hill. Jesper had told him that was where the Ringberg brothers and Mikael Varg met up every weekend.

He followed the road through the birch wood and thought he detected the smell of smoke long before he saw the fires. The hill loomed over the village like a foreboding shadow. Running up the eastern side was a gravel road, so a car could drive right to the top. If you had one, that is. But Lelle chose one of the undesignated paths that skirted the southern side. It soon became overgrown and steep and he had to zigzag between slippery blocks of rain-washed granite.

Smoke from several fires spiralled up between the pine trees, and he could hear voices rising and falling on the wind like a song. It sounded as if there were a lot of them. His calf muscles ached and he paused on an outcrop to get his breath back. He could feel Lina beside him, even though he couldn't see her. They had come up here on the snowmobile every winter, when the Northern Lights danced above their heads and the cold penetrated their lungs. Her eyes had burned as intensely as the sky.

It looks like angels' wings.

Do you think so?

Can't you see them flying?

The memory was as painful as the effort. He ducked between the trees and felt the sky descend on him. Soon the rain came, streaming down his nose and in under his collar. He could hear Lina's voice, urgent through the raindrops.

Go home, Dad. You've no business here.

The sound of howling voices reached him through the downpour like a herd of wild animals, and he felt his throat constrict. He was covering the last part slowly, crouching in the undergrowth like a hunter, when he saw them. They had formed a ring around fires that crackled and flared into the sky, and he could feel the heat on his cheeks. Heavy base notes echoed between the trees and swallowed up the voices. The ground seemed to vibrate under his feet. There were more of them than he had expected, mostly young men with restless bodies, their faces white and ghostly in the firelight. The distinctive smell of hash blended with the odour of damp and the forest. He recognized a few faces from Tallbacka School and thought he saw Jesper Skoog, but couldn't be certain.

Lelle took a deep breath and tried to overcome his reluctance, before walking out from among the overhanging branches. He tried counting them, but there were too many. The whole forest was alive. He strode towards them and stood in the middle of the group, allowing the flames to warm his back, while he looked for someone to fix his eyes on. A few of the youngsters hid their cans of beer under their jacket sleeves and threw joints into the fire.

'I'm not here to gatecrash your party,' began Lelle. 'I'm only looking for the Ringberg brothers. Jonas and Jonah. Have you seen them?'

A young man with staring eyes moved unsteadily up to Lelle. 'You a cop, or what?'

The music had fallen silent and all he could hear was his own heart. They closed in on all sides, like wolves around a prey.

'I'm not from the police,' he said, his voice failing him.

A stocky lad walked up and shone a torch into Lelle's face. 'I recognize you. You're that teacher from Tallbacka.'

Lelle heard an intake of breath from the group. He held up one hand to shield his face from the fire.

'That's right,' he said. 'And I don't give a shit what you're up to. I just want to get hold of the Ringbergs. Does anyone know where they are?'

The lad with the torch came closer. 'What do you want with the Ringbergs?'

'I want to talk to them about a rumour.'

'What kind of rumour?'

'Apparently, they know something about my daughter's disappearance.'

Lelle put his hand into his jacket and brought out the photo of Lina, waving her smile around the group. 'This is my daughter, Lina. As many of you know she vanished from a bus stop in Glimmersträsk three years ago, and if one of you knows anything about her disappearance I'm begging you to tell me. It isn't too late.'

There were only blank faces in response. Rain-washed faces, impossible to read. His fear made him angry.

'Have you really got nothing to say?'

Lelle pulled up his hood and looked around at the pale faces. He noticed the way they avoided eye contact and he resisted the urge to charge at them, knock them to the ground with his bare hands, go berserk among the cowardly, packed bodies. He wished he had his gun. That would have made them talk. When eventually he turned back to the wood his body was shaking with rage. He had just reached the spruce trees when a couple of figures crept up behind him. One of them touched his arm.

'I'm Jonas Ringberg.'

*

Meja's body ached. She had made the trip between the chopping block and the woodshed with a wheelbarrow full of logs at least a hundred times. Loaded and stacked until her shoulders screamed. Carl-Johan said they could go swimming as soon as they had finished, and he had said it with that look that made her chest want to explode.

Suddenly Anita was beside her, her hand protecting her eyes from the sun. 'You've got visitors, Meja. Down by the gate.'

She saw Torbjörn's Ford from a long way off. Somehow the rusty patches made her think of the pecked chicken. They had climbed out of the car, both of them. Torbjörn was pacing up and down like an agitated bull, and Silje had hidden her eyes behind dark glasses and was smoking a cigarette in the nonchalant way that meant she was nervous. Her bare feet were deep in the grass and all she had on was a pair of cut-off jeans and a bleached bikini top. Her hair stood out like a bird's nest on her head.

Meja felt the distaste in her throat. 'What do you want?'

'We want to see how you are doing. Your mother here has been so worried.'

Silje pushed her sunglasses down her nose and looked at

Meja. 'Oh my God, look how dirty you are! What have you been doing?'

'Working.'

'Working? In that case I hope you're getting paid. Your clothes are completely ruined.'

'At least I'm wearing clothes. Unlike you.'

Torbjörn stood between them, his hands raised.

'I think it's time we calmed down a little. We want you to come home, Meja.'

'Svartliden is my home now.'

The crown of Torbjörn's head shone like an overripe lingonberry. 'If this has anything to do with my magazines then I want you to know that's all over. The stuff has gone for good. Thanks to Silje – and you – I've been given the chance to start a new chapter in my life...'

'It's got nothing to do with that. I just want to live here, with Carl-Johan.'

'We don't think that's such a good idea.'

'I don't give a shit what you think.'

Torbjörn turned helplessly to Silje. He looked close to tears.

'But what do Birger and Anita say about it?'

'They've welcomed me with open arms.'

Silje shot her glasses back and lifted her chin, her mouth creasing around the cigarette. 'And how am I supposed to get hold of you, may I ask, now you've got rid of your phone?'

'You can call Birger and Anita on the landline. Just ask for me.'

Silje swayed in the grass. 'Have they been brainwashing you or something?'

'Oh, shut up!'

'Why did you get rid of your phone?'

'I just did. Now you won't have to complain about the bill any more.'

Silje leaned closer. 'Is it some kind of sect they're running out here? Have they used Carl-Johan as bait to get you hooked?'

Meja gave a hollow laugh.

'Go home and sober up,' she said. 'You don't live in the real world. Carl-Johan loves me.'

Silje's mouth twisted into an angry flower. She stubbed out her cigarette on the rusty bodywork of the car and opened the passenger door.

'You know where I am,' she said. 'When it ends. Because it always ends.'

She slammed the car door and the sound reverberated between the pines.

Torbjörn stayed where he was, his eyes pleading. 'You're too young to leave home, Meja. You're not even eighteen.'

'Ask Silje how old she was when she left home.'

'We miss you, you know. Both of us.'

His feet trod the gravel as if he were a drowning man. She felt the prickle of tears, looked towards the woodshed for Carl-Johan and cleared her throat.

'We'll come and say hello, I promise.'

'I certainly hope you will. And don't let Birger wear you out.'

'Don't let Silje wear *you* out.'

He smiled at that. For an instant it looked as if he would hug her, but then Silje pressed the horn and he had to hurry back.

'Call me if she slides into the darkness,' Meja yelled after him. 'Promise!'

*

The young men towered over him, their faces identical and pale under their dark hoods. Lelle leaned his back against a pine as the forest pulsed around him. They had dragged him from the path, taking him deeper into the bushes, where no one could see them. Lelle slid his hand into his jeans pocket and gripped the bunch of keys. His chest heaved and he found it hard to get enough air.

'I don't want any trouble.'

Their eyes glowed in the dim light and the one called Jonas leaned forward and put his face close to Lelle's. He stank of alcohol.

'Who the fuck are you, anyway?' he said. 'Thinking you can go around shooting your mouth off about us.'

He reached round Lelle, found his back pocket and took out the wallet. He pulled out Lelle's driving licence and studied it. Lelle let him, the keys still tight in his hand.

'Lennart Gustafsson.' Jonas looked up from the driving licence and stared at Lelle. 'Sure you're not a cop?'

'I'm not from the police. And I couldn't give a damn what you're doing. I'm here because I've heard you know something about my daughter who disappeared.'

'We don't know nothing about your daughter.'

Lelle took the wallet and the driving licence from him, found the photograph of Lina and held it up like a shield in front of him.

'This is Lina.' His voice shook. 'My daughter. It's three years since she was taken from me – three years! – and I'm prepared to do whatever it takes to find out what happened to her. Do you understand?'

They chewed their lips, both of them, and swayed from side to side as they thought it over.

'Sounds fucking tragic,' said Jonas. 'But we had nothing to do with it.'

'Maybe not, but you've been going around saying you know who did.'

The brothers exchanged a quick look. 'We only heard rumours, like everyone else.'

'What rumours?'

'There's been a lot of talk over the years.'

'Talk about what?'

Jonas turned his face to the sky and sighed. 'Listen mate,

I don't want to pour salt on your wounds, but your daughter was hanging out with a right dickhead.'

'By that you mean Mikael Varg?'

'Could be. Everyone calls him the Wolf.'

'And what makes him a dickhead?'

'He used to buy booze from us. And paid well, to start with. Until his girlfriend disappears, that is. Then he totally loses the plot. Calls every night, wants to buy on credit. Wants other shit, too. You know, tablets and stuff. Parties more than he can afford to. We don't like that kind of thing.'

Lelle thought of Mikael Varg, the way he had staggered over the grass and made an air-pistol gesture with his fingers, and his break-in during the torchlit procession. How he had cried in Lelle's kitchen. A feeling of nausea took hold.

Jonas was standing in front of him, edgily making a roll-up. 'So we pay him a visit to demand the money. That's when he loses it. Starts raving on about what he did.'

'Did what?'

'You know. Kill her.'

Lelle leaned back against the trunk of the tree. His legs felt unsure beneath him. Jonas sounded so nonchalant, as if he were talking about the weather. The other lad stood like a dumb shadow beside him, not looking in Lelle's direction.

'Can you tell me exactly what he said?'

'He says they had this fight and he got mad. Got rid of the body. No one will ever find her.'

Lelle sank to his knees on the wet ground. The words echoed in his head and he felt the need to vomit. He leaned over and retched into the moss, but nothing came up. When he recovered, he looked up at the brothers.

'Why didn't you go to the police?' he asked.

They both snorted. 'We don't talk to the cops if we can help it.'

'But this isn't about you selling your fucking illegal alcohol! It's about the disappearance of a seventeen-year-old girl. If it's true Varg admitted doing it, this changes everything!'

Lelle hauled himself up from the ground and faced the brothers. The rage made him feel straighter, somehow. Taller. There was no time for thinking. He stood so close he could feel Jonas's breath on his face. They glared at each other in a silent battle of wills. Out of the corner of his eye he saw the other lad moving in, felt his own hands clench into fists. They were two to one, but that didn't scare him.

'You gutless wankers,' he said. 'You care more about saving your own skin than a young girl's life.'

Jonas cried out and snatched hold of his jacket with both hands, pulling him close. Lelle tried to twist himself free, but glimpsed the flash of a knife in the other lad's hand. He felt the cold steel against his neck.

'Listen up carefully,' Jonas said. 'You're angry, I get that.

195

If I had a missing daughter I'd be doing whatever I fucking could to find who did it. But we've done nothing and I don't appreciate your attitude.'

'Don't do anything you'll regret,' said Lelle.

Jonas gave Lelle a long look before gesturing to his brother to put down the knife. Then he shoved Lelle away from him, hard, making him fall to the ground. The other lad spat at him.

'Find Varg instead and take your anger out on him.'

Lelle lay still and watched them disappear into the shadows. Their shoes squelched as they started running. He didn't bother following them, there was no point.

His arms started shaking first, then the rest of his body. His limbs were heavy and unresponsive. He dug his hands into the forest floor, sank deeper into the carpet of moss, and let himself be embraced by the cold, damp earth. He didn't hear his own chattering teeth, only the whispering of the pines and the words that still resounded in his head. *Got rid of the body. No one will ever find her.*

Meja had never lived with a real family before and she found herself watching them closely, trying to learn their ways. There was no doubt Birger was in charge. As soon as he stepped into a room everybody suddenly found something to do. And he didn't need to say anything, often his very presence was enough.

He called Anita *my dear* and liked to press his lips against her white head. Even so, it soon became clear that it was a game. Meja had seen that kind of game played many times between Silje and her men and she was disappointed to see it was no different between Birger and Anita, and that they forced themselves to put up with each other. She saw it in Anita's eyes every time Birger was around, that she was thinking thoughts that had nothing to do with love. And then there was the humming. Anita hummed while she worked and you could tell where she was on the farm because of her humming. It was inescapable, floating above the wind and the barking of the dogs. Except when Birger was nearby. Then it stopped.

The brothers also fascinated her with their differences. Carl-Johan was the chatty one, the one who attracted most attention. If families had favourites, then he was theirs.

Pär laughed a lot, a loud liberating laugh that echoed through the house and infected the others. He had a knack with the animals and he collected knives. In the evening he would clean the cutting edges, stick the blades in apples and leave them overnight. They were hardened by the acid, he explained to Meja. *There's nothing worse than a weak knife.*

Göran sought his own company. He went about with his hood up to disguise the damage to his face, the sores that tormented him. They formed scabs, which he scratched off, and then they bled and became even worse. When they passed on the farm, she tried desperately to see beyond the sores and look him in the eyes, but there was also something in his eyes that couldn't be avoided. He looked at her with a kind of thinly veiled fury, as if her presence disturbed him in some way.

She was lying in the clearing when he walked up, her arms and legs outstretched in a sea of white wood anemones. If she squinted they looked like snow. She didn't notice that his were the wrong feet, because of all the white. She held her arms up to the indistinct figure, but there was no response. Not until she propped herself up on her elbow did she see it was Göran. His thin hair was plastered to his weeping skin.

'Did you think I was Carl-Johan?'

'Why did you creep up on me?'

'Was that your mum up by the gate?'

'Yep.'

'She looks so young.'

'She was only seventeen when she had me.'

'Shit.'

The anemones were crushed as he crossed his legs under him. He had a blade of grass in the corner of his mouth. Meja was thankful for the sunlight, causing shadows that hid the scarred face.

'Does she want you to move back again?' he asked.

'Mm.'

'What did you tell her?'

'I said this was my home now.'

Göran ripped up the grass, not caring if he damaged the flowers. His knee brushed Meja's and the skin felt cold, despite the sun.

'Was she sad?'

'My mum's like a kid. I've always been the one to take care of her.'

'But now you've got Carl-Johan. And us.'

Meja smiled down into the grass.

'That's the one thing I haven't got,' Göran went on. 'A girlfriend. Someone to share everything with.'

'Then you'd better start looking.'

'Don't you think I have? No one wants somebody who looks like me.'

He tore flakes of skin from his raw palms. Meja didn't look. She had begun to stretch when she heard Anita's footsteps on the gravel. Her white plait beat against her back and she had a stern expression on her face.

'What are you sitting here for?' she said to Göran. 'Haven't you got a potato field to look after?'

'I was just having a rest.'

'So I see.'

He got to his feet and brushed his jeans. Before slouching off, he winked at Meja, as if they shared a secret. Anita reached down and helped her up. When they were standing beside each other her eyes had turned warm again.

'Well, Meja,' she said. 'My sons are buzzing around you like bees around a hive.'

That made Meja feel embarrassed, and Anita noticed and smiled.

'I was also young and pretty once, believe it or not. So I know what it's like. Sometimes you get tired of all the attention.'

'You are still pretty.'

Anita laughed so loudly it echoed all the way to the stable yard.

'Kind of you to say that, Meja,' she said, when she had recovered. 'But if my boys give you any trouble, let me know. Promise?'

'I promise.'

∗

The madness scared him, the thought that he wouldn't be able to keep it in check. That it would take over. All the time his toes were hanging over the edge of the Maravälta drop and the abyss was calling him. He was woken by a feeling of absolute terror in the pit of his stomach.

Dust motes floated in the sunlight that fell across the wooden floor, and Lina's smile from the mantelpiece seemed twisted from where he was sitting on the sofa. He looked down at himself, at the muddy jeans and shirt stiff against his skin, and the sweat-stained, mismatched socks. The ashtray taunted him from the floor. If Lina walked in now she would turn around on the threshold, thinking it was the wrong house. It was that insight that made him get a grip on himself.

It took all morning to clean the house, and afterwards two full vacuum-cleaner bags were crammed into the rubbish bin. His hands stung from all the washing up and his cheeks itched from the shock of being shaved. Lelle sat at the kitchen table, worn out but showered, his wet hair dripping on to the newspaper cuttings. There was a new article about Hanna Larsson, which didn't have much to offer. The search was continuing in the forests around Arjeplog and the police were appealing to the public for information. Same old story.

The gun lay in its holster on the bureau and the shiny metal kept catching his eye, as if it were calling to him. The cleaning had helped only temporarily. His brain wouldn't give him any peace. Not now.

His jacket hid the weapon and the Laphroaig, and because the garage was still empty he went on foot through the forest. He had been keeping a watch on Varg long enough to know his haunts. The lad seldom left the family home, had never worked and had lost touch with his friends. Fishing and alcohol were the only things that took him outside.

Lelle found him down by Glimmersträsk Lake. Varg was sitting on a rock in the middle of the reeds with his fishing rod in his hand and the lake steaming around him like a witch's cauldron. From the far side came the sound of screams and laughter of children swimming. Varg beat away the mosquitoes with his free hand. He wasn't wearing a T-shirt and his vertebrae protruded like fish scales under the pale flesh.

Lelle hesitated for a long time at the edge of the trees. The blood pounding in his ears was drowned out by the whine of the mosquitoes, but he didn't even try waving them away. The gun was cold against his thigh as he waded through the heather.

Varg didn't hear him coming. He didn't even turn round until Lelle put his feet in the water. He dropped the fishing rod in surprise.

'What do you want?'

Lelle didn't bother to remove his shoes or roll up his jeans. He waded out to the rock and hauled himself up beside Varg, getting rough lichen and bird droppings under his nails. He glimpsed a half bottle of spirits among the gleaming fishing baits in Varg's box. He scanned the lake beach on the other side to make sure the children wouldn't see them among the reeds, before bringing out the whisky.

'Would you like a little snifter?'

Varg blinked, but then reached out for the bottle and swallowed a mouthful without changing his expression.

Lelle tried a smile. 'Don't you think it's about time we buried the hatchet, for Lina's sake?'

'Are you serious?'

'There's nothing to be gained from being at each other's throats.'

Varg handed back the bottle. Lelle took a swig and felt the whisky burn along with his deception. Sweat prickled under his jacket.

'It feels like life came to an end when she disappeared,' Varg said. 'I feel like the living dead.'

Lelle waved the bottle under his nose.

'Drink more. It helps.'

Varg took two deep swigs, wiped his mouth with the back of his hand and looked sideways at Lelle. 'You're not trying to poison me, I hope?'

'Should I be?'

They gave each other a wry smile, squinted over the water where the sun glittered on the waves, and passed the expensive whisky leisurely between them. Lelle felt the alcohol inflame his rage and make his insides boil. The children's laughter and lapping waves only added to it and led his thoughts to Lina.

'I met two of your mates the other evening, up on Glimmers Hill.'

'Did you?'

'Uh-huh. Twins. Like two peas in a pod. Seems they used to do business with you?'

Out of the corner of his eye he saw Varg's jaw tighten and his fingers clench the fishing rod.

'You mean the Ringbergs?'

'Yes, that's the name. Jonas and Johan Ringberg. They had a lot to tell me about you.'

The pulse on Varg's neck became visible. 'I thought you were here to bury the hatchet.'

'And so I am,' said Lelle, holding up his hands. 'Does it look like I've got an axe with me? I haven't come to fight, I've come to hear the truth. From you.'

'What fucking truth?'

Lelle leaned closer, feeling the anger driving him on, giving him courage. 'Why are people going around saying you admitted to killing Lina?'

'How should *I* know? It's a load of bullshit.'

'You boasted about getting rid of the body. Said no one would find her.'

Varg's face seemed to be coming apart at the seams. His voice grew louder. 'That's not true. I would never hurt Lina. *Never.*'

Lelle put down the bottle of whisky and checked again to make sure no one could see. After that everything happened very fast. He pulled the revolver from his waistband and pressed the muzzle to Varg's ribs, seeing the terror in the lad's eyes when he released the safety catch. The fishing rod fell in the water and bobbed on the surface.

'You're fucking insane!'

'True, I am fucking insane, and if you want to get out of this alive I suggest you start talking.'

'But I haven't *done* anything.'

204

'Why do the Ringbergs say you confessed?'

Varg shuddered. The revolver was making a red eye on his skin. Lelle's throat filled with bile, but his finger was calm on the trigger. He could feel the lad give up and almost crumple in front of him.

'I owed the Ringbergs bloody thousands. They were on my case, threatened to break in, steal from my family. Said they'd kill me. I was desperate, I wanted them to back off and feel as afraid of me as I was of them.'

Varg started sobbing. He gasped for breath as if the crying was choking him. His teeth chattered and his joints trembled.

Lelle released the muzzle. It wasn't needed any longer.

'I'm not proud of it,' Varg said. 'And I only said I did it because I was desperate. And weak. Fucking weak. I lied to the Ringbergs, said I'd done it so they would get scared and back off. I reckoned if they thought I was capable of something like that, they wouldn't burgle my home. That they would leave me alone. And it worked! They let me be.'

Lelle rocked up and down, feeling as if he was losing his grip on the world. He brought his face close to Varg's. 'If I understand this correctly, you took the blame for my daughter's death *to gain the respect of some fucking dealers? Right?*'

Varg bent over his skinny legs and was lost in his crying.

Lelle sat there with his rage, letting it wash over him, making him cold. The gun began to wave in his hand

and he pictured himself lifting the weapon towards the sobbing figure and pressing it against his forehead. He saw the birds flying from the trees at the bang, the children's laughter falling silent. He felt the cold steel as Hassan fastened the cuffs, his disappointment in the rear-view mirror as he drove Lelle away. Hassan already thought he had lost his mind. And maybe he had.

It was Lina's voice that brought him back. She was standing at the water's edge, pleading with him to put down the weapon. Eventually he gave up, slid off the rock and waded back to the lakeside and Lina's voice. Varg called out after him, but he couldn't make out what he was saying. He didn't want to turn around. He couldn't. The fear of what he had almost done swept over him and he began jogging through the undergrowth. Away from the lake and from Varg. Away from the madness.

By the time he reached the spruces he was shaking so violently he had to stop. He crouched between the trees and fumbled for something to hold on to while the forest pitched around him. He threw himself over the moss and spewed out the fear. He retched and whimpered until there was nothing left. Nothing but the old, hollow emptiness. Afterwards he walked on trembling legs into a birch wood, where the sun warmed him and the wild grass brushed against his thighs. There he collapsed to the ground and thought he would never have the strength to get up again.

✳

Meja knew they kept things from her, things that only belonged within the family. Things she wasn't yet a part of and perhaps never would be. She could only wait and hope. She knew Carl-Johan wouldn't be the one to tell her. It would be Birger.

One morning, when she was coming out of the hen-house, he suddenly appeared and she saw immediately he had decided that now was the time.

'No eggs?' he asked.

'Not this time.'

'I hope the hens haven't started to get lazy.'

'Oh, no. We have more eggs than we can eat.'

'That's the whole point. We should always have more than we can eat, so that we can have an emergency supply.'

Meja looked at their long, narrow shadows on the gravel and thought they looked other-worldly, somehow.

'We never had food at home when I was little,' she said. 'There's nothing worse than an empty larder.'

'I agree with you, Meja. I've been lulled to sleep by the rumbles from my stomach more times than I care to remember. But most people today have never experienced how hopeless it feels to go without food. They have allowed themselves to trust in the delusion that we will always live with plenty.'

Birger stopped walking and stared down at her. 'I think it's time for you to see our larder.'

'I've seen your larder.'

But he only grinned. He began walking away from the main house and in among the trees, leading her deep into the low-hanging spruce branches. Meja was amazed at how easily he moved, despite his age. In one tangle of bushes he stopped and scraped away the fallen twigs and pine needles with his feet until a hatch appeared. Meja stood breathless beside him and watched as he knelt down in the loose earth and levered the hatch door open. On the inside a ladder dropped down into the darkness. It looked bottomless to her. Birger swung his legs over the edge and began to climb down. He encouraged her to follow him, but she stayed where she was beside the gaping hole.

'I don't like confined spaces.'

He laughed. 'It won't be confined once you're down here.'

Soon all she could see was the downy hair on the top of his head. She looked round, saw the big house with its windows glowing warm in the darkness. She wished Carl-Johan would walk out of the door so she could call him over. If he was with her, she would dare. The fear never took hold of her when he was near.

'Come on, Meja!' Birger called from the bottomless pit. 'Come and see this.'

Slowly, very slowly, she put one foot on the top rung, then the other. Her hands fumbled. It was a long way down and the rungs seemed to go on forever. Raw, cold air hit her and the smell of damp earth filled her lungs. At the bottom Birger was standing by a partly open door. Warm, honey-coloured light seeped through the gap and his eyes shone behind his thick spectacles.

'Get ready for this, Meja my girl.'

Torbjörn and his collection of porn flashed through her mind in the seconds before the door swung fully open. She found it hard to breathe, convincing herself that there wasn't enough oxygen. She felt the dizziness begin to take over.

But then she saw inside the room. It was as wide and as high as a sports hall and well-illuminated, despite the lack of windows. Rag rugs in every colour combination ran in all directions over the wooden planks, bringing life to the huge space. The walls were lined from floor to ceiling with thick shelves packed with food cans, tins and neatly labelled jars of preserves. There were long rows of paraffin lamps, oil stoves and batteries. On the floor, great plastic containers of water slumbered side by side. Three sets of bunk beds equipped with sleeping bags stood against one wall, and there were clothes in every size on hangers, together with shoes, thick winter hats and gloves. Ten gas masks stared down from their hooks and three first-aid boxes stood beside plastic containers of pills and thick rolls of bandages. There were also crutches and a wheelchair.

Further in were the weapons. Ten rifles, muzzles down, and a smaller number of handguns. Hundreds of brown cardboard boxes filled with gleaming ammunition fought for space beside sharp, shining knives and axes, and various other tools.

Birger began pointing and explaining. They had food and water for at least a year, and both battery and sun-powered radios and lamps. Paraffin, fire lighters and other fuel that would last several winters if necessary.

'Nothing and no one can get at us,' he said. 'We are prepared for anything.'

He reminded Meja of the Catholic priest Silje had tried to seduce one summer on Gotland. A man whose voice trembled with conviction and who had chosen God above all earthly desires. He prayed long graces before meals, and denied himself food, sleep and the pleasures of women. But his eyes glowed with his faith, the kind that was contagious and made her want to be a part of it. Meja would never forget the way his lips quivered as he talked about his saints and his God, and how his voice made the porcelain clink on the shelves when he chanted in Latin. She also wanted to experience something that powerful, to believe in something so sincerely that it seeped from her pores and spread to everyone who came near her. It was obvious that Birger overflowed in the same way, that he was also drowning in his conviction. The artificial light threw gold on to his white hair and made her think of angels. The skin on his furrowed face was colourless and slack, but there was an other-worldly aura about him, something that affected her lungs and made it hard to breathe.

'Society cannot offer civil defence or emergency food supplies for very long. But we can. You are safe with us here, Meja. And you will never have to go hungry.'

*

He'd gone too far with Varg. As he ran towards the village he could still feel how tight his finger had been on the trigger. He'd wanted to shoot, that was the worst of it. Wanted to put an end to it all. The lad first, then turn the weapon on himself. Two shots, that was all, then it would be over.

Hassan was on his knees in the flower bed when Lelle arrived. There was a growing pile of weeds beside him and the sound of classical strings floated from an open window. On a nearby bench stood a martini glass with olives in the bottom, and a cocktail shaker glinted in the sun.

Lelle laid his gun gently on top of the pile, as if it were a living thing. Hassan got up and brushed the dirt from his trousers with his gardening gloves.

'What's this?'

'I want you to confiscate it.'

'Is it yours?'

'It isn't registered, if that's what you're getting at.'

Hassan picked up the firearm with his gloved hand and took a good look at it.

'I hope you haven't shot anyone.'

'That's why I want you to have it. Before I do.'

✳

The only way Silje could get hold of her was on the landline, and she rang day and night. Mostly to nag Meja about
coming home.

'It's all this stuff about the missing girls. Torbjörn just
can't relax. He wants you home so we can keep an eye on
you.'

'I'm safer here than I ever was with you.'

'I don't understand why you've got to be so hostile all
the time.'

When she told Birger about Silje's concern he only
smiled.

'The media do all they can to scare the life out of people.
They make mountains out of molehills. Missing girls –
what kind of drivel is that? Youngsters wandering off
without telling anyone where they are, that's nothing to
splash all over the papers. It happens all the time. Anita
and I did the same thing in our day and it didn't do us any
harm. Quite the opposite.'

Even so, he didn't want them driving about at night
any longer. Outside the gates of Svartliden corruption
and unhappiness were taking hold, he said, things they
shouldn't be getting involved in. To be on the safe side he
locked the car keys in the bureau in his office, despite the
protests of Carl-Johan and his brothers.

There was no television at Svartliden. Carl-Johan didn't
know why, he merely said they had never had one. Meja

didn't want to ask Birger, mainly for fear of triggering another lecture. There was a computer, but Birger controlled the use of it with a firm hand. He lost his temper when she tried to check Facebook.

'When are you going to stop being so naive, Meja? Social media is nothing but a means of surveillance!'

They listened to podcasts instead. Birger's favourite was the American Jack Jones, a member of the US air force, who claimed to have insight into the corrupt machinery of government.

In the evenings they gathered in the sitting room, where Birger sat in the armchair, his hands folded on his lap as if in prayer. Anita always had some knitting on the go, and the needles clicked rhythmically and furiously as if they were taking part in a kind of undeclared battle. Göran and Pär lay on the sofa, their arms and legs sprawled over cushions and armrests, while Meja and Carl-Johan chose the reindeer-skin rug in front of the fire, mostly to be left in peace. She liked the way the heat brought the blood to his cheeks and how the flickering flames reflected in his eyes. The podcast and the others were just background noise and it felt as if they were alone by the fire.

When Jack Jones had finished, Birger held court, demanding their attention again.

'Meja, my love, do you know how Anita and I met?' he asked one evening.

His sons groaned and sighed, but it didn't put him off.

Birger's face was affected by an almost imperceptibly small tremor when there was something he was eager to talk about. Meja sat up on the rug. It was always her attention he demanded most.

'How did you meet?'

'Well, you see, once upon a time we were siblings. Brother and sister.'

'Birger, really!'

Anita's needles stopped. Then the room dissolved into laughter. Meja looked at Carl-Johan and saw his face was bright red.

'Not biological siblings, of course,' Birger went on. 'But in our younger, teenage years we ended up in the same foster family, and we were supposed to act like brother and sister. But as soon as I set eyes on her,' he pointed at Anita, 'I knew that would never happen. She's a beauty of the old sort, just like you, Meja. A classic femme fatale, who can turn the head of the most cold-hearted man without even having to try.'

Anita's face blushed over her knitting.

'So, naturally, even our foster father took a liking to her. Damned lucky the house was small and you could hear everything that went on, so he couldn't get away with it. I caught him at it in the laundry room, when he was trying to put his hand up her skirt...'

'*Birger*,' warned Anita. The needles worked faster and faster in her hands, building up to a crescendo.

Birger rested a hand on her shoulder and continued: 'I smacked him so hard he fell and hit his head on the tumble dryer. We thought the man was dead. So we packed our things and fled, determined to steer clear of the authorities and look after ourselves. I was seventeen and Anita sixteen, and it was us two against the world. Ten years it took, to save up for this piece of land. And the rest is history.'

Birger leaned forward in his chair and fixed his eyes on Meja and Carl-Johan. His chin jutted out as he smiled. 'All you need to succeed in this life is a true partner. Someone you can share everything with. If you've got that, you can do anything. Just look at us.'

Meja thought of Silje and the way she had always pursued love, but never managed to hang on to it. How unhappy and troubled her life had been, with the seeking and the loneliness. She leaned her head on Carl-Johan's shoulder and promised herself she would never be like that. She would hold on to love.

Lina was always lying in water when he found her, cold and ashen under the black surface. Her thin body was swollen when he got her on to land. It was always the same procedure: he ripped off his jumper and wrapped it round her wet body, but water continued to stream from her scalp, her mouth and her eye sockets. Lelle tried to cover the leaking cavities, but it was no good, the water gushed out of her like a river swollen with meltwater. She drained away from him every time. And when he woke up the bedding was damp around him.

It was the thunder that dragged him out of the dream. In the flashes of lightning he saw his wounds: scratches and bruises from nights in the forest, and swollen mosquito bites around his ankles and hairline, bloody from where he had scratched them in his sleep. His whole body itched and stank. In the shower, memories from the day before came back to him, how he had held the gun to Mikael Varg's ribcage and been ready to shoot. The image made him shiver, despite the hot water. He leaned against the tiles and sobbed uncontrollably. He didn't stop crying until the power cut off and he had to feel his way to the kitchen for a candle, the water dripping from him. He had only just found the candles when his mobile rang.

As always, Anette's husky voice hit him hard in the stomach. 'I phoned the landline, but there was no answer.'

'I was in the shower.'

'I see.'

There was a heavy silence that didn't bode well. Lelle lit a candle with his free hand, walked to the table and sat down. He could hear her breathing.

'I phoned because I have something to tell you, and it might come as a shock to you – God knows it was a shock to *me* – I was almost sure I was too old by now, but obviously not...'

'Just say what you've got to say.'

'I'm pregnant.'

A deafening crash of thunder distorted her words. Lelle pressed the mobile closer to his ear. 'What's that you said?'

'I'm pregnant. Thomas and I are having a baby.'

'You and Thomas are having a baby?'

'Yes.'

Lelle gave a laugh, even though there was nothing at all funny about it. Lightning flashed around him and threw flickering shadows over Lina's chair. He looked towards the office. In the light he saw the door was ajar. How long ago was it they had made love in there, he and Anette?

'Are you sure it's Thomas's child?'

'Of course I'm sure.'

'Because if I remember correctly we happened to...'

'That's all over and done with, Lelle. What we did that day doesn't matter.'

'Oh, right. I see.'

The candle flickered and shadows moved across the wall.

'What about Lina?'

'What do you mean?'

'You already have a child, a child who has been missing for three years. All our energy should be spent looking for her, don't you think? Or is this a way for you to move on, get a new child instead of the one you already have?'

Anette's voice trembled at the other end.

'I hope you'll be happy about it one day,' she said. 'When you've come to your senses.'

Later that morning he got his car back. Hassan was apologetic when he handed over the keys and told him that no human blood had been found. Lelle didn't make things difficult, he was too keen to get back out on the road.

He set off almost immediately, smoking with the window closed until the air was thick and ash whirled over the dashboard and cup holder. He didn't care. He thought about the first time Anette had told him she was pregnant, how she very nearly hadn't said anything at all. They had only recently moved in together and he had boiled some eggs and bought fresh rolls for breakfast. Anette was dead to the world and, when he woke her, she complained that the eggs smelled revolting. Anette, who had always loved eggs. She had sat there in her old dressing gown, saying the coffee was making her heave, and he was worried they had made a mistake, moving in together so soon. She was standing with her head out of the balcony door when he crept up behind her, slipped his hand inside her dressing gown and cupped her right breast. It was merely a playful gesture, with no urgency or desire, but Anette shrieked as if he had stabbed her. Then she started crying. Through the sobs he discovered that an abortion was planned for the following Monday. She had held up the letters from the local surgery. That's how he found out.

He had insisted on taking her there. He wanted to be

with her. Anette's lips were a tight red line as she sat with her gaze fixed on the passing fir trees to emphasize her need for silence. In Frostkåge she complained of nausea and wanted to get out and be sick. Lelle smoked as she retched into a ditch.

'And you think you're ready to be a father,' she sneered at him. 'Smoking like a chimney.'

'I'll stop smoking right this minute if you keep the child.'

He had held up the cigarette between them. Anette straightened up and walked towards him, bile still running down her chin. She stood so close, the cigarette almost touched the tip of her nose. They had looked at each other in a kind of fury. Eventually, Anette had wiped her mouth and relaxed her shoulders.

'Stub it out,' she said. 'I want to go home.'

Since that day he hadn't smoked once in seventeen years, and here he was now, ash over his lap like a blanket. He tried to work out how many weeks had passed since that morning in the office, but he couldn't. All he could remember was Anette scrambling eggs afterwards. She certainly did love eggs. He wound down the window and dropped the partly smoked cigarette on to the road. Then he picked up the packet and threw it in the same direction. Anette could say what she liked. He still knew it was his child.

PART II

The silence was worse than the darkness. She heard no wind, no rain, no birdsong. No footsteps or voices, almost as if there was no world outside. She pressed her ear to the walls and listened, but the only sound was her heartbeat. The scratches on her arms grew deeper in the dim light. Here and there were old bruises that had turned yellow and faded with time. She didn't fight any more. She couldn't be bothered. Her veins were swollen under her loose skin as if she had aged too early, as if the very life was seeping out of her.

The bulb hanging from the ceiling cast her shadow on the wall and she found herself waving at it from her bunk. She saw the tall, thin figure wave back, in their fight against the isolation.

The room was a perfect square. It was like being in a box. Along one wall was the bed and a side table with the untouched food: a cheese sandwich wrapped in cling film and a flask of soup. She smelled the soup when the hunger became unbearable, but retched as soon as she took a mouthful. Her body refused. It was as if her insides protested against the captivity.

On the other wall, beside the metal door, was one bucket intended for use as a toilet and another filled with water. She avoided both of them as far as possible. She ate so little she hardly even had to pee, and she didn't have the energy to wash herself. Her hair hung in thick, matted strands over her shoulders and left greasy marks on the pillow, and she guessed she stank, even if she couldn't smell it herself. She hoped she stank. It might keep him from touching her.

She tried to sleep away the dead hours, to sleep away time. When the restlessness came she walked round and round until her legs ached. She tapped her knuckles on the walls, searching for hollow sections, and concentrated hard to hear anything other than her own breathing. She couldn't help listening for sounds that didn't exist. Without daylight it was hard to know how many days she had lost. Hours ran into each other and were defined only by sleep and exercise. And listening. For long periods of time she watched the door. Her own blood had dried like rust on the light grey metal. It was a long time since she banged on the door, but her fingers were still red raw, as if the skin wouldn't heal in the enclosed space and the darkness. He had offered to put plasters on them, but she had rolled herself into a ball and turned to face the wall, like a hedgehog with its prickles out. The last thing she wanted was for him to touch her.

*

Lelle sipped his coffee and looked at the bent heads of the students in front of him. All that could be heard was the scraping of pens. There must be a trend for long hair, judging by the number of boys constantly pushing it out of their faces. The girls were more particular. One of them had pink highlights in her fringe, another had a wide, shaved strip just above her ear. They were so young and healthy and bored that it made him catch his breath.

Lina was older than them now. She would be twenty soon, but he found that impossible to imagine. She had talked about it so much, all the countries she would visit. Thailand, Spain, maybe America. She had mentioned working as an au pair.

What do you know about kids?

How hard can it be?

He liked to daydream about it. Lina, driving on a highway in California, with a couple of American kids on the back seat. That she wasn't missing at all.

The darkness had returned and another summer had passed him by. Autumn terms felt like a death sentence these days, forcing him to give up the search and sit in the classroom. The new students knew who he was. He saw the looks they gave him, a mixture of fascination and sympathy. It made his stomach turn. But they never asked questions. When he introduced himself to the new class he didn't mention Lina. They knew anyway. Everyone in Glimmersträsk knew. People were afraid, and the youngsters at their desks had to live with that fear. They'd had to learn never to walk alone and always be on their guard. He doubted any of them had stood alone at a bus stop, waiting for a bus that didn't arrive on time. Their parents had learned from his tragedy and certainly weren't going to make the same mistake. Hanna Larsson's disappearance had added fuel to the fire, yet another reminder of everything that could go wrong and how vital it was to keep your children close, even in a small community like Glimmersträsk.

The kids were easier to deal with than their parents. When lessons finished and they slouched past him and through the door, he sat for a long time in the silence they had left behind. It was the staffroom he worried about, the colleagues with their strained expressions and empty, well-meaning remarks.

He flinched at their bursts of laughter, and walked straight to the coffee machine, busied himself there, stirring his mug even though he didn't take milk or sugar. He hid behind the clink of metal against china. Through the slats of the blinds he saw the birch trees that had begun to turn yellow and drop their leaves. A fragile layer of ice covered the puddles outside.

Claes Forsfjäll, one of the sociology teachers, came and stood next to him and started talking about the moose hunt.

Lelle listened dutifully, but didn't shift his gaze from the frozen puddles outside. Forsfjäll's breath smelled

226

disgustingly of banana and liquorice throat sweets when he leaned closer and put a hand on Lelle's shoulder.

'You know, we always think of that daughter of yours when we're out in the forest.'

Lelle turned to look at Forsfjäll's pasty face and felt a shiver run down his spine. 'And what makes you think she's out there in the forest?'

Forsfjäll shut his mouth and his face turned red above the knot of his tie. 'I didn't mean it like that. I just meant we think about her. That we keep our eyes open.'

Lelle bowed his head, suddenly conscious of the hard floor under the soles of his shoes and the weight on his feet from the effort of keeping himself upright.

'Thanks,' he said. 'That means a lot.'

Forsfjäll moved away to sit with the other teachers, the ones who could relax and cross their legs and knew how to make conversation. Lelle saw Anette sitting on one of the wooden chairs, talking and waving her arms about like she always did when speaking to a group of listeners. She was wearing a tight dark jumper, which made it impossible to miss the hard little bump above her jeans. He put his hand on the windowsill as his legs turned to jelly, and he heard his coffee slop on the floor and then the rustle of their shirts and blouses as they turned to him with their sympathy. The floor rocked under his feet as he hurried away. He thought he could hear them shouting after him. *Poor devil! How do you cope?*

*

She had no warning when he came, only the squealing hinges and the door that clanged against the toilet bucket. If the light was off he pulled the cord and peered down at her, and his stare burned through her eyelids, even when she pretended to be asleep. After he had convinced himself she was alive, he reached for the buckets and left. She had time to see a staircase behind him, but no daylight. He always emptied the dark urine from one bucket and filled the other with fresh water before returning. It left dark pools on the cement.

The door locked automatically. She never heard any keys. Right at the beginning, when she was stronger, she would try to attack him as he came in with the buckets. She would stand by the door and hurl herself at him as he stepped over the threshold, and the water would splash everywhere. He had struck out and hit her on her back with the metal bucket with such force that she couldn't stand up afterwards. She couldn't even protest when he lifted her back on to the bunk and stroked her with his disgusting hands. He patted her as if she were an animal that had to be calmed down before the slaughter.

His face was covered by a balaclava and through the holes his eyes looked pale against the black cloth. She had never seen his hair and got the idea he didn't have any, that his head was bare and misshapen underneath.

It was difficult to judge his age. She guessed he was

younger than her father, but couldn't be sure. He dominated the little room. His back and shoulders loomed over the raw concrete walls as he stood by the door. But she couldn't be sure if he really was a big man in the outside world. His movements were light, despite his thick, workman's boots, and he always smelled of sour new sweat, as if he had been running. His voice was like velvet when he spoke, and low, as if his vocal cords sat deep in his stomach.

'Why aren't you eating?'

He impatiently gathered up the uneaten food and replaced it with vegetables that were still steaming, and a shiny piece of meat. The nausea attacked her immediately. Despite her hunger. Her stomach was a yawning hole.

'I can't eat. I throw up as soon as I try.'

'Is there anything special you want, something you really like?'

She heard he was trying hard to be kind, even though the rage was vibrating under his artificial voice.

'I've got to have fresh air. Just for a few moments. *Please!*'

'Don't start that again.'

He unscrewed the beaker from the thermos, filled it and handed it to her. The steam felt gentle against her flaking lips. It smelled sweet, like fruit.

'Rose-hip soup,' he said. 'Get a few mouthfuls down and you'll feel better.'

She raised the beaker to her mouth and pretended to

drink. Her eyes fell on his boots, where a small yellow leaf was stuck.

'Is it autumn out there?'

He visibly stiffened and began backing to the door.

'When I come back I want that food to be gone.'

∗

'I dreamed you were pregnant.'

Carl-Johan had pulled out of her, leaving her lying in the damp patch. Meja pushed the duvet aside and got out of bed.

'Sounds more like a nightmare.'

'You were so beautiful, with your huge belly!'

Meja disappeared into the bathroom and shut the door behind her to stop him following. She brushed her teeth and hair and put on some mascara. There was no time for anything else. When she came out again he was still lying there, grinning. She walked over to the bed and leaned over him, put her lips on his and felt the warmth radiating from his body. He reached out both arms and drew her down on the bed.

'Do you really have to go? Can't you stay here with me?'

He hugged her tight and then ruffled her hair with both hands.

Meja twisted free. 'Why do you have to ruin my hair?'

'Why does it matter? Who are you making yourself gorgeous for?'

Carl-Johan and Birger didn't like her going to college. They thought it was a waste of time. Meja had to explain over and over that she had promised herself she would pass her exams and do well in life. Better than Silje, at least. Silje, who left school when she got herself knocked-up.

'Your mother didn't miss out on a thing,' Birger had told her. 'Bringing a child into the world is considerably more important than being brainwashed by the most manipulative of all the state lackeys.'

It would have been easy to give way, because she didn't even like school. She had never lived in one place long enough to get used to it. As soon as she started to feel at home in a classroom, the bags were packed and ready in the hall. Silje didn't care if it was the middle of term. If it was time to move, they moved. And that's what motivated Meja. Being someone different. Being herself.

It was three kilometres to the Silver Road and the bus stop. *You won't like it when November comes and it gets dark*, Birger had warned her. But it was already dark. The forest was a mass of shadows around her and she kept her eyes firmly on the gravel to avoid seeing the movements among the trees. The code for the gate was a combination of numbers she had to learn by heart, because they wouldn't let her write it down. She found out later it was the date of Birger's birthday. The gate whined in the silence and she could feel Birger's eyes staring at the back of her neck. She was careful to shut the gate after her and then began jogging, past the sad-looking grey pines and naked birches. The ground squelched and crackled under her feet and she thought she could smell snow in the air, even though the first frosts hadn't arrived yet.

Her throat was stinging as she reached the road, and she had to stand well away from the verge so the bus driver could see her. He was a short, florid man who drank coffee from a flask and spoke so abruptly she could barely understand what he said, other than that he asked after Birger.

The bus gradually filled up with students from the surrounding villages. She rarely saw any houses, just the signs that pointed in among the trees. The kids stood by the roadside and waited. Meja could see rosy cheeks and their breath in the chilly air. She shut her eyes and leaned her head against the cold glass when they got on. She felt them looking at her. Her eyelids burned with their curiosity, but they left her alone.

Tallbacka School was in Glimmersträsk and consisted of a single-storey red-brick building that was more like a barn than a school. The windows were draughty and most people in her class kept their coats on. Inside the swing doors were rows of green lockers. Meja hung her jacket on its hook inside her locker and ran her hand along the bookshelf until she felt the blister pack. She broke out one of the blue tablets and swallowed it without water. When she shut the locker door there stood Crow with her spiky pink hair.

'Your parents don't know you're on the Pill, right?'

'I've moved in with Carl-Johan.'

Crow's eyes widened. 'And he doesn't know?'

Meja smiled.

'He wants to get me pregnant.'

*

When he came next time she had drunk the rose-hip soup. She smelled the cold air and rotting leaves. The smell of autumn was clinging to his clothes and she didn't need to ask if summer was over.

'It makes me happy when you eat.'

He had milk and cinnamon buns with him. The aroma lay like a truce between them.

'Stay for a while,' she pleaded.

He stiffened, his eyes moving cautiously in the balaclava, and then he sank to the ground with his back to the door. He scratched his covered cheeks as if there was an itchy beard hiding underneath.

She gave him back the bag of buns and sat down on her bed.

'It's so boring, eating alone.'

He took a bun and the black mask came alive as he chewed. She couldn't eat one herself, because of the fear that lurked inside her and had a stranglehold on her throat. She put on an act instead.

'Can't you take the balaclava off?'

'When are you going to stop asking the same stupid questions?'

He grinned, as if he was teasing her. She felt a spasm of hope inside and searched her mind for something that might make him relent.

'Have you baked these?'

'No.'

'Are they shop-bought?'

'What have I told you about being nosy?'

He took another bun and wiped the crumbs from his chest. He was wearing a dark Helly Hansen fleece that sagged over his stomach. A hint of irritation in his voice made her press her shoulders up against the cold wall. He didn't like it when she asked questions.

He stood up, clenched one hand over the other and approached the bed. It creaked under his weight. She shut her eyes as he reached out his arm, and felt his fingers glide along her collarbone, over her T-shirt and down over her chest. He tapped his knuckles on her ribs.

'You've got to eat. You're fading away in front of my eyes.'

'I'm not hungry. I need fresh air.'

She forced herself to meet his gaze and tried to swallow her fear. The whites of his eyes were bloodshot, either from drugs or lack of sleep. Enlarged pupils that didn't reveal much. He still smelled of the chilly air outside. Perhaps he interpreted the eye contact as an invitation, because an instant later he leaned over and pulled her towards him.

She tried to wriggle out of his grasp, but he held her even tighter and slid a hand under her top. She clawed at his cold fingers and tried to knock them away. She felt the fury boiling inside him. When he let her go, he hit the wall so close to her head that she could feel the rush of air.

'You should learn to show a little gratitude,' he said. 'For everything I do for you.'

She didn't look as he left. There was the slam of the door behind him, and then the loneliness.

*

It had already begun to get dark when Meja walked out of the school doors. Crow stood hunched under a birch tree, making a roll-up. Her tongue piercing showed as she licked the paper, and her pink hair was frizzy in the damp air. She cocked her head at Meja.

'You coming for a pizza? My treat.'

'I can't. My bus leaves soon.'

'Isn't it boring out there at Svartliden?'

'No, I think it's lovely and peaceful.'

'Yeah, well, you've got Carl-Johan to help you pass the time.' Crow looked around, sucking her roll-up suggestively. 'What's he like? In bed, I mean?'

'None of your business.'

'God, you're so boring!' Crow cackled. 'Judging from the colour in your cheeks I'd say he lives up to expectations.'

Meja pulled up her collar.

Crow went on: 'I've always thought he was hot. A bit distant and weird, but hot.'

A car pulled up beside them. Meja recognized it immediately from the rusty paintwork and felt a knot in her stomach. Torbjörn had wound down the window and was leaning over the steering wheel. He was alone, there was no trace of Silje. He smiled broadly under his moustache and said hello to Crow, who answered by blowing smoke rings in his direction.

'Meja, have you got a minute?'

She pulled a face at Crow, before walking round the car and sliding into the passenger seat.

'Something happened?'

'No, no. All's well.'

He closed the window and lowered the volume on the radio. The dashboard was littered with tobacco pouches and sweet wrappers. Meja propped her backpack on her lap and took a look at the clock. Her bus was due to leave in ten minutes. She wasn't going to let Torbjörn drive off with her.

'What do you want?'

'It's Silje. She sleeps all day and won't eat.'

'Has she stopped painting?'

He sighed and she interpreted that as a yes.

'Make an appointment. But not the local surgery. You'll need a psychiatrist.'

'What do I do if she refuses?'

'You take away the wine until she agrees.'

He pulled at his moustache and looked at her with hangdog eyes.

'To be honest, she's missing you, and I've got this damned guilty conscience, because I drove you away.'

Meja turned to look at the school's red bricks.

'You didn't drive me away.'

He drummed his grimy fingers on the steering wheel in time to the swish of the windscreen wipers.

'How are you getting on at Svartliden?'

'Good.'

'Everything OK with Birger and family?'

'Yep.'

'What's it like, living together?'

'Fine.'

'So you don't regret it?'

Meja squinted towards the birch tree. Crow's hair looked unnatural in the greyness.

'Nope.'

'Because it's nothing to be ashamed of. Changing your mind, I mean. You're very young, both of you.'

'I haven't changed my mind.'

Torbjörn's sour breath filled the car as he exhaled.

'Then come and have a meal with us one day, won't you? You and Carl-Johan? We miss you. Both of us.'

'Mm.'

He looked at her with his pleading eyes.

'I want so much to be a dad to you, if only you'd let me.'

Meja hugged her backpack to her chest and reached for the door handle.

'I don't need a dad.'

*

She lay on the bunk, playing with her own shadow and making plans with the gangly shape on the wall. She was going to have the toilet bucket ready for when the door opened. He would get his eyes so full of urine he wouldn't see as she raised the little table. She would bring it down on his head with all her strength. Knock him unconscious, or at least off balance enough to be able to run past him and up the stairs. She didn't know what was waiting up there, whether there were any more locked doors, but she was prepared to take the risk.

Sometimes it was several days before the man came back. She had only her own brain to keep track of the hours and days, but she could tell from the food how time passed. It solidified and turned mouldy. Then she was afraid the door would never be opened again. It was a strange feeling, being afraid of something and longing for it at the same time. She realized her fear of being left to rot alone was greater than her fear of him.

She put the plate of dried-up food on the floor and practised lifting the table. The wood was bulky and heavy and the effort made her chest hurt. She saw the shadow arms tremble on the wall as if all her strength had drained away.

'We must eat,' she said to the shadow. 'If we are going to do this.'

She was woken by flashes from a camera. He was standing over her, taking pictures, and the hand around the lens was coarse from cold and hard work. She pulled the blanket over her and hid her face in her hands. The flashing continued. He jerked the blanket off her and ripped the front of her T-shirt, exposing her stomach and bra. Not until she started crying did he finally stop. He breathed deeply as he paced the floor.

'You've hardly eaten anything! Are you trying to kill yourself or what?'

'I'm not well. I need a doctor.'

He threw her a look, a silent warning, before he started frantically emptying the dried-up food into a bin bag. Then he laid out more: sausages, potatoes and grated carrot. Two flasks and a bar of chocolate. The silver paper shone up at her. She watched the shadow on the wall become eager.

'I thought you were never coming back.'

He smirked.

'So you missed me?'

She reached for the chocolate and fumbled with the paper.

'You smell of winter. Is it cold out?'

'I won't say what you smell of. Haven't you seen the bucket of water and the soap? Can't you wash?'

She broke off a square of chocolate, put it on her tongue and let it melt along with her tears. He reached out his hand and stroked her hair.

'Shall I help you wash your hair?'

She pulled up her knees and saw the shadow imitate her. Her nose was running. The chocolate tasted of salt.

'Why did you take pictures of me?'

'Because I want to see you even when I'm not here.'

'Do you live alone or have you got a family?'

'Why, are you jealous?'

'Only curious.'

'Curiosity can be dangerous.'

His hand moved from her hair to her cheek. She sat as still as she could, struggling not to flinch. His thumb stroked her lips.

'Family or not, you are the most important thing in my life.'

*

She stood alone at the bus shelter, waiting, a hazy circle of street light above her head and blonde strands of hair showing from under her hood. It was the hair that made him react. And the fact that she was standing there alone.

Without thinking Lelle skidded across the left-hand lane and drew up at the bus stop. He wound down the passenger window and beckoned her over. He was disappointed it wasn't Lina, even though he knew.

The girl was called Meja and was new to the school. In his class she sat by the window and spent most of the lesson drawing spiral patterns in the margin of her writing pad. He left her alone, because she was new and because she seemed lonely. Now the girl was taking a few steps towards him and he could see her narrow eyes shining under the hood.

'I'm on my way home. Want a lift?'

He saw her glance up the road in the direction of the bus that never came.

'It's over ten kilometres to Svartliden where I live.'

'That doesn't matter. No one's waiting for me.'

He saw her hesitate, clearly weighing up the offer. Then she took two quick steps towards the car, opened the door and slid into the seat beside him. She smelled of rain, and wet strands of hair dripped on to her hoodie. Lelle steered out on to the Silver Road, going north.

'You can't rely on that bus, anyway,' he said.

'It's always really late.'

At the top of the hill he switched to full beam and looked at the grey forest. It would be white soon. The trees would stoop like old people under the weight, and the ground and everything concealed below it would be forgotten. Another winter. He didn't know how he would get through it. He felt Meja looking sideways at him and he looked back, but her eyes slid away.

'So you live at Svartliden?'

'Mm.'

'With Birger and Anita?'

'Do you know them?'

'I don't know them, exactly. Are you related?'

She shook her head.

'Their son, Carl-Johan – he's my boyfriend.'

'Well, I'll be damned.'

People liked turning up their noses at Birger Brandt and his family, even though nobody knew them very well. Or perhaps that was why. They were rarely seen in the community, and no one knew how they made a living out there at Svartliden, whether it was hunting or their farm that kept them going. There had been a hell of a row when they refused to send their boys to school. They said they wanted to home-school the boys, the way people used to. Lelle didn't know how that had turned out, whether social services had agreed or not. But he had never seen them at Tallbacka.

'Do you smoke?' Meja suddenly asked.

'Only in the summer.'

Of course, the car reeked of smoke. It got into the upholstery and Lelle hadn't bothered cleaning it. There was a thick carpet of ash all over the instrument panel. But he wasn't embarrassed.

'Do *you* smoke?'

'No, I've given up.'

'Good. Cigarettes are crap.'

'Carl-Johan says tobacco is a conspiracy of the state. To get rid of the weak.'

Lelle looked at her.

'I've never heard that before. But cancer isn't a benefit to the state, surely?'

Meja sighed.

'A weakened population gives the state more opportunity, so Birger says.'

'Oh, does he?'

Lelle cleared his throat to disguise his bemusement. He didn't want to laugh at the girl. He had searched for Lina on Birger's land, that first summer three years ago. They had all helped – Birger, his wife and their three lads. Given him keys to outhouses and root cellars, and guided him along the forest tracks that criss-crossed their land.

He studied the girl out of the corner of his eye, noting the blonde hair and the sprinkling of freckles from the summer. Her shoulders were drawn up to her ears and she seemed fragile, like the first shards of ice before winter took hold.

'How long have you lived at Svartliden?'

'Since the summer.'

'Where did you live before that?'

'Here and there.'

'You sound like you come from down south.'

'I was born in Stockholm, but I've moved about.'

'What do your parents think about you living at Svartliden of all places?'

'I've only got Silje, and she doesn't care.'

He could tell she didn't like his questioning. Her fingers drummed restlessly on her jeans and picked at the seams. He thought of Lina and how hard it had been to have a conversation with her. It got worse as she got older, as if the years came between them and made them strangers. Everything he said resulted in grimaces and eye-rolling. It had made him frustrated then, but he missed it now.

Meja lifted her arm and pointed as they were getting close, and through the gloom he could see the wooden sign between the spruce trees.

'You can drop me off at the drive.'

'I'll take you to the door.'

She squirmed in her seat as if that bothered her, but Lelle wasn't put off.

He wondered why a young girl would willingly move to such a desolate place, and whether teenage love could be enough. Svartliden had nothing but dense ancient forest and a sad little lake to offer.

At the gate he stayed in the car, while Meja ran to punch in the code.

'Birger Brandt's boy must be one hell of a charmer,' he said out loud to himself, before she came back.

Behind the gate the large farmhouse stood flanked by black forest and the lit-up windows seemed to burn in the darkness. Meja sat on the edge of the seat, playing with her hair. She pulled it back in a ponytail, only to undo it and start again. It made him nervous.

Birger was standing on the top step as they drew up. The old man held up his hand and quickly bounded down the steps. When Meja got out of the car he patted her as if she were one of his bitches. Brisk, but affectionate.

'Well, well, Lennart Gustafsson, it's been a while!' He leaned in through the passenger window. 'You'll stay for coffee?'

＊

The shadow on the wall danced, waving its spindly arms and legs, headbanging and sending drops flying from the wet hair. The smell of soap was alien to her nostrils and made her sinuses hurt, but both the wash and the chocolate had given her energy. Enough energy to lift and turn the small table eight times in a row. Afterwards she put her hand on the wall and high-fived the shadow. She felt stronger now than for a long time.

When the man came the food was gone. Most of it had come back up in the bucket, but if he noticed he didn't say anything. He went out and emptied it and was soon back, filling the room with autumnal air and his own breath. His eyes shone behind the mask.

'You've had a wash!'

She sat with her back to the shadow. The wall was rough against her shoulders. Immediately she became afraid of what he would do now she was clean. She looked as he moved across the floor, watching his hands as he took fresh food out of the backpack. Thick slices of blood pudding, lingonberry jam. The side table creaked as if it also shrank from him.

'Pity I haven't got the camera with me,' he said. 'Now you've made yourself look so pretty.'

The bunk protested on her behalf as he lowered himself beside her. She was numb and silent. All she could hear was her own rasping breath as he touched her. He stroked her hair with his fingers and slid them down her neck.

'Why have you chosen today to make yourself pretty?'

Her chest heaved and it was hard for her to speak.

'I thought maybe if I ate something and cleaned myself up, then you'd let me go outside for a while and get some fresh air.'

His hand tightened impatiently round her neck, and he lifted her face to his.

'Kiss me and we'll see.'

The balaclava was damp against her face as he pressed his mouth to hers. She screwed up her mouth and turned away. She watched the shadow struggle as he started to tear at her clothes. The spidery arms clawed and hit until he started hitting back. Warm blood ran from her forehead and into her mouth as he forced her down on the bed.

She floated up to the wall as he did what he wanted, joining the shadow and gritting her jaw so hard it made her teeth ache.

Afterwards he pulled on his jeans and dabbed her

bleeding eyebrow with his own T-shirt. He pressed hard with his whole hand. She breathed with her mouth to avoid his smell. The hood had ridden up on top of his head and she resisted the impulse to pull it off. She understood from the way he was touching her that his anger had turned to regret. She took her chance: 'Why can't you take off that mask?'

'You know what I've told you about that.'

'But I want to see you.'

He let her go, crumpling the stained T-shirt in his hand.

'One of these days I will take it off and we'll walk out of here together, hand in hand. But you're not ready. Not yet.'

The blood began to pound in her eardrums. She leaned closer to him, suddenly eager. 'I am ready.'

He left her there on the bed. She watched the shadow reach out towards the door as it swung open, as if it had plans of its own to slip out when he did. But the door slammed, leaving both of them with the whirling dust and the taste of blood.

They remembered him, naturally. Anita, the wife, made coffee and stared at Lelle from under her fringe. She seemed agitated and her chapped hands shook as she laid the table. She wouldn't sit down. She stood hunched by the stove. That's what happens, Lelle thought, when you never get out and see people.

Birger had aged since he last saw him. Lines on his forehead and sunken eyes. He looked at Lelle in concern.

'No news of that girl of yours?'

Lelle shook his head and looked outside to the driveway lit by a single lamp. He could see the wind had picked up. The trees and shadows were moving, making it hard to focus.

'Nothing new,' he said.

'What about the police? Are they doing anything about it?'

'Sod all,' he said.

The skin on Birger's face quivered as he nodded.

'Incompetent numbskulls, that's what they are. If you want anything doing, do it yourself, I say.'

'I haven't given up. I'm going through the whole of Norrland with a fine-tooth comb.'

'That's good,' said Birger. 'That's how you'll find her.'

Lelle stared down at the table and blinked until his eyes were clear again and he could make out the dents in the wood and the grains of sugar on the cakes Anita had served. The crying still came out of nowhere, but he had mastered the art of not giving in to it.

'I'd like to thank you for giving Meja a lift home,' Birger said. 'We worry about her.'

'Do you?' said Meja.

'Yes, of course we do.'

Lelle lifted his head and looked from Birger to Anita.

'I guess you've heard about the girl who disappeared from Arjeplog in the summer?'

'We certainly have,' Birger said. 'And the police don't seem to be much help there, either.'

'No,' said Lelle. 'Not much is happening.'

Anita bent over the oven and a cloud of smoke poured out as she opened it. The loaves had a black crust as she lifted them off the baking tray. She flapped the tea towel and he could see the perspiration stains under her arms.

'No,' said Birger, opening the window. 'A wise man looks after himself. The police are nothing more than a pack of bungling idiots.'

Lelle's lips puckered. The coffee was incredibly bitter.

'I don't know if I'd go that far,' he said.

Birger was about to answer when the front door opened. Three young men came in with a cold blast behind them and stamped wet earth from their boots. When they caught sight of Lelle they stopped in their tracks.

'Here are my lads!' said Birger, beckoning them in. 'Don't stand there like idiots, come and sit down!'

They were fair-skinned and red-cheeked, with wiry bodies and dirt under their fingernails. Birger presented them one by one. Göran, the eldest, had red-blond hair and a face covered in acne scars. He didn't seem especially chatty. The middle son, Pär, was growing a beard and his cheeks glowed as he scratched it. His handshake was cold and firm. Carl-Johan was the youngest, tall and thin, and he hurried to sit down beside Meja. Birger's flabby cheeks shone with pride.

'I have succeeded with three things in this life, if nothing else. Now all we're waiting for are the grand-children.'

'It stinks in here,' said Pär. 'Are you trying to burn the house down?'

'I burned the bread,' said Anita, and that was the first thing Lelle had heard her say.

She looked small standing there, at least a head shorter than her sons. Lelle felt the young men's energy, their closeness. It made him feel exhausted. The tiredness lay like a yoke across his shoulders and he stood up so suddenly his cup clattered on the saucer.

'Thanks for the coffee,' he said. 'I must be off before my eyes get too tired.'

There was a heavy silence, before Anita found her voice. 'Yes, you must. Goodness me, how dark it's got.'

Meja thanked him for the lift and he felt their eyes on the back of his neck as he went. Birger accompanied him to the car and put an arm round his shoulder as if they were old friends.

'I hear you left the hunting team?'

'They gave me the push.'

Lelle slid behind the wheel. A light rain pattered against the windows and settled as mist over Birger's glasses as he stood beside the car.

'You're welcome to hunt with me and the lads if you feel the urge.'

'Thanks, but I think I'm done with moose hunting. I'm after bigger prey.'

Birger smiled, tight-lipped.

'I understand, and I want you to know that we would be happy to help look for your girl. Just say the word. We have good equipment and my boys don't give up easily.'

'Thanks, I'll bear that in mind.'

Birger slapped the car.

'Take care, now.'

'You too.'

Lelle turned in the drive, taking the curve carefully and waving his hand. He kept the lights on full beam and drove as fast as he dared between the spruces lining the drive. The coffee was still burning his throat and he held his breath until he reached the gate. He sat there with the engine ticking over and looked back at the farmhouse, watching the shapes move behind the lighted windows. It felt like an eternity before the gate rattled and swung open.

* * *

'Why did that teacher give you a lift home?' Carl-Johan asked.

'I was waiting for the bus and he offered.'

'And you said yes, just like that?'

'What should I have done?'

'I think he seems a bit shifty, that's all. Best you get the bus.'

Meja glanced at him. 'Are you jealous?'

Carl-Johan's laugh blew warm air on to her neck. 'Not of that old man!'

Meja broke free of his arms and the duvet and climbed out of bed. The warm stickiness ran between her legs and it occurred to her that she missed sleeping alone. Having a bed to herself.

'I feel sorry for him. He seems so alone. So abandoned.'

Carl-Johan reached out for her. 'He's not the only one to feel abandoned.'

Meja went into the bathroom and peed. She tried wiping away the pee and the stickiness with toilet paper, but gave up and turned on the shower. She pulled off her top and stepped under the cold stream of water. Soon Carl-Johan's shadow appeared on the other side of the shower curtain. She heard him lift the toilet seat and pee noisily. She should have locked the door. He didn't seem to have a clue about respecting another person's space. It took a long time for the water to run warm and she stood completely still, letting it flow over her. She wished it was morning, so she could go to school. Through the water she could hear Carl-Johan brushing his teeth. She shut her eyes to avoid seeing him, but then the shower curtain swung aside and he stepped in beside her, pressing up against her and taking most of the water. His eyes shone through the steam.

'I think you should keep away from that man.'

'He's my class teacher.'

'That doesn't mean you have to ride around with him out of school.'

'He wanted to be kind and he gave me a lift home. That's not so strange considering his daughter disappeared waiting for a bus.'

'I think you should be careful. And Mum and Dad don't like people coming here.'

'You never told me that.'

Meja jerked the shower curtain aside, stepped past him and grabbed a towel from the hook. She quickly wrapped it round her, ignoring the water dripping everywhere. Carl-Johan called out something, but it was obliterated by the noise of the shower. Meja walked to the window, leaned her wet head to the narrow opening and inhaled deeply.

Anita was walking down below. Meja squinted at the shrunken figure with the tired shoulders. Her short legs raced over the gravel and she was holding something tightly to her body, as if she were afraid of dropping it. A black cat followed her over the drive like a shadow, winding itself between her legs. Anita kicked out at it and it leapt into the flower bed. A moment later she looked up and her eyes met Meja's. In the dusk her face looked like dough, her cheeks drooping as she raised a hand. Meja waved back and stayed where she was with her fingertips against the glass. She wondered why Anita had kicked the cat. Wondered who she was really angry with.

*

Light became scarce, days shorter. Even so, time was a lonely eternity. Lelle felt sick in the mornings and had to take his coffee in small sips, all the time trying not to throw up. He forced himself to look on social media, even though it only increased his feeling of nausea. On Lina's Facebook page Anette had posted an ultrasound picture and written: *Hurry home, Lina. Soon you'll have a little brother or sister waiting for you.* The picture had two hundred and thirty-two likes and over a hundred comments, all with exclamations of delight and pastel-coloured hearts. Lelle sucked the coffee between his teeth and grimaced.

At school he walked around in the usual daze, taking whole lessons without being able to say what he had talked about. The students' faces were like A4 sheets of paper, blank and unrevealing. In the staffroom he kept to the standard small talk about the weather and the approaching weekend. He drank coffee and ate bananas on autopilot. He avoided Anette and her growing stomach as much as he could. No one asked about Lina any more, and that made him angry if he allowed himself time to think about it. The school nurse was the only one to ask how he *really* felt and even that annoyed him, the fact that she couldn't find the words to ask what she wanted to know. She seemed to enjoy putting her head on one side and touching him with her cold fingers, and at times he made a U-turn by the coat hooks if he saw her sitting in the staffroom.

Outside the fluorescent lighting of the brick building the world was in constant dusk. It was dark in the morning and dark again in the afternoon. Sometimes he went out in the lunch break and walked among the puddles and cigarette butts, the sticky blobs of chewing gum and the rustling leaves. The clouds were at bursting point, but it wasn't cold enough for snow. Not like when he was a lad, when the snow was deep already in October. He had tried explaining that to Lina, that winter wasn't as real these days. Only a few bitingly cold, record-breaking weeks, which made people lose their grip. Not like before, when it was the norm and no one would even think to moan. Lina liked the winter, especially fishing through the ice and rides on the snowmobile. The last time they were out fishing there was coffee in both flasks. She had outgrown the hot chocolate. It felt such a long time ago.

The only one he looked out for was Meja. She seemed so alone as she sat, pale and huddling at her desk, always with her jacket on as if she were constantly cold. She seemed to find it hard to make friends. He thought he ought to reach out to her, ask how she was feeling. *Really* feeling.

The opportunity came when he was on his way home.

Meja was sitting on one of the rotting school benches by
the car park, her feet in a pile of leaves and her hands
deep in her pockets. Her breath was white in the cold. She
wasn't wearing suitable clothes, only a black hoodie. No
hat or gloves. He walked over to her without thinking. The
scrunching leaves made her lift her eyes and look straight
at him. In fear, it seemed, as if she had been found out.
Lelle tried to smile.

'Well, so here you are.'

It sounded stupid. He was almost expecting her to roll
her eyes. Close up she wasn't particularly like Lina, but
even so his heart leapt and he found it hard to breathe.

'Is it OK if I sit here for a while?'

She shrugged, moved up the bench and made room
for him. The mouldy wood was damp and he felt it soak
through his jeans when he sat down.

'How are you getting on here at Tallbacka?'

'OK, I guess.'

'Have you made any friends?'

She scowled. It was clear his questions bothered her.
Lelle racked his brain for better words. That feeling of
fumbling in the dark was all too familiar.

'You said you had a mother. Where does she live?'

'Here, in Glimmersträsk. With Torbjörn.'

'Torbjörn Fors?'

Meja nodded.

'No way.'

He filled the gap between them with white breath and tried to hold his tongue. So Hassan was right, Torbjörn Fors had found himself a woman after a lifetime of living alone. That was a miracle if nothing else.

'How come you live at Svartliden? Shouldn't you be with your mum and Torbjörn?'

'Silje and I don't get on. I'd rather live with Carl-Johan.'

'What about Torbjörn? Do you get on with him?'

She shrugged again. 'He's a bit weird, but he's always nice to me. It wasn't because of him I moved out. It was time, that's all.'

Lelle nodded as if he understood, hoping she would say more.

Meja turned and looked at him, her eyes wide, as if he scared her. 'Is it true your daughter went missing?'

Now it was his turn to be on guard.

'That's right.'

'But you're looking for her?'

'I'll always be looking for her.'

He dug in his pocket for his wallet and took out the dog-eared photograph of Lina. He handed it to her. She was wearing chipped pink nail varnish, he noticed, and her fingers were white with cold. She looked at the picture of Lina for a long time.

'She's like that other girl who disappeared,' she said after a while. 'The girl on the posters.'

Lelle nodded slowly. When she handed back the picture

with her cold hand he resisted the impulse to take it between his and warm it, the way he had done with Lina when she was small. He left his wallet on his lap.

'You'll find it hard to make friends now you live at Svartliden. It's so isolated.'

She turned her head away and kicked at the leaves with the toes of her shoes.

'I've always found it hard to make friends, so that's nothing new. I've got Carl-Johan and his family now and that's all I need. Birger and Anita make me feel really welcome.'

'Sounds good. But I want you to know that I'm here, too, just in case. I know it isn't easy, starting a new school, especially in a small community like this where everyone already knows each other.'

Meja looked at him sideways, her chapped winter lips open.

'Thanks,' she said. 'But I'm used to it.'

Lelle could see the shiver run through her thin body when she stood up and rubbed her palms over her wet jeans.

'I've got to get the bus.'

Her knees knocked as she walked away, as if they needed supporting between the steps. She was so thin it hurt him to look at her. He hoped at least they had the good sense to feed her up at Svartliden. She stood in the bus shelter and hugged herself, patting her arms with her gloveless hands to get warm. Lelle was also cold, sitting on the damp

258

bench, but he stayed there until the bus came and he was sure she had got on.

*

She was woken by him standing over her. The light bulb swung on its cord behind him, giving the impression the whole room was swaying. His breathing was like sandpaper. She propped herself up on her elbow and saw he was holding out something that glittered in the space between them. Slowly, slowly, she saw a pair of handcuffs take shape, dangling from one of his hands. In the other he held a dark-coloured scarf.

'What is it?'

'I'm putting these on you.'

He tied her hands behind her back and fastened the cuffs so tight it hurt. Then he covered her eyes with the scarf. She felt the draught when he pretended to slap her, to convince himself she couldn't see. Panic came over her immediately, a metallic taste in her mouth and a shuddering down her back that she couldn't hide. She was afraid he was going to attack her in some new kind of vile game. Her fear irritated him.

'Why are you shaking?'

'I don't know.'

'How many times do I have to tell you that you don't have to be afraid of me?'

His face was so close that she could feel his breath on

her cheek. She clenched her teeth and tried to steady herself. He pressed himself close to her and rubbed her arms with his hands, as if trying to warm her. When she carried on shivering, he took a firm grasp of her waist and began dragging her across the room.

'Where are we going?'

To her surprise she heard the door open and then felt the cold draught of wind from somewhere above her. His hands pushed her in front of him. Steps felt unfamiliar after such a long time and were even trickier to negotiate with her hands behind her back. When they reached the top she was gasping for breath as if she had just climbed a mountain. She heard him unlock another door and then there was a rush of cold air like a wave over her body. His fingers dug into her arms as they walked over a threshold and suddenly everything was wonderfully alive. She heard fallen leaves crush under their feet and the wind tearing at the treetops. There was a powerful smell of forest, leaf mould and approaching winter.

They walked a short distance while she gulped the fresh air deep into her lungs, feeling it strengthen her. Through a gap in the blindfold she could just make out the bumpy forest ground under her feet and the darkness of night. Thoughts whirled in her head. This was her chance. She must break free and run. Scream and fight. But his grip on her was as unrelenting as the handcuffs. She didn't have a chance. Not yet.

Then a new fear struck her. He was going to kill her. It was over. Perhaps he had tired of her. Perhaps he couldn't go on keeping her alive any longer. Perhaps it had all been a mistake and his only way out was to get rid of her once and for all.

She came to a halt. The cold air was getting under her skin, but she felt the warmth radiating from the man, as if not even the weather could get at him.

'Where are we going?' she whispered.

'You've nagged about getting fresh air, so here it is. Make the most of it for as long as it lasts.'

She breathed deeply, trying to conceal her shivering. She stood absolutely still and listened, but all she heard was the wind sighing in the pine trees. She wondered if anyone would hear if she called out and felt the cry take shape in her chest, but she didn't dare let it out. Not when he was standing so close. Perhaps he felt her stiffen, because he started to pull her again.

'OK, that's enough. You're getting cold.'

'Just a little while longer.'

'I'm not letting you get ill.'

The disappointment was like something black and swollen inside her as he took her back to the little room. There were livid red marks round her wrists when he removed the handcuffs. She sank on to the bunk and let him wrap a blanket round her. The regret hammered in her head. She should have run, she should have screamed.

261

Instead she was back in this stinking hole. And it really did stink. She smelled it now as she returned from the freedom. It smelled rotten. Like a grave.

'Now you can't tell me I don't do anything for you,' he said. 'Every single thing I do is for you.'

Impulses. Since Lina disappeared it was the impulses that controlled him. He did things, his body took him to new places and his brain couldn't catch up. There was no warning.

After the conversation with Meja on the damp bench he found himself on Gammelvägen, going through the village. The road that went to the southern edge of the lake came to an end in a turning point at Torbjörn Fors's property. He realized he was on his way there when he glimpsed the dilapidated house between the pine trees. He stopped the car by an overgrown ditch and sat for a while. They were acquaintances, he and Torbjörn, nothing more. Two lone wolves each on his own side of the forest.

He found it hard to get his head around the fact that Torbjörn had met a woman. Torbjörn, who had lived alone since his parents died and had collected porn as a substitute for real relationships. There had been a lot of talk about his habit through the years, that he sent money to women he met online, while his own home fell into disrepair, and that he liked to watch girls swimming in the lake. Lelle knew he worked in forestry and liked his drink as a youth. But he had never had a woman.

Torbjörn was supposed to take the same bus as Lina that morning she disappeared. Lelle could almost picture him standing there, pulling at his moustache.

She wasn't there when I arrived. I was alone in the bus shelter. Ask the bus driver. We never saw her.

The police had judged him credible. In Lelle's mind nobody was worthy of that description.

The house certainly was run-down, sagging on one side and weeds growing up the windowsills. The front door was half-open and a scrawny dog lay stretched out on the top step of the veranda. It managed a few wags of its tail, but made no attempt to move. Lelle knocked sharply a few times.

'Hello! Anyone home?'

A few minutes passed before a figure appeared in the dim light inside. It was a woman, wearing a faded dressing gown and matching slippers. Her hair was like a lion's mane around her head and her cheeks were smeared with make-up. Her eyelids seemed heavy as she blinked at him.

'Who are you?'

'My name is Lennart Gustafsson.'

He was about to reach out his hand when he noticed she was holding brushes and a palette. The paint was dripping on to the floor.

'Have we met before?'

There was a pungent odour of rubbish and cigarette smoke coming from inside the house.

'I don't think so. You must be Silje. I'm your daughter's teacher at Tallbacka School.'

She stared.

'Has something happened to Meja?'

'No, no, nothing's happened.'

'Meja doesn't live here any more. She's moved.'

'I know. That's partly why I'm here.'

Silje made a gesture with the dripping paintbrushes. 'Come in. You don't have to take off your shoes.'

Lelle stepped into the hall and dodged the shoes, clothes and rubbish scattered on the floor. He breathed through his mouth as she led him into a sitting room where an easel was set up by the window. Beside it was a fraying sofa with red wine stains and a low table littered with empty glasses, ashtrays and dirty plates. A window was open, despite the rain and cold, but not even the smell of pine needles could cloak the foul stench inside. She hadn't fastened the dressing gown and he could see she was almost naked underneath. He glimpsed her breasts and lacy pants in the opening. He realized he was feeling embarrassed and looked down at the filthy floor.

'Do you want a glass?' she asked, clinking with the wine bottle.

'No, thanks. I'm driving.'

He watched as she downed a couple of mouthfuls and clicked a lighter. The smell of the smoke was almost refreshing in the rank air of the room. There was no trace of Torbjörn.

'Meja has moved in with her boyfriend.'

'I heard.'

'We tried to get her to come home, but it's like she's been swallowed up, we can't reach her.'

The cigarette hung loosely from her mouth as she slowly dabbed paint on the canvas.

Lelle cleared his throat.

'Where's Torbjörn?'

'Working, in the forest.'

'Working with what?'

'No idea, but he'll be back soon.'

Lelle leaned over to take a look at the canvas.

'Meja told me you moved here last summer.'

'That's right.'

'And you like it here?'

Silje stopped painting. The black make-up made her eyes look enormous. 'I wouldn't say like. But you do what you have to do.'

'What about Torbjörn? He's treated you well, I hope.'

'Torbjörn is the kindest man I've ever met.'

'So he didn't drive Meja away?'

Silje took a last drag of her cigarette and dropped the glowing end into an empty beer can on the windowsill. She wasn't old, but her hard life had already etched deep lines around her eyes and mouth. Her lower lip trembled as she looked at him.

'No one drove Meja away. It's that Carl-Johan, he's turned her head. We've tried to get them to visit, both of us. We drove out to that godforsaken dump and begged and pleaded with her to come home, but she wouldn't listen. Neither of us can get through.'

'She's too young to move out without your permission. Have you talked to social services?'

She snorted. 'Social services and I don't get along. They've never done anything for Meja and me.'

'I know a guy who's a police officer,' said Lelle. 'He's good at talking to youngsters.'

'I don't want to get mixed up with the authorities. They'll only end up taking Meja away from me and I wouldn't survive that.'

Stained tears began running down her cheeks and the paintbrush waved erratically in her hand. She reached out for the wine glass and drained it.

'Meja knows I need her. She knows I can't cope. She'll come back eventually.'

Lelle looked around at the dirt and the mess, and at the scantily clad woman in front of him.

'Isn't it the case that Meja needs *you*?'

Her face crumpled behind her hands.

'I'm sick,' she said. 'That's why we need each other. I was

the same age Meja is now when I had her. Since then it's been the two of us against the world.'

Her voice broke into sobs that wracked her body. Lelle stood awkwardly by the wall. He thought about Meja sitting in the cold, alone and with no warm clothes. Something flared up inside him.

He cleared his throat again.

'I know you've moved about a lot and I believe the most important thing for Meja now is stability and that she feels she has a home. A real home.'

'I tried! I've already told you that.'

'My police officer friend can drive out and talk to her. He doesn't have to write a report...'

'No, I said: I don't want the bloody police involved!' Silje swayed slightly. She held the paintbrush like a weapon between them. 'I think it's best you go now. I mustn't get upset.'

Lelle held up his hands and backed out through the untidy hall and on to the veranda. His legs felt heavy as he walked through the overgrown grass and he felt his fingers tense up and the anger pulsate in his head. If it was up to him he would get rid of the lot of them – all these parents who didn't fight for their children, who were too wrapped up in their own suffering to care.

He had just put his hand on the car door when she stuck out her head and called after him: 'Tell Meja I miss her!'

*

'It's all about the breathing. To feel at one with your weapon you must breathe together.' Birger's boots crunched patiently behind Meja on the golden carpet of fallen leaves under the birches. Meja was kneeling down and she felt the damp soak through her jeans. The rifle wouldn't keep still in her hands. The black plastic vibrated in her fingers. She felt their eyes on the back of her neck, Birger and the boys. One by one they had demonstrated how to fire a shot. They had peppered the target with lethal black holes to the heart and head, and shown her how to breathe out slowly as her finger pressed the trigger, as if the very shot were coming from deep within her. But Meja tensed up, ready for the recoil, and her muscles and lungs wouldn't obey. The shots were too high and disappeared in among the trees. And it got worse the more shots she fired. The weapon remained cold and alien, and it scared her.

'We've been shooting since we were little,' Göran said. 'Just be patient, it'll come.'

Pär was the champion marksman. They threw up clay pigeons and his bullets shattered them every time. He could run from tree to tree and take up a shooting position in seconds. Meja thought his face took on a sharp, predatory expression when he had a gun on his shoulder. He stood with his hands over his ears, relieved when her attempts were over.

Birger patted her. The air was full of the smell of

propellant and the autumn chill had bitten into his cheeks. It was evident he was enjoying himself.

'I don't think you're ready for the moose hunt this year, Meja love. But you'll be the one bringing down a bull next year.'

They carried the rifles on straps over their shoulders. Carl-Johan turned into someone else in his camouflage gear. More serious, more grown up.

'Pity it gets dark so early,' he said. 'Otherwise we could practise every day, just you and me.'

He moved nimbly through the low lingonberry bushes and the fallen leaves and didn't notice she was lagging behind. For the last stretch she was alone with Birger. The setting sun was pouring through the trees and casting long shadows behind them. He stopped often, bending down and touching fungi and the remaining berries. He lifted his head and sniffed the air, as if he had picked up the scent of something. Every time their eyes met he smiled.

'I'm glad you came with us today, Meja. Everyone ought to know how to use a firearm.'

'Wouldn't it be better if people didn't use weapons at all?'

'Now you sound just like those leftie newspapers. You mustn't be so naive. You know the state has cut back on civil defence, even though the world today is so unstable. The ability to defend yourself has never been more important than now.'

Birger grinned down at a ring of toadstools. 'In this country they don't like us arming ourselves, because armed civilians are a threat to a dictatorship, you see. That's why we've got more weapons than they'll ever know. Because we refuse to dig our own graves.'

'Is it legal to have so many weapons?'

He smiled. 'We put our own survival and freedom above arbitrary Swedish laws. In the long run, that's all that counts.'

They could see the house beyond the forest. The white smoke rose up in the dusk sky and welcomed them home. Meja felt the old hunger begin to claw at her stomach and she longed for the warmth and the smell of food in Anita's kitchen. But Birger put a heavy arm round her shoulders.

'The most important thing I can teach my sons is the art of survival. Learn our ways, Meja, and no one can ever trample on you again.'

She was back in the boot. The car bumped over the badly surfaced road. There was the drone of voices and singing from the radio. She chewed on the gag and the corners of her mouth stung. One hand had gone numb behind her and her throat still hurt from where his fingers had held her. When the boot slammed shut she was certain he had made a mistake, that he hadn't noticed she was still breathing.

Her lungs ached when she woke up, as if she had been

running in her sleep. Slowly but surely the rectangle took shape before her eyes. The damp walls, the white glow of the light bulb. She ran her fingertips over her throat, felt her heartbeat underneath. Turned to the shade and rested two fingers against the wall as if she were taking its pulse too.

'So far we are alive,' she whispered.

She forced herself to eat a few slices of the blood pudding, although it felt like glue between her teeth. She rinsed her mouth out with warm milk from the flask and stretched, making her stiff joints creak. Then she sank to the floor and struggled through a few weak push-ups, before lying down with her cheek on the cold cement. It was harder than she thought to keep her strength up. Her body refused and her thoughts worked against her the whole time. The fear of what he would do to her if she failed.

She caught sight of the leg of the bed. There was something wound around the dirty metal. It looked like a thin rope of some kind. When she reached for it she saw it was a hairband, a purple hairband that someone had threaded on to the leg of the flimsy bunk. Her chest heaved as she pushed herself up with her tired arms, put her shoulder under the bed and lifted it up to pull the hairband off the leg. She held the purple material up to the bulb and in the light saw some fine strands of fair hair, several shades blonder than her own. Almost white. The realisation was crushing and it took her breath away. She pressed a fist to her mouth to keep back everything that started to come up.

When the man came she had the hairband threaded around her wrist like a bracelet. He seemed agitated and left muddy footprints after him as he moved around the room, emptied buckets and put out fresh food: cooked potatoes with their skin on, and dark sausages. It seemed everything he gave her was made of blood. She avoided looking at the food and tried to catch his eye instead.

Perhaps he felt her challenge, because he soon stopped what he was doing. The winter jacket made him look even bigger than he was. His throat reddened where it showed just above the collar, as if he were boiling inside.

'What's the matter? What are you gawping at me like that for?'

She tried to swallow her fear, to breathe it away. 'Has there been someone else here, before me?'

He grabbed at the balaclava, as if he had been caught off balance, and pulled down the top of the jacket zip. 'What do you mean?'

'Has anyone else lived in this room?'

'Why are you asking?'

'Because it feels as if someone has been here.'

He shoved a hand under his jacket and scratched his chest. His eyes searched the walls and the corners of the room.

'What have you found?'

'Nothing.' She pulled her sleeve down over the hairband. 'Just a feeling.'

'I haven't got time for this. Eat your dinner and try to get some sleep, instead of imagining things you know nothing about.'

She saw his hands tremble as he reached for the door handle, and that gave her courage.

'Where is she now? What did you do with her?'

He stopped, slowly turned his head and fixed her with his eyes. 'If you don't stop asking questions I won't come back again. And you'll rot down here.'

Late autumn mornings were the worst, when the air was freezing and raw and made its way through doors and inside collars and made him feel cold all the time. When he arrived at school it was pitch-black outside the windows and the stubble on his chin was wet with melted frost. Lelle could feel it dripping. The classroom smelled of damp down jackets and cold skin, and the students' faces looked sickly in the fluorescent light. Noses ran and lips cracked. Black eyeliner smudged in the biting wind.

Meja was in her place by the window with a scarf wound all the way up to her mouth and her hood up. He felt a jolt of relief when he saw her sitting there. Or was it pure happiness? The marker pen felt light in his hand as he wrote up the calculations. He understood now why she had ended up at Svartliden. He could hear Silje's voice echoing in his head: *She knows I need her!*

At lunch break he found her on the rotting bench. Lelle handed her a mug of steaming coffee, which she took without protest.

'I didn't know if you wanted milk with it.'

'Doesn't matter, I can drink it black.'

She moved along to make room for him.

'I heard you went to see Silje.'

'That's right.'

'Why did you do that?'

'Because I care about you.'

She exhaled and looked over at the football pitch, where the grass was wilted and defeated in its wait for the snow.

'Because I remind you of your lost daughter?'

'No,' he said, a little too quickly. 'Maybe,' he said, after a while.

She gave a lopsided smile over the coffee mug and he smiled back. The silence between them wasn't easy, but it wasn't uncomfortable either, and he tried not to think about what passers-by would make of them sitting there together, a middle-aged man and a seventeen-year-old girl. It was the kind of thing that got tongues wagging.

'Was she drunk when you were there?'

'A bit.'

She looked at him sideways from under her hood. 'Do you drink?'

'Sometimes. But I've noticed it makes things worse.'

'Alcohol is forbidden at Svartliden. Birger and Anita hate alcohol and drugs.'

'Do you hate alcohol?'

She shrugged. 'It's nice coming home knowing people are sober. With Silje you never know what to expect.'

'I can understand that.'

The coffee had gone cold already, but Lelle sipped his for the sake of appearance. He tried to formulate the words in his head before he let them out of his mouth.

'How are things with Carl-Johan?'

'OK, I guess.'

'What happens if it finishes between you? Where will you go?'

She pulled a face at the coffee. 'It won't finish.'

'It's hard living together, especially when you're young and need to find out who you are. It's easy to smother each other.'

There was a swift exchange of glances, and he saw she understood. Lelle stood up and crumpled the empty paper mug in his hand. He pointed towards the Silver Road, shining like fish scales in the dead light.

'I live just a couple of kilometres north, Glimmersträsk 23, a red house. If ever you need anything or want to get away for a while, my door is always open. Svartliden isn't your only alternative.'

She stared at him, but she didn't speak.

'Think it over.'

When he stood up to go the sweat was running inside his jacket, despite the cold.

Meja stayed where she was on the bench and watched him go. She held back from the bright corridors and the laughter. The rain had turned to sleet and it stung her cheeks and turned puddles into shiny glass. Meja crushed the ice under her feet, but withstood the impulse to jump on them like a child, in case anyone saw.

Crow's voice came from nowhere: 'So what was that all about?'

'What?'

'You and Lelle Gustafsson.'

'Nothing. He wanted to talk, that's all.'

'Are you two sleeping together?'

Meja couldn't help laughing. 'You're sick.'

Crow smirked. 'Want to hang out with me?'

She was wearing a black coat and a bright red knitted hat that shone like a lingonberry. Her made-up face looked glamorous even in the sleet, as if the weather had no hold over her. They started walking away from school, towards a clump of birches wrapped in frost. Piles of leaves shimmered in the twilight.

Crow smoked cigarettes and tapped at her mobile with frozen fingers. Tiny skulls grinned up from her black-painted fingernails.

'What are we hiding from?' asked Meja.

'We're not hiding. We're waiting for someone.'

Crow peered in among the trees. A path snaked ahead of them and disappeared among some pines. Soon they heard the harsh rattle of a moped.

'Who are we waiting for?'

'Just some guy I buy dope from.'

Crow pulled her in among the trees and glanced back at the school. Soon a red moped appeared, ridden by a gangly youth in a leather jacket with wind-blown hair. His helmet hung nonchalantly on the handlebars. He switched off the engine, but stayed on the seat and jerked his head in Meja's direction.

'Who's she?'

'This is Meja,' said Crow. 'She's cool.'

'You know what I've said about bringing people.'

'Meja isn't people.'

Crow laid a protective arm round Meja and smiled as if they were best friends.

'This is Micke, but we call him Wolf. Despite the name, he's as harmless as he looks.'

Wolf hit out with his helmet and grinned. Crow handed him some creased notes, which he quickly stuffed inside his jacket. He took a swift look towards the school, before bringing out a small plastic bag which he gave to Crow. She hid it in her clenched fist and her red lips smiled. It was all over in seconds.

But Wolf stayed, his sleepy eyes fixed on Meja.

'You look familiar. I think I've seen you before.'

Meja pulled up her hood and shrank into it. 'I don't think so.'

'I could swear it. You look fucking familiar.'

'All blondes are the same to you,' Crow interrupted. 'We've got to go. Unlike you, Meja and I have plans for the rest of our life!'

'I don't think dope whore counts as a career.'

Crow gave him the finger.

Wolf laughed as they left.

When they had walked for a short while Crow linked arms with Meja and leaned her head on her shoulder. The red wool tickled Meja's cheek.

'There's a lot of bollocks going around about Wolf, but I've known him all my life,' she said. 'He's like a brother to me and I'm not turning my back on him like all the other village idiots.'

'Why have they turned their back on him?'

Crow straightened up and looked at Meja. 'Because he was with Lina before she went missing. People want someone to blame.'

Meja felt a prickling sensation at the back of her neck. She thought of Lelle, his sad face in the car, his arms leaning heavily on the teacher's desk as if to stop himself falling down.

'You don't think Wolf has got anything to do with her disappearance?'

Crow's lips twitched.

'Never asked him. Not sure I want to know.'

*

Not until autumn did he make up for the lost sleep. Time and again the exhaustion caught up with him and he gave in to it as often as he could. He would park by the roadside and recline his seat, rest his head on his arms at his desk, find himself on the sofa at dawn, cold, muzzy and with unbrushed teeth. Already by early afternoon the darkness returned, forcing him to submit. Memories of the midnight sun and long nights behind the wheel seemed unreal now, when every hour he had to struggle to stay awake. He saw his reflection in the dark panes of glass and knew he was sitting alone at the dinner table. But in his dreams she was there.

Lelle was sleeping when the patrol car rolled up the drive. He didn't hear the car door slam or the heavy steps on the gravel. Not until the ring of the doorbell turned to hard knocking did he finally wake up.

'Shit, were you asleep? It's only six.'

A light rain was falling outside and Hassan's hair curled on his forehead.

'Has something happened?'

'No, I just want to see how you are. Any coffee going?'

'Of course there's coffee, but take off your shoes before you come in.'

Lelle staggered into the kitchen. The tiredness made him unsteady on his feet. He nodded towards the thermos jug on the table. Hassan fetched a cup for himself. Lelle couldn't recall when he had brewed the coffee, but it couldn't have been that long ago because it was still steaming. He knew Hassan was looking at him from over by the table.

'Have you been to work today?'

'Of course I've been to work.'

'Are the kids wearing you out?'

'I'm just tired, that's all.'

Hassan leaned on the table and gulped his coffee. 'Why don't you ever have anything to eat with your coffee at home?'

'There's a loaf of bread.'

'I don't mean bread. I mean things like pastries, biscuits.'

'Do you eat that stuff? I thought you had your figure to worry about.'

'Get lost.'

Lelle put the loaf and a tub of butter on the table. He removed the lid, so Hassan wouldn't see it was three weeks past its sell-by date. There was no cheese.

'You're the one who should be eating. How much weight have you lost?'

'Forget about me. I want to know what's happening with the police and the Hanna Larsson investigation.'

'You know I'm not working on that case.'

'But you must have picked up some snippet of information.

Are they working on the basis of a connection between Lina and Hanna's disappearance?'

Hassan reached for some bread and looked suspiciously at the dry slice.

'We're not ruling out a connection, but the two incidents are pretty far apart. That complicates things.'

'Yes, it must be very bloody complicated, seeing as you never seem to get anywhere.'

Hassan didn't bother answering. He finished his coffee and poured out some more.

'Haven't you got a home to go to?'

'I'm working.'

'Anything happening in the villages this time of year?'

'More than you could imagine.'

Lelle reached for the coffee jug and poured himself a cup. He was thirsty and had a bad taste in his mouth. He tried smoothing his hair and felt the greasiness under his fingers.

'Come here, I'll show you something,' he said.

He led Hassan to his office, on the way taking an apple from a bowl and switching on every lamp to ward off the mocking darkness. He walked up and down in front of the growing collection of information on one wall. Every newspaper article that had ever been written about Lina was pinned up there, along with printouts from the internet that could be useful. He had even added cuttings concerning Hanna Larsson's disappearance from Arjeplog. Photos

281

of the girls were pinned side by side and it took his breath away every time he looked at them. They were so alike. They could be sisters.

Hassan stood in the doorway. He had brought his coffee cup with him, but wasn't drinking from it. Lelle took a large bite of apple and nodded at the photos.

'And you still don't think there's a connection?'

Hassan scratched the back of his head and kept quiet. Lelle rapped his knuckles on an article written by a journalist from *Norrbottens Kuriren* who had drawn parallels between the cases. The headline screamed: ALARMING SIMILARITY IN THE CASES OF THE MISSING GIRLS.

But Hassan stayed stubbornly in the doorway. 'What is it you're trying to say?'

'That there is a connection between Lina and Hanna's disappearance. I can see it. The journalists can see it. I just want to make sure the police can see it as well.'

Hassan's uniform creaked as he crossed his arms. Now he was the one looking tired.

'Believe me,' he said. 'We can see it.'

*

He was always kind after he had hit her. That was when she could ask for things. The green first-aid box was open on the floor and he insisted on bathing the cuts in antiseptic.

'They can get infected,' he said, when she backed away. 'Especially when you insist on being so filthy.'

She hated having him so close to her, hated his hands and the sweet, sour smell he gave off. It was like rotten fruit. If she never saw his face, she would recognize him from his smell. It stayed in her nostrils long after he had left.

'I need fresh air, otherwise they'll never heal.'

'It's cold out.'

'I don't care. I just need to breathe.'

'Not now.'

'Please.'

'Not now, I said! You won't get anywhere if you keep going on about it.'

He flared up, but not enough for her to back away. There was still room for negotiation.

She leaned closer, trying to make her voice meek: 'We don't have to go far. I can just stick my head out, fill my lungs.'

He stuck a plaster on her forehead and smoothed it out with his thumb. Then he jerked his head towards the plate on the side table. Thin, dark slices of bread and gleaming pieces of cured salmon.

'I made it myself,' he said. 'Eat it while it's fresh and we'll see if there's time for a walk.'

She reached out for the bread. The bitter taste of dill made her stomach heave, but she took a big bite. The salmon melted on her tongue. Her jaws didn't need to work hard and she was grateful for that. Even eating drained her energy.

He crouched over the first-aid box and meticulously put everything back in its place. She looked at his bowed head and wondered if she would be able to kick it hard enough to make him defenceless. Her foot dangling over the edge of the bed was so close she felt the tingling in her toes. She would have time for one kick, possibly two. In the beginning he had never turned his back on her, but now he was starting to get careless.

He raised his eyes and saw she was struggling to swallow the bread and salmon.

'You're dreaming of escaping from me, aren't you?'

'No,' she said, her mouth full of food.

'That's why you want to go out.'

'I just need some air.'

He sat beside her on the bunk and put his heavy arm round her shoulders.

'Eat up and we'll see.'

*

Lelle hated Fridays, when all his bright-eyed colleagues were on their way to their well-lit homes and their taco suppers and cosy evenings. Home to kids and partners and that feeling of temporary fulfilment. He remembered the feeling of having someone to go home to. Lina and Anette, and lighted candles on the dinner table. A film, maybe. Simple, everyday luxuries that seemed foreign to him now.

The house was cold and in darkness when he walked

in, but he didn't bother putting on any lights. He kept his jacket on and went into the kitchen, where there was a smell coming from the fridge. Or was it the sink? Anette wanted to buy a dishwasher, but he was tight-fisted. He had put his hand to his heart and declared he would be responsible for all the washing up from now on. *Who needs a machine when you have your own two hands?* He had been an idiot even then.

He put the coffee on, mainly wanting the aroma of it to fill the kitchen, and leaned heavily against the draining board until it dug into him. The thirst was on him. The craving, burning on his tongue. A cold sweat broke out on the back of his neck. He had drunk his way through the first winter, when the snow lay thick and they had spells of minus forty. He couldn't have done any searching anyway. The police couldn't either, whatever they might have said. Everything was buried in the cold and the snow. Anette had retreated into her drug-induced sleep and he rarely went upstairs, let alone to bed. Where had he slept? He couldn't recall.

He was sitting in the darkness when the doorbell rang. The palpitations were so immediate that his head swam as he lurched into the hall. A quick look through the window shocked him. There outside was a thin little figure with a hood up and blonde hair escaping from under the black fabric.

Lina, Lina, my beautiful, darling child. Is it you?

She pulled down her hood as the door opened and Lelle felt the heavy blow of disappointment. They silently blinked at one another for a few moments. A film of rain had settled on her face and her eyes flashed with apprehension when she saw him.

'I missed the bus. Am I interrupting anything?'

'No, no. Not at all. Come in.'

He put on the lights and was ashamed of the mess and the bad smell, which he still couldn't identify. Meja kept her jacket on and when he asked her to sit down she pulled out Lina's chair. He wanted to protest, but didn't, somehow. Instead he poured out the coffee and laid the table with the same sad-looking bread, thinking about what Hassan had said about cake. He wished he'd bought some.

Meja's eyes wandered around the room, the dirty dishes, the magnets on the fridge door, the pictures of Lina.

'Nice house you've got.'

'Thanks.'

'The houses are so big up here in Norrland.'

'That's probably because no one wants to live here.'

She smiled, revealing a gap between her front teeth that he hadn't noticed before. It struck him that he had never seen her smile this way.

'I want to live here,' she said. 'I didn't at first, but now I like it here.'

'Do you like it at Svartliden?'

'I like it in Norrland.'

'So do I.'

Lelle began spreading a slice of bread and she copied him.

'If I'd known you were dropping by I'd have made sure there was something else to offer you. I don't get many visitors these days.'

'Haven't you got a woman?'

'We divorced two years ago. She's got a new man now.'

'Oh, shame.'

'Yes, you could say that.'

Meja's forehead creased and Lelle dunked his bread in the coffee. His hand was steady and he realized this was the first time he had mentioned Anette without getting upset. He didn't feel bitter or depressed. Rather the reverse. It made him feel exhilarated to be sitting here with someone young. Someone who could be his daughter.

'Can I ask you something?' he said, after a pause.

'What?'

'What's it really like, living at Svartliden? I've heard the Brandt family don't even have a TV.'

'We listen to podcasts in the evening.'

'Podcasts?'

'Yes. Americans, mostly, talking about the New World Order and stuff.'

'The New World Order?'

He watched her blush and avoid his gaze. 'It's mainly Birger who believes in it. And Pär.'

'Not Carl-Johan?'

'He grew up at Svartliden, he doesn't know any different. But he can change if he sees more of the world.'

'So is that your plan, to show him more of the world?'

Meja sighed, looking down at the table. 'He wants us to get married and have children.'

'Not yet, surely? You're so young, both of you.'

She raised her head and peered at him with a mischievous dimple in each cheek. 'I'm on the Pill, but he doesn't know.'

They sat in a warm circle of light, while the world outside was in darkness, but branches whipping about in the wind were a surly reminder that they couldn't sit there forever. *She isn't Lina. You haven't got your daughter back.*

Meja was the one to stand up first and leave the circle of light. He heard her rinse her coffee cup at the sink and walk back across the floor behind him. When he turned his head, he saw she had stopped in front of the fridge and the photos of Lina. Ten Lina faces smiled out at them from the stainless steel: a naked baby with a Midsummer crown of flowers, an eight year old with a gap in her teeth and riding a red scooter, and the very last picture, from the end of the summer term at Tallbacka. Lina in a white dress and her hair piled on top of her head. Meja put her head on one side and looked closely, as if there was something in Lina's face she was searching for. It was several minutes before she turned back to Lelle.

'It's getting late, I'd better phone for a lift.'

'I'll give you a lift.'

The spruce trees bowed low over the wildlife fencing as they drove past. The Silver Road was shiny and deserted ahead of them and Lelle found himself driving slowly, as if he wanted to draw out the time. Meja had been very quiet in the passenger seat. Quiet and still. When he swung on to the gravel road to Svartliden she pulled up her hood.

'You can drop me off here.'

'No, I'll drive you to the door. The wind is biting out there.'

'It doesn't matter. I want to walk.'

She spoke quietly, but there was an edge to her voice, so he slowed down and did as she asked, despite the howling wind, which was whipping up the gravel. When he stopped, she turned and hugged him abruptly, her cold cheek against his stubbly face.

'Thanks for the lift.'

Then she flung open the door and disappeared into the storm. Lelle kept his eyes on the meagre shadow until she was swallowed up by the darkness. He sat there for a long time with the wind whining around him and a growing emptiness inside. It was no coincidence she had sought him out, he knew that. There was a reason. It had been so obvious, there at his kitchen table in the pool of light, that something had brought them together.

✳

The night pressed up against the window panes and threatened to stifle her. Meja recoiled from her own reflection in the murky glass. The farm became a solitary light in the darkness and the forest loomed behind the house like a black curtain. Anita had given her a headtorch to guide her way to the chickens. The cold darkness found its way in there, too, and the chickens had their feathers fluffed up when she went to them. They weren't laying well at the moment. Meja was lucky if she found two a day.

The evenings fell quickly and drew them all together. Meja sat curled up in front of the fire with Carl-Johan and his brothers. As usual it was Birger who fed the fire, while Anita sat in an armchair, squinting at her knitting. Her hands had a life of their own and the yarn never seemed to run out. Meja wished she too had something to focus on, something other than the brothers' lectures about an imminent war and the end of the world. As usual, Birger wanted her attention. He stood with his back to the fire and stared hard at Meja, as if he wanted to reassure himself that she was listening.

They want us to flee from reality. They want us to have our heads buried in our mobiles and screens. They don't want us to look around and start questioning what is actually going on in the world.

She had no room of her own, no little corner to escape to. They buzzed around her, all of them, like flies. Göran and Pär also wanted to sit close to her, given the chance, touching her and putting their heavy arms around her as if they were feeding off her. She had always dreamed about a real family, brothers and sisters. But now, when they surrounded her all the time, she found herself longing for the solitariness she had before. To be able to breathe. And she began to realize, although she didn't want to admit it, that it wasn't only the darkness that was suffocating her.

Carl-Johan pushed open the door without knocking and stuck his head in the gap. 'What are you sitting in here for?'

'I just want to be on my own for a while.'

He frowned. 'We're going to listen to that guy from Texas, and Mum's made a cake.'

'I've got homework to do for an assessment tomorrow.'

He stayed in the doorway. She saw the annoyance on his face and it made him ugly.

'I'll come down when I'm ready.'

But she didn't go down to the others, and when nighttime came and he crept in beside her she breathed deeply and hoped he would leave her alone. They had lived under the same roof for a few months and already it was making her feel anxious. She wondered if she suffered from the same restlessness as Silje. Perhaps she would never be able to put down roots. During the summer she had been so sure of what she wanted, sure that Svartliden would always be her home. Now when the darkness and everyday life had crept up on her, that idea seemed almost ludicrous. She thought about what Lelle had said, that it was hard to live with another person while you were still trying to find yourself.

When she was certain he had fallen asleep she got out of bed, one leg at a time. She clutched her clothes tightly until she had shut the door on Carl-Johan. Behind Göran and Pär's doors it was silent and dark. They were not night owls, their hard labour on the farm saw to that. She dressed hurriedly and awkwardly. As she went down the stairs the whole house creaked and sighed, but if anyone heard the sound they didn't bother checking what it was. The double doors leading to Birger and Anita's room were closed and only darkness seeped through the cracks.

Stepping out into the autumn night was like taking a dip in Glimmersträsk Lake. Every muscle came to life instantaneously. The gravel drive was illuminated by the sliver of moon and she had no trouble finding the henhouse. Immediately she wished she had her phone with her, so she could call someone. Silje, maybe, or Crow. Or Lelle. He was probably the one she really wanted to talk to. But she didn't have her phone. She had to be content with the hens.

They slept huddled together and didn't seem to mind her joining them in the middle of the night. Meja sank down on the sawdust, ignoring the dirt. She laid her hand on the bullied chicken. The tar had gone and soft new feathers had started to grow where the old ones had been pecked away. She sat there, trying to untangle her thoughts. She may even have cried a little, but not enough to upset the birds.

She was on the point of falling asleep when the sound of voices jerked her awake. Her first thought was that it was Carl-Johan, looking for her. Perhaps he had woken Pär or Göran. None of them seemed to get it that she needed time alone. Whoever it was, they were speaking softly, almost whispering. She leaned closer to the door and held her breath to hear better.

First there was a man's voice, mumbling something she couldn't make out, closely followed by another voice, high and unfamiliar. A female voice.

That evening he sat at the kitchen table in the same pool of light, opposite Lina's place, but she was not the only one to occupy his thoughts. He didn't want to admit it was Meja he was waiting for, but even so he was waiting. Sitting stiffly on the flattened seat pad, listening. He could still see her wide-open eyes as they scanned the walls, as if she were impressed by his untidy old house. She had found the photographs of Lina and that's where her eyes had stayed. Longingly. Like a hungry dog under a dinner table she had looked at Lina, from her chubby baby cheeks to the sharp teenage face. Ten pictures crowded together on the steel surface, ten moments he would never get back, but which he could still devour. The rest of the world had lost its smell and taste. He no longer took any photographs. Everything he had experienced and that meant something was attached to his fridge door with dreary magnets, staring back at him and silently demanding *Do something, Dad. Don't just sit there.*

In the end he called Hassan. When there was no answer, he left a brief message: *I'm worried about a new student of mine, Meja Nordlander. She's seventeen. Her mother is the woman who's moved in with Torbjörn Fors. Silje, she's called. I want to know more about their background. Grateful if you can help. You know where I am.*

He sat for a long time with his mobile in his hand. He got a weird feeling down his spine when he thought of Meja. She had never had a real home or a real father. She had probably never adorned a fridge door.

Meja peered through the bars of the henhouse. Two figures were moving at the edge of the trees. Her first thought was that someone was trespassing on Birger's land, but the dogs were quiet in the pens. And one of the figures was recognizable. Although she couldn't see his face, she knew it was Göran. There was something about his movements, the way he swung his arms, as if he wanted to protect himself from the world or go on the attack.

The shape beside him was small, far too small to be one of the brothers, and considerably thinner than Anita. It was a girl. A young girl, in fact, perhaps even a child. When she turned in the moonlight Meja could see the blonde hair down her back. She walked oddly, with her shoulders raised and her head bent down, as if she had a pain somewhere.

They were talking to each other, more heatedly now, almost as if they were arguing. Meja ducked under the low door and got closer to them, her back pressed to the hen-house wall. She crouched behind the wheelbarrow and in the light from the lamp on the drive she watched as Göran held the girl up against a tree and put his hand over her mouth. It looked as if he had something over his head to hide his face, and the black cloth moved as he talked.

'I've done everything for you,' he said. 'And this is the thanks I get.'

The girl in his grip cried. Meja felt a vile taste fill her mouth. She wanted to scream at him, but her tongue wouldn't obey. Göran brought his face close to the girl's.

'The last girl I had was just as stupid as you,' he said. 'She tried to leave me, even though I saved her from every-thing – *everything!* And believe me, you don't want to know what I did to her.'

The girl moaned. He took his hand from her mouth and she sucked in air and coughed.

'I want to go home,' she stammered. 'Please, I only want to go home.'

That only made him angrier. Meja saw him lift her up and shake her like a rag doll. 'You *are* home. Don't you get that?'

He rammed the thin body against the tree trunk and held her in a stranglehold. The girl's widening eyes were white in the dim light and her legs struggled helplessly beneath her. She kicked and trampled the air. She let out a gurgling sound and Meja heard herself scream.

That made the dogs howl in the pen. Göran turned his head, but his hands stayed around the thin neck, and Meja saw the girl's legs fall still and her body dangle. Meja started running over the dark earth to Göran, where she began beating and tearing at the wiry sinews of his neck and his tense shoulders, so much stronger than hers. Perhaps it was astonishment that made him loosen his hold, and the girl dropped to the ground with a nasty thud. Coughing and spluttering, she crawled towards the trees.

Göran pulled off the balaclava and looked at Meja with eyes she didn't recognize. She could see his scalp was bleeding and a dark gash ran over his cheek and down to his throat. His shoulders rose and fell as if he couldn't get enough air.

'Don't interfere, Meja. We're only playing.'

Behind him she saw the girl get to her feet and run into the trees that were only shadows in the darkness. She ran like a white wraith among the low branches, in the direction of the lake.

'What are you doing? Who is she?'

Göran didn't answer. He only looked her over, up and down. His breath filled the gap between them and she could almost hear the thoughts whirling in his head. Suddenly he threw himself at her, grabbing her with both hands, but he only managed to get hold of her sleeve. Meja pulled herself free and started running. She ran so hard over the damp ground that earth flew up into her mouth. She ran to the dark farmhouse.

She was on the veranda steps when she realized Göran hadn't followed her. She scanned the barn and the edge of the forest, but couldn't see anything moving. Both Göran and the girl had been swallowed up by the darkness. The effort and the fear burned in her lungs as she hammered on the door of Birger's room.

It was Anita who opened. Her hair shone silver in the dull light and her nightdress was ghostlike around her ankles.

'What's happened?'

Meja supported herself against the doorframe. Inside the room she could make out the shape of Birger, reaching for his rifle.

'It's Göran. You've got to come.'

She didn't need to say more. Birger and Anita threw on some clothes and when they raced out of the house Birger was still clutching the rifle.

They found him down by the lake. The water was motionless under its coating of ice and everything was quiet. Göran was clinging to a twisted birch and it was impossible to see where the branches ended and his arms began. His face was as pale as the moon, apart from the blood that ran from his scalp. His eyes were wide as he saw them coming, and small bubbles of saliva ran from his mouth as he breathed. He let go of the birch tree and clung tightly to Anita instead, winding his arms around her back and neck. The blood ran down to his throat and Meja could hear him whisper, 'Sorry, Mum. I'm so sorry.'

'My darling boy, what have you done?'

'I never meant to hurt her. I never meant it. We were only playing.'

Birger swept the beam of his torch over the bushes and the trees were grey and ugly in the light.

'You wretched boy. Where is she?'

Göran leaned over the frozen water and threw up. Anita stroked his back and glared at Birger.

'It's your fault,' she said, in a sharp voice that hung in the air among the trees. 'You refused to let him get help.'

Birger didn't answer. The only sound was the crushing of bushes under his feet as he searched. He waved the torch like a weapon in front of him. Meja stood to one side, her teeth chattering. She could smell the sweat, the vomit and the blood. A cold rush of fear hit her as Göran stood up and pointed into the forest.

'She's lying in there,' he said.

Birger shone the torch. They saw the hair first, then the splayed legs. She was face-down in the moss and the metal of a pair of handcuffs glinted in the white beam of light.

It didn't look as if she was breathing. He ran up and turned her over. Her neck muscles had given up and her head flopped. Streaks of blood had coagulated over her mouth and chin. Anita began screaming to the sky: 'Not again. Oh, good God, not again!'

Birger sank to the ground and put his ear to the girl's parted lips. He had dropped the torch and the rifle and now he opened her mouth with trembling hands and blew as hard as he could to fill her lungs with his own air. He threw himself over her and pressed his hands to her frail ribcage.

'I didn't mean to, I didn't mean to,' Göran said, over and over. 'She was the one who attacked me.'

Birger blew and thumped so hard that he threatened to break the lifeless bones. 'You wretched boy,' he wheezed. 'You'll be the ruin of us.'

When the girl started to cough Birger didn't seem to notice and he carried on thumping her chest in a kind of frenzy. Meja heard herself shout at him. She ran on unsteady legs over the bumpy ground and pulled him off the girl, who rolled over on to her side and began gasping for air. Birger's shirt was damp under Meja's hands and his lungs rattled from the exertion.

'We must call an ambulance.'

Birger wiped his face and looked up at Meja, as if he had only just noticed she was standing there. His eyes were streaming. He heaved himself up and grabbed her, pulling her tight to his chest. She could feel him trembling under the wet shirt and feel his fear mixed with her own.

'We're not calling anyone,' he said.

Meja tried to wrench herself free of his hold, but he clamped one hand round her wrist and picked up the rifle with the other. All she saw was the weapon lifted into the night sky, high above her head, and his white fingers round the rifle butt, before the world exploded.

✳

Lelle was woken by the crunch of gravel outside. A string of saliva ran from his mouth to the leather sofa and his cheek felt flattened as he levered himself up. There was a rapid knocking on the door, before he had time to look out through the window. The bright markings of a patrol car were visible through the venetian blind. Lelle clutched his head.

'Bloody hell, Lelle, don't you ever do anything but sleep?' Hassan placed a pink carton in his hands and pushed past him. 'I know it's Saturday, but it's nearly eleven o'clock.'

'Who gives a toss? I'd sleep for the rest of my life if I could.'

Lelle lifted the lid of the carton and saw two almond croissants dusted with icing sugar staring back at him. Hassan kicked off his shoes and went into the kitchen.

'Don't you get tired of living in a pigsty? You do know there are things called cleaning firms, don't you?'

'I'm not in the mood for your humour.'

'Then put the coffee on and act like a civilized human being.'

Lelle put the croissants down on the table and did as he was told. Hassan unzipped his uniform jacket and sat down at the table, avoiding Lina's chair.

'Have you got any news for me or have you just come to sympathize?' Lelle said, as the coffee machine began to splutter on the worktop. Hassan already had his mouth full of croissant.

'Both, I'm afraid.'

The ground swayed beneath Lelle's feet as he put out the cups and milk.

'Let's hear it.'

'That girl you phoned me about, Meja Nordlander. I've made a few enquiries into her background. It seems social services have been involved in her life ever since she was born. There are files full of notes.'

'Really?'

'Things I shouldn't be telling you.'

Lelle stood by the coffee machine. 'You know I won't say anything.'

Hassan wiped crumbs from the corners of his mouth.

'She's had a complicated life, to put it mildly. She and her mother – Silje, right? – have lived at over thirty addresses in the seventeen years of Meja's life. No mention of a father, and a lot of trouble with the mother. Drug problems and psychological diagnoses. Enquiries into suspected prostitution. The girl was taken into care a couple of times, but Silje always managed to get her back.'

'Shit. Hardly surprising she's ended up at Svartliden. She must be profoundly fed up of being dragged around by her mother.'

Hassan pushed the remaining croissant in Lelle's direction.

'It looks as if she's searching for a permanent place to settle,' he said. 'Someone or something to become attached to.'

✳

'Lie still. You're bleeding.'

Meja squinted up at the figure leaning over her. The girl had bruising around her eyes and a cut above her mouth, and blood was oozing from it, thick and glossy. She pressed a wet cloth to Meja's forehead. Her voice was hoarse as she spoke.

'Try to relax. You've been hit.'

'Who are you?'

'I'm Hanna.'

Above her collarbones, beneath the strands of blonde hair, were livid bruises. Meja's heart sank when she saw them. She ran her eyes around the dark walls. The room was small, with a single light bulb hanging from a cord in the ceiling. It cast long shadows around them. The air was dank and stale and the acrid smell of urine filled her nostrils. Meja looked at Hanna again, struggling to speak.

'Where are we?'

'We're underground, that's all I know.'

'Where are the others?'

'There's only us here.'

Meja raised herself up on to her elbows. There was a blinding flash of pain behind her forehead and the walls shifted. She shut her eyes and slowly sat up, fighting the nausea that welled up in her throat.

'I think you should lie down,' Hanna said, dabbing her own mouth. 'You've been hit really badly.'

'Who hit me?'

Hanna tried to make her voice work.

'I don't know. There were several of them out there.'

She took the blood-stained cloth from her face and dipped it in a bucket of water, then wrung it out and went on bathing Meja's forehead. The wet fabric stung her skin.

'Can you hold it there yourself, do you think? You're still bleeding a lot.'

Meja put her hand on the cloth. Her fingers didn't feel like they belonged to her, but she pressed as well as she could. She blinked up at Hanna's face and her heart lurched as the realization struck her.

'I've seen you before,' she said. 'On the posters.'

'What posters?'

'The posters everywhere. People are looking for you.'

Hanna's lower lip began to tremble.

'I've been here,' she said. 'All the time.'

Meja looked at the door and breathed deeply, fighting the impulse to vomit. Then she prepared herself and sat up. There were angry black flashes before her eyes and a stab of pain in the back of her head. She put a hand to the wall to support herself. Hanna's voice sounded distant.

'Lie down before you faint.'

But Meja leaned heavily on the rough wall and shuffled towards the door. A couple of images floated across her mind and she saw the icy lake glittering in the night and Birger's hand stretching out for his rifle, on his face an expression she had never seen before. She reached the door and put her free hand on the handle. When nothing happened she let the cloth fall to the floor and started pulling and beating on the door with both hands until the light grey metal was covered in her bloody handprints. She screamed for Carl-Johan, for Birger and Anita, screaming until she began to vomit and her legs gave up and she sank to the cold floor.

Hanna helped her back to the bed and laid the wet rag over the mess she had left behind.

Tears ran down her dirty face, but her voice was level.

'There's no point shouting, nobody can hear us.'

Meja's breathing was fast. 'It was you I saw with Göran,' she said. 'Up there.'

'So you know who he is?'

'He's my boyfriend's brother.'

'Your boyfriend?'

Meja nodded her aching head and put a hand to her shuddering chest. There wasn't enough air in the confined space and she instantly felt so cold her teeth started chattering. The realization that they were shut in a bunker crept up on her. A small, dark bunker, made for hiding in when your worst fears became reality. There was no doubt this was Birger's work. Or one of the son's. The metal door, the suffocating feeling of being locked in – it was all their doing.

She found Hanna's wrist and gripped it tightly. 'How did you get here?'

'We were camping, me and my friend. I went out to pee during the night. That's when he appeared – he came from nowhere. He put his arm round my throat and squeezed so hard everything started swimming before my eyes. I tried to hit out, tried to break free, but I couldn't. He just held on, pulling at me. Trying to strangle me. I was convinced he'd kill me...'

Hanna's voice broke. Meja could feel the thin body shuddering beside her.

'I must have fainted,' she whispered. 'Because when I came round I was in the boot of his car. I can't remember how I got there.'

'What did he look like?'

305

'His head was covered. It was always covered. I've never seen his face.'

Meja thought of Göran, of his pockmarked face, his acne sores, and his fingers that couldn't stop touching and scratching them. His look when he saw her and Carl-Johan in the grass. The intensity of his jealousy, as palpable as the weather. She remembered the glade and the way he ripped up the wood anemones and said he wanted what Meja and Carl-Johan had. She took a deep breath and Anita's words echoed in her head: *If my boys give you any trouble, just let me know.* She pictured Birger's hands round his rifle and Anita's nightdress flapping over the frosty meadow. Göran cowering by the lake, not far from the body. His face as he cried and pointed.

She was still holding Hanna's wrist and could feel her regular pulse under her fingers.

'When I saw you by the house, you and Göran, had he let you come out?'

'No. I hit him.'

Hanna nodded towards the small table in a corner of the room.

'I hit him over the head and ran. But I should never have done that.'

*

He had overslept yet again. Lelle only had time to splash his armpits and brush his teeth. His hands shook with the caffeine all the way to Tallbacka. Then it was a quick dash to the staffroom for another cup. He walked with his eyes on the newly mopped floor to avoid making small talk, leaving a trail of coffee behind him. He didn't have time to worry about it, and anyway nobody would have said anything. People made allowances for someone who had lost everything, the same as they would with the elderly or very young children. They left them alone.

He was only seven minutes late. The students sat sleepily at their desks and glanced up at him as he arrived. A few grunted in disappointment.

'Anyone got any questions before the assessment? Or have you all got a good grasp of Pythagoras's theorem?'

He demonstrated two examples on the board and finished his coffee before he noticed Meja's chair was empty.

'Where's Meja today?' He got only blank stares in return and a few shrugs in reply. 'Does anyone know?'

'She hasn't been in all week,' said a voice at the back.

'She's probably sick,' said another.

Lelle scratched his stubbly chin. It itched so much he could hardly bear it, but he was forced to control himself with all the eyes staring at him.

She wasn't there on Friday, either. He looked in on Gunhild, the school nurse, after lunch. She spoke so quietly you had to hold your breath to hear what she said. No, Meja hadn't called in sick.

'Is everything all right?' she asked.

'She's missed a few lessons, that's all.'

'Is everything all right with you, I mean. You look tired.'

Of course, she saw him as one of her cases. Lelle felt the irritation like an acid reflux in his throat. What a bloody stupid question. A year ago he had roared out no, nothing was all right and he would look tired for the rest of his lousy life, so they might as well get used to it. But now he had learned to swallow that feeling and not give them what they wanted.

'I'm alive,' he said. 'You can't ask more than that.'

Meja talked about Carl-Johan, the way he had taken the cigarette from her mouth and said that nice girls don't smoke. She talked about Anita and Birger and how they seldom left Svartliden. Everything they needed was behind that gate. And there was more. She described the animals grazing in the country idyll. And the huge bunker that could keep a whole family alive for five years, maybe forever. Hanna sat with her back to the concrete wall and listened intently.

'I never saw anyone else. It was always him who came.'

'Göran must have made it on his own, in secret. Or else I've been totally blind.'

'I hit him on the head,' said Hanna. 'I hit him as hard as I could. But it wasn't enough. The next second his hands were round my throat. I thought he was going to kill me.'

Meja pictured the way Birger had thrown his mouth and hands over the lifeless body. The memory of it made her dizzy. She put her fingers to her own throat to check that her pulse was still beating.

'We will survive this,' she said. 'No one's going to kill us.'

They slept side by side on the bunk, leaving a gap that closed during the night. When Meja woke she found their arms and legs entwined, as if they were sustaining each other. There was no food, only lukewarm milk in a flask that they shared. Meja's stomach growled loudly in the silence.

'Mine has stopped protesting,' Hanna said. 'It gave up long ago.'

Meja walked round and round the damp floor. Her head ached if she moved too quickly, but the dizziness had gone. Carl-Johan would be missing her. He would never let them hurt her. Perhaps he didn't even know what they had done and was running around searching for her? He must be. And they would miss her at Tallbacka School if she stopped coming. Lelle would notice, she was sure of that. And Silje. She used to phone on the landline several times a week to complain about Torbjörn. It would take a while, but sooner or later they would get concerned.

'People know I'm here,' Meja said. 'It won't be long now.'

'What if they kill us first and get rid of the evidence? You know, make sure there's nothing left.'

Hanna's voice was as sombre as the shadows in the corners.

'Don't talk like that.'

'I'm not the first. Someone else has been here. I found evidence.'

Hanna pulled up her sleeve and showed Meja the purple hairband with its strands of blonde hair.

'You see? Someone else was here before I came.'

Meja turned her head away.

'They know I'm here,' she repeated. 'Both of them. Silje and my teacher.'

They were sleeping when the door opened. Meja only had time to see a shadowy figure in the doorway and an object shoved across the floor. By the time she reached the door it had already closed. A basket of food steamed on the floor and the smell quickly spread in the small space. Meja screamed through the closed gap and beat the door with her fists until the scabs on her skin broke open and started bleeding again. Then she sank down and turned to look at Hanna, who was still lying on the bed, her eyes like glittering stars in her battered face.

'I told you there was no point.'

*

Lelle didn't need to open his eyes to know it was snowing. He could tell from the silence. Now everything would be buried and rot and become unrecognizable. He could

trample paths through the forests and still not sink deep
enough to come up against anything hidden underneath.
In the classroom Meja's chair had been empty for two
weeks and he couldn't wait any longer. He couldn't live
with two empty chairs. Not now the snow had come.

Lina was nearly born in the snow. They had been visit-
ing Hassan's cabin up in the fells that Easter, even though
Anette looked as if she would burst any moment. They
had spread out reindeer-skin rugs in the snow and sat
with their faces turned to the sun. Such a bright light, it
made their eyes water. The spruces were weighed down
under thick, white blankets that had started dripping
at the edges. They could unzip their winter jackets and
Anette took his hand and placed it over her jumper, so that
he could feel the baby kicking. They had laughed in the
sunlight, laughed and yearned and felt apprehensive. But
a second later Anette's face had twisted in agony and she
pressed her woollen mittens to her groin. The child wasn't
content with kicking, it wanted to come out, out on to the
dripping snow and the flames licking the sky. Out to those
who were longing for her. Dark stains appeared on the rug
under Anette and all they had was the snowmobile. Lelle
had been the one to drive her to the local hospital, although
he remembered nothing about it afterwards. Nothing
apart from the light and the snow and his streaming eyes.

Ten cigarettes left over from the summer. The tobacco
had dried out and lost its aroma. It hissed unpleasantly

when he waved the lighter under it and inhaled. He couldn't hear Lina's protests. He couldn't see her either, only his own haunted look in the flecked mirror. His face had gone flabby – he wondered if she would recognize him, the day she came home. Or whether both of them had changed beyond recognition.

He was still smoking as he scraped the ice from the car windows, his steaming breath and the smoke like a cloak around him. He thought he heard his neighbour call out on the other side of the hedge, but he went on scraping and then climbed in behind the wheel with the glowing cigarette between his lips. The falling snow had already begun to weigh down the spruce trees, but it wouldn't stay. Out on the Silver Road cars had cut dirty tracks through the white and he dropped the cigarette out of the window. Once winter had been beautiful, but now he saw only ugliness.

The sign to Svartliden had a tall hat of new snow. There was a pure white covering over the gravel road that led to the gate, with no trace of a car or feet. No one had been here since the snow started falling. He left the engine ticking over as he rang the entryphone. He stamped his feet and peered towards the house, and then Birger's voice boomed out of the loudspeaker: 'Who's there?'

'It's Lennart.'

There was a pause, before he heard an answer.

'Please come in.'

The gate swept a ridge of snow ahead of it as it swung

open. Occasional flakes were still falling and heavy clouds lay over the trees, so he could barely make out any daylight behind them. Soon darkness would descend again. He didn't have long.

Birger received him in the kitchen, like last time. A large pot was boiling on the stove and a strong aroma of stewed meat filled the room. There was no sign of Meja or the boys. Lelle stood in the doorway with his hat in hand, like a schoolboy. His clothes were dripping and his nose was running. He wiped it with the back of his hand. He wouldn't take his jacket off, he had promised himself.

'I won't stay. I've just come to ask after Meja.'

'You'll have a cup while you're here?'

Birger poked his head into an adjacent room and called for Anita. There was an impatience in his voice, as if he were calling a disobedient dog.

'Please don't go to any trouble,' Lelle said.

But Birger reached out for his jacket. Lelle didn't hand over the bag containing the maths assessment. He had been clutching that tight since he stepped into the meaty smell and the warmth. The cleft in Birger's chin widened as he smiled.

'Well, here she is at last. Winter. All we can do now is bow our heads and grit our teeth.'

Lelle whistled. 'Yep, she's back.'

'I had no idea you teachers made home visits these days.'

'I was out driving, so I thought I'd check up on Meja. She

hasn't been to school for some time, so I thought something serious might have happened.'

'She's got flu, poor girl. She's been wiped out by it.'

Birger shook his head, making his cheeks tremble. He would have resembled a dog if it hadn't been for his eyes. There was nothing dog-like in that gaze.

'Has she seen a doctor?'

'No, but she's over the worst now. She'll be fine in no time. And the wife is looking after her. She's better than any so-called doctor.'

The smell of meat was so intense that Lelle could practically taste the moose that was cooking on the stove. Despite that, his mouth was dry as he held up the plastic bag.

'Could I see her for a moment? I've got the mid-term assessment here, which she missed, unfortunately, and I thought I'd give her a chance to do it at home. I don't want her grades to suffer.'

Before Birger had time to reply, Anita appeared in the doorway. She looked wild, with her staring eyes and white hair flowing over her shoulders.

'There you are,' said Birger. 'Can you go up and see if Meja can manage to come down for a while?'

Anita looked from Birger to Lelle as if she didn't quite recognize either of them. She held a hand to her chest as if she had a pain somewhere.

'Of course,' she said, and left.

Birger pulled out a kitchen chair for Lelle.

'It's good of you to come all the way out here,' he said. 'Not many teachers would.'

'I don't know about that.'

Lelle unzipped his jacket and took a sip of the coffee Birger had given him. It was hot and bitter and made his stomach protest. The whole room seemed to be boiling around him. From the floor above came dull thuds and Lelle held his breath to hear better. Birger kept his watery eyes on him and stopped smiling. Lelle felt the sweat trickle down his back.

'The rest of you didn't get it?' he asked. 'The flu?'

'We are made of sterner stuff,' said Birger. 'Not much affects us.'

Lelle nodded. Outside the window dusk was stealing over the farm and everything was still. There were a few sporadic barks from the dog pens, but otherwise no sign of life. Birger rested his hands on the table. He had rolled up his shirtsleeves, revealing his ageing skin and thick wrists. It was clear he wasn't a man to shy away from hard work.

'Meja has talked about leaving school,' he said.

'Really? She never mentioned that to me.'

'She says school isn't really for her,' Birger went on. 'She would rather work.'

'Well, I hope you advised her against that. School is important.'

Birger grunted. There was black under his fingernails. It looked as if he had been digging in the earth with his bare hands. Lelle sat on the edge of his chair and wanted to ask about the sons, but somehow couldn't, so he sat in silence with Birger's eyes on him and the moose stew bubbling on the stove.

They were still sitting like that when Anita came down the staircase, alone.

'She's fast asleep, poor girl. I haven't the heart to wake her.'

Lelle raised his eyes to the ceiling as if he could summon up Meja simply by thinking about her. The bag rustled against his jeans as he stood up. He took a sideways look at the staircase and then at Birger, who was smiling widely.

'Leave the assessment here and we'll give it to her when she wakes up.'

The handles of the plastic bag were tight around his fingers and Lelle hesitated a while, before handing it over.

'Ask her to call me if she has any questions. About the assessment.'

Soon he was out in the falling snow again, breathing deeply to get rid of the taste of meat and the feeling that the world was about to cave in on him again. A layer of fresh snow had settled on the windscreen and he brushed it off with his jacket sleeve. He took his time, glancing up at the illuminated windows and hoping he might catch a glimpse of her. He didn't want to leave her with those people. Images of Lina alone at the bus stop floated across his mind. Behind the kitchen window Birger waited to see him leave. The rear tyres skidded a little in the snow and the gate was already wide open and inviting.

✳

He woke up in Lina's room and it was a whole blessed minute before he realized she wasn't beside him. He had his head at the foot end and the patchwork quilt felt wet underneath him, as if he had sweated his way through his dreams. Lina's room faced north and the window was always richly decorated in winter with ice crystals and icicles that hung metre-long from the roof. Posters of bare-chested young men stared back at him from the walls, and books were crammed on a shelf: the well-worn *Lord of the Rings* trilogy that she had read time and again stood next to some books with black spines about vampires sparkling in the sun. She had loved those books.

Anette had taken Lina's diaries, along with her clothes and jewellery. And no doubt she had read them, because she had poured out things neither of them should have known, about how Lina was no longer a virgin and how she had tried hash at a university party in Luleå. Personally, he didn't want to hear Lina's secrets. He was happy with whatever she chose to tell him. The things she wanted him to know.

He got himself into a sitting position and sat stroking the patchwork gently with his rough hands, as if it were an old dog. It was mainly after he had been drinking that he ended up here and he didn't like it, the way his own smell took over and drove hers out. The smell of Lina had been so strong to begin with, it was in her clothes and hairbrush and the very walls. But by now he had spent so many hours and nights in here that he had erased hers with his own. It was unforgivable.

He tried to remember why he had taken to the bottle, but could only blame the winter. The darkness that engulfed the windows and scorned him as he sat there. The constant cold that bored deep into the ground and strangled the life out of everything. He couldn't bear the thought that she was out there, freezing. That was why he drank. It was an avoidance tactic.

Back down in the kitchen he stood leaning over the sink for a long time, fighting the nausea. He kept taking sips of water until he felt strong enough to measure out the coffee. It was dark outside, even though the snow brightened things up a little. He tried to look beyond his own reflection in the glass. That was what he hated about the darkness, always being forced to see himself. The way everything was turned inwards.

He found Birger Brandt's number on Eniro and called without thinking, only aware that he wanted to hear Meja's voice. But he was answered by endless unanswered ringing tones. He hung up and tried again and again, sitting there until his coffee got cold and a grey, midday light made its way into the room.

He barely gave himself time to get dressed before he left. The same jeans and socks as the day before, and then his jacket over the T-shirt he had slept in. His hair felt like wire wool and he knew what he smelled like: unwashed body mixed with whisky oozing out of the pores. He opened the side window a crack and let in the cold air. Frost clung to the birches that stretched their naked frames to the sky. He thought it was a wonder they weren't suffocated by the cold. It seemed illogical to think they would ever come into leaf again.

He felt a cold sweat prickling the back of his neck as he swung on to the road that led towards Svartliden. He tried calling again on his mobile, but still no one was answering. He was driving so fast he hardly had time to brake at the gate. The damned gate, that towered indistinctly above him in the dim light. The car skidded slightly to one side. He looked up at the snow-covered metal and wondered if he would be able to climb over, but they had probably seen him by now.

Birger's voice was loud at the other end when he rang the entryphone.

'What is it now?'

'I'm here to talk to Meja.'

He heard the static in the silence and then the gate swung open. On the other side the drive had been ploughed and the snow lay hard-packed and glistening. Smoke rose from the chimney of Birger's house and the red walls stood proudly among all the white. Like a Christmas card, if you were that way inclined. He peered up at the first-floor windows, but was met by closed curtains.

Birger waited for him in the hall.

'A hell of a lot of visits you're making all of a sudden.'

'I've only come to collect Meja.'

In the kitchen Anita was surrounded by steam and the smell of blood. A bowl of glutinous, blood-coloured batter stood before her on the work surface and her hand was dripping as she raised it in a greeting.

'We're rather busy here, as you can see,' Birger said.

'I won't stay, I'll just wait for Meja.'

'There must have been some misunderstanding. Meja isn't here.'

Lelle stopped in the doorway, trying unsuccessfully to breathe through his mouth and avoid the stench of pig's blood. He felt under his belt with one hand, where the holster usually sat. But he had given the gun to Hassan and now all he had was Lina's warning cry in his ears: *Leave, Dad. Turn around and go.*

'You said she was sick, that she was sleeping.'

'Ah, well, she left this morning.'

'Do you know where?'

Birger shook his head.

'She went through the gate at the crack of dawn,' he said. 'Maybe her mother was going to pick her up by the road. She wouldn't say anything to us. I think she and Carl-Johan have had a tiff, you know what youngsters are like.'

It sounded so normal. Birger's unperturbed expression made his flesh creep.

'And you let her go in this weather? Couldn't you have given her a lift?'

'She wanted to walk. Meja isn't a child, Lennart. We don't have any control over her.' Birger pulled out a chair, but Lelle remained standing. Anita's neck was very red as she bent over the blood pudding. He could see the pulse beating under her delicate skin, and her fear triggered his. The sweat streamed under his jacket. He began moving towards the door, but Birger followed him, grinning and baring his gappy teeth.

'Come in and sit down, Lennart. It looks like you need it.'

'No, I won't bother you any more. You must excuse me bursting in like this. I don't know what got into me.'

He opened the front door and stepped out into the cold air. Barking echoed across the driveway and over by the barn he saw a movement, as if someone had ducked behind a corner. He got in the car and it swerved in the snow as he drove away.

He had to sit and wait for the gate to open and his fingers ached as he gripped the steering wheel. When nothing happened, he drove so close he was practically touching the metal. Suddenly it felt absolutely essential to leave, to get as far away as possible from these people.

But the gate remained closed. Furious, he got out of the

car and began waving his arms and shouting for them to open up. Back at the house Birger appeared. He straddled a snowmobile and set off with a screech that sent the birds flying up from the trees. A tail of powdery snow followed him as he drove towards the gate. Lelle felt himself tense up as Birger skidded to a halt in front of him.

'The frost has got to the mechanism,' Birger said. 'But I can open it manually.'

He climbed off the snowmobile and took hold of something that looked like an iron bar.

Lelle stepped aside to let him pass.

'Can you push on it?' Birger said.

Lelle walked over, put both hands against the cold metal and pushed as hard as he could. Beside him Birger stood with the iron bar, prodding the gate where it should be opening. Clouds of cold air came from their mouths as they strained, but nothing happened. The gate was unyielding. Lelle felt the panic rise at the thought of being trapped at Svartliden. He stood back and tried again, pushing with every muscle. His eyes closed with the effort and he didn't see Birger raising the iron bar, ready to bring it down on his head. Flashing white pain shot up and down his backbone and then the darkness came.

Meja recognized Anita's food. The home-made bread and the blood pudding. Butter she had churned herself, that tasted of cream and salt and melted on the tongue. The lingonberry jam was on the runny side and the coffee left a heap of grounds at the bottom of the mug. All of it was Anita's work.

Anita, with her silver hair and her nightdress dancing over the frost. Meja recalled her dark expression when she discovered her with Göran in the glade. The sharpness in her voice as she sent him away. Her wiry arm around Meja's waist. *If my boys give you any trouble, let me know.*

When she saw the food she knew they had betrayed her, all of them. Göran, Birger, Anita – possibly even Carl-Johan. He did everything Birger told him, without question. She thought of his pride when he talked about them: *I'd be nothing without my family.*

The rage burned inside her as she spread out the familiar items, but she was too hungry to refuse to eat it.

Hanna was still lying on the bed. It was hard to tell if her eyes were open or shut in the murky light. Bruises and shadows merged together. Her thin body was barely discernible under the dirty sheet. Meja felt afraid.

'Aren't you going to eat?'

Hanna pulled a face. 'Is there any rose-hip soup?'

There were two flasks, one with coffee and one containing something sweet. Meja unscrewed the cap and breathed in the steam.

'It's hot chocolate. Would you like some?'

'I'll try.'

Hanna managed to sit up and watched as Meja poured the hot chocolate. It was made from fresh milk that frothed and was smooth in their throats. Meja put her rage aside and let the hunger take over. She devoured two sandwiches and two mugs of chocolate, while Hanna only sipped hers.

'Have you lost your appetite?'

'Yes. I think it's the lack of fresh air. My body hasn't got the strength.'

Meja curled up close to Hanna, sleepy all of a sudden. She laid her head on the bony shoulder and felt a new kind of calm descend on her. They would get out, one way or another. As soon as either Anita or Birger decided to come down to the bunker she would talk them round.

She wanted to tell that to Hanna, but her tongue wouldn't obey. Her mouth had become thick and unresponsive and her lips couldn't form the words. She tried to reach out for Hanna, and although their hands were almost touching she couldn't seem to lift her fingers. Her joints were heavy and paralysed.

She made a guttural noise and saw Hanna drop her cup. Hot chocolate spilled over the sheet and on to her jeans, but neither of them moved. Instead they sank closer together, fumbling with hands and fingers that had become stiff and useless. Meja desperately fought against her drooping eyelids. Hanna had already given in. Her neck muscles had relaxed and her head was lolling over her chest. Meja saw it and wanted to yell at her to wake up, but she was too far gone herself.

So this is what it feels like to die, she thought, before the world floated away.

∗

They had tied his hands and the rope was so tight it made his wrists bleed. The pain in his head came and went in waves of consciousness, and the periods he was asleep he dreamed that his cranium was too small and brain matter was about to leak out. When he awoke, his cheek was resting on cold cement and the pain was a second heartbeat in his right temple.

There was water for him in a bowl and he leaned across and lapped like a dog. After that the pain subsided and he became aware of the silence, and all he could hear was himself. His lungs straining, his heart beating. Nothing else. He propped himself up against the wall and rested his ear against it, but there was nothing. No voices, footsteps or wind. There was no window and no natural light, only the cold white glare of a naked bulb hanging in one corner. Either he was very deep underground or someone had put a lot of effort into making this space soundproof. In which case, this was its sole purpose: to keep a person imprisoned without fear of hearing their screams.

He thought of Lina and suddenly he was fighting for air. He hyperventilated so much the walls flickered in front of his eyes. Just one tiny pinprick of light far away and everything else drowned in darkness. It was this he had been afraid of. That she had been bound and locked up in absolute silence. Buried alive. It was the windowless walls he had seen in his nightmares; it was what had driven him out on his searches. And now it was his reality. He realized his face was wet and he licked the salty tears with the tip of his tongue, so nothing else of his would be lost.

When Birger came the pain had returned. Lelle lay in a foetal position with his bound hands protecting his face. He didn't hear the footsteps, only the door that swung open with a sigh, and then there was the figure of Birger with his back to the light. The bulb etched dark lines into his face. Lelle sat up.

'What the hell's going on, Birger?'

The old man sank down on a simple wooden chair. His tongue licked his upper lip as he deliberated on what he was going to say.

'Lennart, you more than anyone know that we have to do everything we can for our children. If they suffer, we suffer. It's the natural order of things, to protect our children. We fight for them, to the last drop of blood if necessary, because in the end they are all we have.'

Lelle spat black tears on to the dirty floor and struggled hard to keep calm.

'Where is Meja?'

Birger's eyelids flickered in the dim light.

'Don't worry about Meja. And you will get your answer, if you listen.'

'I'm listening!'

Birger gave a faint smile. He crossed one leg over the other, before going on: 'Everything we do, we do for our children. I think we can agree on that, Lennart. I bought this piece of land because I wanted to create a safe place for my children to grow up in, as far from the clutches of society as possible. We have worked our fingers to the bone for years, Anita and me, to ensure our children will never have to rely on the corrupt jungle outside the gates of Svartliden...'

'Untie me, Birger, for fuck's sake!'

'I'm afraid I can't do that. Not yet.'

Birger leaned closer, resting his hands on his knees.

'Do you know why I revile the world?' he asked.

Lelle spat again and struggled with the rope.

'I revile the world because I have been a victim of it ever since I was born. I was unwanted, my parents didn't want to know me. So the state became my tender, loving mother and gave me foster parents and carers and other legitimized sadists. I won't bore you with all the violence I suffered as a child. All I will say is that my faith in the state and its citizens died long before I reached the age of majority.'

'I'm not interested in your sob stories.'

Birger gave a mirthless smile.

'I think you are. Because unfortunately one sob story

leads to another and they spread like weeds, killing flowers. Grief is an infectious illness, Lennart. It spreads from one person to another whether we like it or not.'

Lelle grimaced. 'What has all your crap got to do with me?'

'The pieces will soon fall into place, I promise,' Birger said. 'This story is about our children, and I want to tell you about my son Göran.' He stopped, took his glasses from his face and breathed on them, making them mist over. 'Göran isn't like the others, you see. He's ill, mentally ill. We realized early on that he carried a kind of darkness inside him. Even when he was little he would attack the animals with sticks and stones and set fire to the dog pens. He showed the kind of disturbed behaviour that can only be cured with a firm hand and plenty of love.'

'Sounds to me like he needs a psychiatrist.'

'Anita and I know our son best. It wouldn't occur to us to hand him over to a stranger, not after everything we have experienced ourselves. We know what it means to have no power and be made to feel worthless. We would never, ever expose our own child to that.

'We looked after Göran here at home, taught him to respect the animals and control his impulses. And we succeeded. He calmed down. Until he became a teenager. You know what they say about teenagers, eh, Lennart? A blasted cocktail of hormones and other things that makes all common sense fly out the window.

'Unfortunately, things weren't made any better by Göran's appearance. It's always been against him. He wanted to meet a woman, naturally, like all young men. He started driving around the villages, putting out feelers, trying to charm someone into going out with him. But nobody took the bait and in the end he got frustrated, poor lad. He looked for other solutions.'

Lelle felt the hairs on his arms stand on end. 'What do you mean by that?'

'He started to take things into his own hands, you could say. Of course, we knew nothing about it, me and Anita. It wasn't until our other sons told us that we realized Göran's illness had come back. And that it was worse than any of us could have imagined.'

'His illness?'

'His dark side got him into a heap of trouble. He started molesting girls. He was tired of being turned down all the time and that led to the physical abuse. We're not proud of it and we tried as hard as we could to put a stop to it. We set him to work, tried to get him to take out his frustration in a more positive way. And it succeeded. To start with. He spent a whole year building his own bunker down by the lake. He didn't want any help. Naturally, I had taught him all the basics. We already had two bunkers on our land, but Göran wanted one of his own. And of course, we didn't have anything against it. We were proud of him, proud of the initiative he had taken. Never could we have guessed what it would lead to.'

Lelle leaned back heavily against the wall and tried to keep his head still to avoid the nausea. Birger pushed a fat finger under his glasses to wipe his eyes.

'It took several months for us to realize what he had done. Göran has never been able to tell the difference between humans and animals. He can't see any difference between hunting moose and hunting girls. To him they are prey to be caught. He doesn't understand that people can't be had by brutality.'

Birger's face became animated, while Lelle sat frozen against the wall. The feeling of unreality seemed to have wrapped him in a thick daze. He didn't want to hear more, but his tongue wouldn't let him speak.

'It was my other sons who came and told us that Göran had a girl in his bunker,' Birger continued. 'It came as a total shock to us, as you can imagine. It was around mid-summer three years ago, and by now you have probably realized that it was your daughter he had taken. Your Lina.'

Lelle heard the scream, a primal howl that made his guts freeze. He heard it, but it took a long time for him to realize that it came from him.

Birger got up from the chair and began moving towards the door, away from Lelle. A weapon Lelle hadn't noticed before glinted in his hand. He waited until it was quiet.

'I hate to say this, but we lost her last Christmas. Göran told us it was an accident, a game that went wrong. He didn't mean to kill her. I'm sorry, Lennart. From the bottom of my heart.'

The walls began to beat in time to his heart and the whole room spun. Then came the retching. Lelle crawled to a corner and spewed up a stinking pool of bile and utter despair. His body began to shake and something ruptured deep inside. He felt it. The very life was running out of him.

His eyes played tricks on him, he couldn't keep them focused. But he saw Birger by the door, one hand on the handle and the other holding the gun, as if he was afraid. Lelle hoped he planned to shoot him. He crawled as close as he could.

'My daughter died last Christmas, you say? So you let her sit in a bunker for two and a half years, like some kind of toy for your deranged son?'

'We had no choice, Lennart. You have to understand that. The damage was already done. If we had let Lina go we would have lost everything. Our whole life's work, ruined. And I can't let the state take our son. Over my dead body.'

Lelle's heart felt like it was exploding, as if it couldn't take any more. He clasped his hands to his chest and pictured Lina as he closed his eyes.

'I want to see her. I want to see my daughter.'

'I'm afraid there isn't much to see. But you will be buried side by side, I promise you.'

*

Lelle didn't know if he was alive or not. Neither his body nor his head would obey him. Time had stood still and become something else, something duplicitous and intangible. He could hear Birger's voice right beside him, but it wasn't to Lelle he was speaking.

Soon they were over him. Tall, thin figures who put their hands under his arms and round his ankles and lifted him as if he weighed nothing. They lugged his body between them down a corridor and up a flight of stairs, where every step felt like an axe in his ribcage, and out into a winter night that seemed blinding after hours in the dark.

Lelle was slung about roughly in their hands. Outside, the stars burned above and the cold that got in under his clothes cleared his head. He could see their pale faces under their winter hats – young men, that was all, but with gritted teeth and eyes that avoided contact with his. He heard himself swear at them, saying he would murder them all. The tallest of the three had a smile on his pitted face and Lelle made a grab for him with his tied hands. That only made him smile even more.

They carried him into the forest. The tops of the pines swayed restlessly above his head and a cold winter sun had made its way above the trees. They put him down in a clearing, on his knees in the fresh snow. A large hole gaped at him from the ground and the dark, iron-rich earth inhaled the cold. It seemed to be waiting to swallow him.

Raw damp had soaked through Lelle's jeans, but he wasn't cold any more. He looked around, saw the pile of earth and the spades and the white faces surrounding him. Birger and his sons. Vapour from their mouths and agitated feet crunching the frozen snow.

Birger stood behind him, still with his pistol in his hand. Lelle could hear him releasing the safety catch. His voice was thick when he spoke.

'I'm sorry it had to be like this, Lennart. God knows how sorry I am.'

He ought to protest. He ought to be begging and pleading for his life, but instead he knelt there with his head bowed. He visualized Lina and Meja. He heard himself whisper their names under his breath.

One of the boys got impatient. *Come on, Dad, shoot him.*

Time stood still and only the pines were alive and moving. Lelle was sitting at the kitchen table, looking at Lina, seeing her eyes under her fringe and her uneven teeth when she made a face at him.

What are you waiting for?

This is where she is, Lelle. Your daughter.

It wouldn't hurt, he wouldn't feel anything at all. His blood would stain the snow and his body would rot and send up dandelions in the spring. And he would never again drive along the Silver Road with a cigarette in his mouth and his eyes on the forest, because now he had found her. The years of searching were over.

He shut his eyes and waited. He felt the pressure of the muzzle on the back of his neck, and then the shot came, a dull whine in his eardrums as if he had lost his hearing. His muscles gave up and let him go.

When he opened his eyes he saw that Birger had fallen on his face with his hands clutching his chest. Behind him, with the rifle still raised, stood Anita, blinking, her snow-white hair like a fur collar around her shoulders. She waved the rifle at the young men who backed away in terror.

'Drop your weapons,' she said. 'That's enough now.'

Anita was still holding the rifle when the police arrived. She had forced Lelle and her sons to sit round the kitchen table, united in their silence. Birger had been left out in the cold and whether he was alive or not didn't appear to concern her. She stood with her legs apart, aiming the muzzle of the rifle at them to ensure their obedience.

The oldest boy swore and argued, ripped the scars on his cheeks and accused her of destroying everything. Anita wiped her tears with the back of her hand, but didn't relent. It was as if she wasn't really with them, as if she had only one thing on her mind. The other two sobbed like children, with their faces behind their hands.

Lelle was so cold he was shaking, despite the warmth of the kitchen.

'Where's Meja?' he wanted to know. 'Is she alive?'

Anita's answer was to turn the rifle on him. Her face was red under the white hair.

'We never meant for anyone to die,' she said. 'Birger promised me it would all work out, that in the end it wouldn't matter. When the world came to an end the girl would be grateful to be safe underground. Alive. That was what we thought.' She wiped her eyes. 'But there is something wrong with my boy, and we can't help that.'

The darkness was soon filled with flashing lights. The police brought new chaos in the form of heavy footsteps and the static of radio communication. Shrill voices that didn't quite reach them. Anita put down the rifle and clasped her chapped hands.

'He's out in the clearing. It was me who shot him. The girl is also there.' She pointed at Göran. 'He's the one you've got to take care of. He'll never be like other people.'

Everything happened very quickly, but also in slow motion. When they put the cuffs on Anita, Lelle saw her crumple, as if in relief that it was all over. It was Göran who put up some resistance. When the police approached him he started shouting and threatening them with his hunting knife. His eyes burned black.

'You've got no business here,' he hissed. 'This is our land!'

It was his brothers who made him give up the knife. They closed in on him and made some kind of manoeuvre they must have practised often enough through the years. They got him down on the floor and one put his knee between his shoulder blades while the other twisted the knife out of his hand. They were both pale and weeping.

Lelle sat completely still and watched them being led away, first Anita and then the boys. There were so many police officers and they dragged in snow and cold air, which made it hard for Lelle to speak through his chattering teeth. A policewoman asked him what had happened, but he still couldn't get any words out. Someone put a blanket round his shoulders and a mug of hot soup in his hands. Lelle let the steam warm his cheeks, but he didn't even realize the soup was for drinking. Outside the window black, shadowy shapes crowded together in the darting beams of torches. More police cars arrived. The gate was wide open now. Someone stood over him and put a dressing on his head. He knew he smelled of blood, but he wasn't in pain anywhere.

'They killed my daughter.'

That was all he could say. The smiling officer didn't seem to understand, but then all of a sudden she was in a hurry.

'You'll have to excuse me,' she said, and disappeared out into the cold.

Lelle followed her on to the veranda, staggered slightly in the slush and had to sit down again. There was a group of police officers and excited voices.

'We've found the girls!'

*

The policeman had kind eyes and if he judged her he didn't show it. He made her forget the hospital bed and the drip. Meja wasn't used to anyone listening to her so intently, unused to being able to explain anything from beginning to end. She hesitated and stumbled over the words at first, but soon the words were stumbling over each other in haste. The policeman was called Hassan and he didn't seem to mind that it was past midnight. He didn't look at the clock at all.

'Take it from the beginning,' he said.

Meja told him about the train journey to Norrland, how they had sat up for the whole journey, because they couldn't afford a berth. Over ten hours with nothing to do but stare at each other. They had moved many times over the years, but never this far. Torbjörn had been kind, even though he smelled and collected porn magazines, but Silje stayed the same. It didn't matter how far they moved, Silje was always Silje. She told him about her loneliness in the triangular room and how it drove her out into the forest. That was where she met Carl-Johan, by the lake. She stopped smoking the very next day. It was love at first sight.

She thought of his special smell, the way it smoothed everything out. All the talk about war and destruction had stayed on the periphery. Perhaps that's what made love dangerous. Not because you became blind, exactly, but because you didn't heed the warning signs. She wondered what Lelle would say about that deduction, whether he would agree.

Hassan wanted to know if it was love that took her to Svartliden, but she denied that. She wanted to get away from Silje, wanted a life of her own. She had always dreamed of a real home, a home with food in the larder and parents who didn't drink or smoke or walk around naked. Parents you didn't have to be ashamed of. Birger and Anita were weird in their own way, with all their talk about the coming end times, but she had chosen not to believe all that.

Her cheeks reddened when she told him about the survival bunker and all the weapons, the glitter in Birger's eyes when he showed her everything they had collected. And Göran with his injured face – her stomach hurt when she thought he had caused all that pain himself. She thought Carl-Johan was jealous when he said he didn't want her to be alone with Göran. In actual fact he had been afraid he would hurt her.

'I knew they were weird, with all that stuff they believed in. But I didn't have much to compare it with. I've never had a normal family. I was just grateful they wanted to take me in.'

Hassan nodded as if he understood. When the grey dawn began to filter through the venetian blind and her speech became slurred with tiredness, he went and bought two cups of coffee and two sandwiches, which they devoured instantly. Birger was dead, he explained. The others were in custody. And Hanna was going home to Arjeplog as soon as the doctors had given their approval.

Meja tried to imagine Birger dead. Pale and staring under a white sheet. She couldn't. And she didn't feel any grief, either. She wondered how Anita would cope in prison, without her saucepans to stir or bread to knead. And how would things turn out for Carl-Johan, who had never left Svartliden?

'Have you found Lelle's daughter?' she asked.

Hassan's eyes welled up, but he didn't cry.

'We have found a body. It hasn't been identified yet, but everything suggests it could be Lina.'

Meja felt exhausted as her head lay on the pillows. Unreal. She thought of Lelle, the drooping shoulders and the tousled hair, which seemed to be protesting about life itself. What would happen to him now, if the worst was confirmed? Would he cope? Her eyes stung when she thought of it, but she didn't give in to the tears either.

'The media will be desperate to talk to you,' Hassan said, when they had finished their coffee. 'But don't let them. I think you should concentrate on getting some rest. You've had a severe shock. And according to the doctor you've been given enough sedative to knock out a horse.'

'I'm ashamed,' Meja said. 'Ashamed I lived with such people.'

'Don't be so hard on yourself. You haven't done anything wrong.'

He brushed the breadcrumbs from his shirt and stood up. That made her afraid. Afraid to be alone, afraid of what people might say and what would happen now. Perhaps Hassan noticed, because he put his head on one side and looked worried.

'Do you want me to get your mother?'

Meja bit her lip so hard it hurt.

'No. But maybe give Lennart a call?'

✳

They had exhumed her remains from the clearing, but occasionally he went there, in the summertime. Svartliden was like an abandoned fort now, in the middle of the ancient forest. Fallen branches and pine needles covered the ground and graffiti spread like ugly sores over the rotting walls. The animals had been auctioned off to farmers in the neighbouring villages and a sour smell of forgotten hay rose over the empty stalls. Lelle smoked cigarette after cigarette and left the ash where it fell.

Meja was living with him now. They drove along the Silver Road with the windows down and let the scent of the forest fill the space between them, while Lelle pointed out the places where he had searched. They stopped at lay-bys only for a breather, and when the rain pattered on the roof she switched off the radio. She didn't like it when there was too much noise.

Silje phoned on Sundays. She had a room in an institution

by a lake, where she could paint as much as she wanted. She was done with self-medication and was getting proper help. She would learn to look after herself, without a man and without Meja. That was what she had said and Lelle could see her daughter's shoulders relax with relief now that she no longer had to bear the responsibility.

Lina had been strangled to death. Göran denied it, but his mother and brothers had been witnesses. He had strangled her and left her in the bunker to rot. When Birger found out he insisted on a burial. But no one said anything about raising the alarm.

Lelle and Meja didn't talk much about Svartliden or the Brandt family. Göran and Anita were waiting for their trials. Meja had received a few letters from Carl-Johan that she hadn't answered. He had been sent to stay with a family far away in Skåne. The prosecutor had decided not to charge him or the other brother. Their upbringing was considered mitigating circumstances, which gave the evening press a field day. Lelle avoided mentioning him, because that made Meja withdraw. She found it hard to forgive herself for voluntarily going to stay with a family that had blood on its hands, as she put it. And she hated herself for not having picked up on anything. She imagined she could have rescued Hanna earlier if she hadn't been so naive.

Hanna phoned occasionally and the conversations usually wiped the anxiety from her face. They had only spent a couple of weeks together in that wretched bunker, but that time had meant a great deal. Hanna was tough. She had told Lelle about her time in the bunker and what she had endured, and he had listened as far as possible. For Lina's sake. Because he didn't want to run from her suffering and because he needed to know. Hanna had given him the hairband, Lina's hairband, and he wore it round his wrist as a bracelet. He would never take it off as long as he lived.

Lina's grave could be seen from a long way off, surrounded by fresh flowers and burning candles, and signs and cards filled with sad messages in black felt-tip pen. Two figures were standing with their backs to them when they walked up. Lelle felt Meja draw closer to him and their feet marched in time over the gravel path. Anette was holding her child. The crinkled face was resting on her shoulder and it made the ground sway beneath him. He stopped in the middle of the path with Meja a shadow beside him. When Anette caught sight of him she placed a hand over the child's bare head. Thomas, in turn, put an arm around her. They looked from Lelle to Meja as if they couldn't work out their relationship with each other, or why. Lelle noticed streaks of mascara on Anette's cheeks as they approached. None of them said anything for a long time, there was only the babbling of the child in the silence. Eventually Anette held out a free hand and drew him towards her. They hugged awkwardly with the child between them. Lelle felt the downy hair on his nose and breathed in the baby smell and it made his eyes brim with tears.

'Thank you,' Anette whispered. 'For bringing home our daughter.'

They stood for a long time at the grave after Anette and Thomas left. Lelle knelt on the cold earth and felt his muscles begin to contract from his neck all the way down to his fingertips. Meja watered the flowers, pulled up the weeds and lit the candles blown out by the wind. Everything was as it should be when she took a step back. She didn't notice the rage overtake him, how he shuddered and spat. Not until he began lashing out with his arms and legs did she notice. He hit and kicked and tore at all the beautiful things, extinguishing the candles and sending the petals flying on the wind. He dug up the earth with his fingers until his hands were black, until he ran out of breath and energy. Meja didn't move until it was over and he had become still. Then she held out her hand and helped him up.

In Arvidsjaur they stopped at the filling station and drank coffee with Kippen. He had finally been able to take down the poster of Lina, although he hadn't gone to the trouble of cleaning away the dirty frame that had built up around it. Lelle could still picture her smiling face as he walked past. Kippen wasn't one to dwell on past sadness. He preferred instead to fill the silence with tales of moose hunting and hockey matches and other things that were not so sensitive. Meja ate an ice cream, despite the cold.

'I'd like to shoot a moose,' she said, unexpectedly.

Kippen chuckled and clapped Lelle on the shoulder with his massive hand. 'Looks like you'll have to teach your daughter to hunt, Lelle.'

It was an innocent slip that led to a lengthy silence.

She's not my daughter. My daughter is dead.

It was on the tip of Lelle's tongue, but then he saw the worried look on Meja's face and the ice cream running down over her wrist.

'I'll teach her all I know,' he said. 'Even if that isn't much.'

On the way home he let her take the wheel, even though she didn't have a licence and dusk had begun to fall over the Silver Road. He knew it like the palm of his hand. He shut his eyes, but still saw it winding ahead of him, stretching out and carving its way like meltwater across the ground, creating a link between people, for good or bad, and eventually running into the sea and disappearing. If it hadn't been for the breathing beside him he would probably have been overwhelmed by the old despair. But now he realized he would no longer need to journey endlessly.

The search was over.